From
Stumbling Blocks
To
Building Blocks

From Stumbling Blocks *To* Building Blocks

A 21st Century Perspective On the Moral
Decline of America And How to Fix It

Dr. Alveda King

To order additional copies of this book, contact:
Xlibris Corporation
1-888-795-4274
www.Xlibris.com
Orders@Xlibris.com
113114

CONTENTS

LIBERTY

AND THE PURSUIT OF HAPPINESS

Compiled by Dr. Alveda C. King
A King for America Anthology

ACKNOWLEDGEMENTS

All honor, glory and praises are due to God. Each contributing author in this book shares this sentiment in his or her own way. Authors, you willingness to share original chapters or allowing the privilege to "reprint" previously published works is deeply appreciate. Thank you all for adding to this collection of works which will sustain future readers for generations to come.

Dear readers, as your authors, we collectively acknowledge and affirm the leaders—grandmothers, grandfathers, church mothers and fathers, relatives and countless others—who lobbied for life, liberty and the pursuit of happiness in their families, churches, and communities. Theirs is the legacy that inspired King for America to compile this anthology.

Our prayer is that we will continue to pursue the Kingdom of God, the Love of Christ and the Power of the Holy Spirit to ensure that people are led to Jesus; and also to work with a passion to rescue the unborn and restore the family in the hopes of impacting future generations; to enhance the lives of people spiritually, intellectually, morally, physically and economically.

A stumbling block is a hindrance or an obstacle which causes us to err or to stray from the truth. Casting a stumbling block in one's way is the opposite of being one's brother's (or sister's) keeper.

"Cast ye up, cast ye up, and prepare the way, take up the stumbling block out of the way of my people".
(Isaiah 57:14).

A building block is a foundation upon which something solid can be established.

"And your ancient ruins shall be rebuilt; you shall raise
up the foundations of many generations; you shall be called
the repairer of the breach, the restorer of streets to dwell in."
Isaiah 58:12

INTRODUCTION

**"Have I now become your enemy because
I am telling you the truth?" Galatians 4:16**

In 1998 a dearly departed friend, Angel Rocker and I wrote a little book we named LORD, REMOVE THESE STUMBLING BLOCKS. In those days, our platform of "school choice" led us to confront the startling statistics of how America's failing school systems were crippling the youth of our nation, with African American youth experiencing the highest levels of crisis. Our mission to defend the educational rights of the families let me to proclaim that "school choice was the most pressing civil rights issue of the decade." Then, at the turn of the 21st century, the mission expanded, and for me, defending the right of all human beings to be born and to live out their natural lives became "the most pressing civil rights issue of the century."

In the nineteen seventies and eighties, I served as a Georgia State Legislator, performed on stage and screen as an actress, wrote and produced some songs and books; and in general "spread my wings" and "reached for the stars." I was also married, with six living children; and by the time the late nineties rolled around, I perhaps thought I "had it made." As far as I was concerned, my "quality of life" was at its peak. I didn't realize it, but the best was yet to come.

King for America was founded about a year before LORD REMOVE THESE STUMBLING BLOCKS was published. At that time the "Prolife Movement" was reaching a new peak of outcry in America. While I had been teaching that "school choice was the most pressing civil rights issue" of that decade, I quickly realized that too many babies were dying from abortion, and that if they were not allowed to be born, we would never have the chance to educate them.

So my platform expanded to include the message of "life from conception/fertilization until natural death." Along the way, my circle of associates expanded as well, and I began to meet wonderful people, freedom fighters and abolitionists who were dedicated to preserving life, liberty, the pursuit of happiness and justice for all people regardless of skin color and natural human conditions.

You will meet some of these friends between the covers of this book. We are by no means the only voices who are crying out in the wilderness. We are working with many others, including many of our readers, to clear away the stumbling blocks that deter the dreams of God's beloved creations and replace them with building blocks for a brighter future.

The world is experiencing a "poverty of spirit." In order for us to be blessed, we must admit that we are "poor in spirit." We need redemption so that we can recover and experience regeneration for what has been dying. There can be no revival in the land without repentance preceding revival.

It takes a proud heart and stiff neck to refuse to admit that we have something to repent for, even if the truth is staring us in the face. Prayerfully, as you read our chapters, you will find not only what the problems we are facing are; you will also be motivated to understand that you too hold the keys to successful resolution, and you are a part of the solutions.

The long and short of it . . .

Some of the chapters in this book are long, some are short. Some are excerpts and some are reprinted with permission. An anthology can take on the personality of the compiler. It has been the desire of this compiler to give the readers a generous sampling of contemporary thought for the 21st century. Dear reader, you must be the judge of the success of meeting the goal.

God bless you,
Dr. Alveda King
Founder of King for America
www.kingforamerica.com

FAITH, HOPE
AND LOVE

HOW GOD USED A CUP TO INCREASE MY FAITH

Dr. Alveda C. King
www.kingforamerica.com

"Have faith in God." Mark 11:22

God gives us many blessings in life. Among the countless blessings experienced in my now 61 years of life on earth are the lessons learned from my four favorite mentors. Three of them are elders from my bloodline, and from them I learned to receive God's miracles, to have a compassionate heart and that love never fails.

My father, Rev. Alfred Daniel Williams King, I (A. D.) taught me to believe in and later to experience the miracles of God. When I was a little girl, I would sit in the pews of churches where Daddy preached and listen to his sermons on the miracles of Jesus. When Daddy preached, I actually believed that Jesus walked on the water, turned the water to wine, rebuked the winds and the waves, multiplied the fish and the loaves and healed the sick and raised the dead.

When Granddaddy (Dr. Martin Luther King, Senior) preached about how we have to have "faith, hope and love," and the compassion of God, for the prisoners, for the sick, for the elderly, for the widows and for the children, my heart went out to "the least of these."

When Uncle M. L. (Dr. Martin Luther King, Jr.) preached about the love of God, my heart learned to know God as my loving father. Most people know that Uncle M. L. was a famous civil rights leader, but my best memories of him are as a loving family man and preacher.

My daddy and uncle in the nineteen sixties went to Heaven when they were both killed in the 20th Century Civil Rights Movement. Granddaddy lived to see his "first three great-grandchildren," my first three children born alive. He went to Heaven in the mid-nineteen eighties; just about two years after I was "born again" in 1983.Daddy never saw one of his grandchildren. I try and help them to know Daddy through my memories.

I miss them all so very much. They were my family, my protectors, my heroes, my mentors and my first Bible teachers. God in His infinite wisdom gave me another mentor, Pastor Theo Allen McNair, Senior Pastor of Believers' Bible Christian Church in Atlanta, GA. He has been my Pastor and mentor for almost 25 years. It is to him that I gave my first symbolic cup to a prophet.

In 1987, two women mentors had both directed me to "a little church on Campbellton Road", where" the Pastor there was beautifully saved." When I first went to what was then BBMOC in 1988, I had no idea what was in store for me.

Soon, I enrolled in the School of Ministry. By then, I was the mother of six living children, with the youngest at my breast, two in my arms and three young adults. I just can't tell you how blessed this time was! Then, twenty years ago, during the 1992 Christmas season, God allowed a series of what I considered at the time to be unfortunate events to alter the course of my life. Let me be very clear, I went through some more hard times, even though I was born again. The consequences of my pre-born again choices were still pursuing me. I was a "new creation in Christ," but I was still a babe in Christ, with a lot to learn.

That Christmas of 1992 found me facing foreclosure, cut off utilities, little or no food in the cabinets, and no presents for my family and friends. I was still active in my new church home, paying my tithes and offerings (against the naysayers who were telling me that I needed to be paying my bills and let God wait.) I was too ashamed and too prideful to ask people for money back then. I was determined to make it on my own.

After I paid most of the bills, but not my mortgage, I had $35 left. Yes, $35.I had two choices, actually three. I could call around and start begging for help. I could break down in tears and cry and curse God. Or, I could grow up and learn how to use my authority as a believer.

I chose the latter. I got mad at the devil that day, just a few days before December 25, 1992. I started praying the best I knew how, and decided to trust God. I remember saying: "You know what Mr. Devil. I may not have a lot of money, but I do have Jesus, and you are not going to spoil our Christmas! We will celebrate the birth of our Lord!"

I took that $35 dollars to the dollar store. My children, my mother and my pastor were on the top of my list. I didn't even stop to think how pitiful those presents would probably look to those who I would give them to. I was just too determined to have Christmas no matter what. I bought 33 items, including a bag of bows and two boxes of Christmas cards. In the basket was a Christmas cup. I remember thinking, "he who gives a cup of water to a prophet in the name of the prophet will receive a prophet's reward." That was a scripture I was studying at the time.

Well, my Pastor is a prophet so I gave him the cup. I should have also bought him a bottle of water. I gave out the gifts and the cards, and over the years, I've had many occasions to remember that season of breakthrough in my life. It was almost instant. The day before Christmas, the children's "spiritual godfather" called and asked me what I was buying the children for Christmas. Not wanting to speak outside of my newfound faith, I answered, "God will provide."

Well, wouldn't you know he read between the lines, and came over just in time to take me shopping for new clothes for the children? With his gifts and my dollar store toys and books, they had Christmas. I decided right then, when I was putting the bow on that cup, that for the rest of that year, I would dig in my heels, take out my notepad and study everything my Pastor was teaching, because I knew he had something that I needed.

Over the next few years, I graduated from our school of ministry, was delivered from a "fiery bed of affliction" in an intensive care unit, delivered from bankruptcy into a brand new home with no down payment, received new cars, mission trips around the world, new books, the launching of King for America, abortion healing and so much more.

Today, Pastor McNair, my mentor, is one of the world's best Bible teachers. Along with many well seasoned ministry gift guests invited to speak at our church over the years, he teaches his flock the Word of God in such a way that we are becoming doers of the word, believers of the word and he encouraged me to launch my own ministry, King for America. Our foundation scripture "Have faith in God," is found in Mark 11:22. I also serve as Pastoral Associate with Priests for Life, and remain in the music ministry at BBCC and am on the teaching staff there.

Giving my pastor that cup was an act of faith, a little bit like the widow's mite, at least that's how it felt back then. Today, God makes all grace abound to me, so that always having, I am able to give gifts without reservation. I am so glad that Jesus is Lord. My friends, "HAVE FAITH IN GOD!"

FAITH: YOU ARE WHAT YOU BELIEVE!

Angela Stanton
www.dontaskjusttell.org

"Have faith in God!" Mark 11:22

Dr. Alveda King is my mentor. She and her family encourage and support me in life. My two books, LIFE BEYOND THESE WALLS, and LIES OF A REAL HOUSEWIFE are inspired in part by my faith and the encouragement of those who have gone before me.

Life is hard. As a matter of fact no one has ever told me that life would be easy. Even though I have heard & truly believe that life is a gift from God; what we do with our lives more importantly is our gift back to God.

What gives us the strength to keep pressing after severe heartache, how do we find the muster of hope that we need to get us through to the next step in life? Quite simply, you are what you believe!

As a mischievous child I often got into trouble trying to discover the world around me and I made many, many mistakes. And I often found myself believing the negative reports of my on lookers. Whenever I did the wrong thing or made the wrong decisions they would say, "you will never amount to anything, you're worthless." Their words weighed heavily on my mind and stayed at the tip of my thoughts.

Whenever I was faced with adversity I never stood a chance because in my mind I was already defeated. Eventually I stopped believing the negative report and began thinking of the reactions that I had gotten from my parents on numerous occasions. When the world around me despised me for my actions, my parents continued to encourage me and speak life! "Angela you can be whatever you want to be in this life, we all make mistakes, quitters NEVER win."

Mama King says her pastor Allen McNair taught her that we all have a "believer." We also have the power to believe what we choose to.

The day that I decided to change my thoughts and remove negative thinking from my brain was the day that I became a winner! Whether you believe you can or you cannot . . . Mama King, you're right! You are what you believe!

HOPE: WE WERE BORN TO SHINE BECAUSE WE BELIEVE

By Ruth Stafford
www.wewereborntoshine.com

"Now, faith is the substance of things hoped for, the evidence of things not seen."Hebrews 11:1

Dr. Ruth Stafford shares her hope for the future in this passage. She concludes by sharing a poem from one of her readers.

HOPE:

What is the solution for the many people who continue in their discontent? We have hope. Our hope is built on nothing less than Jesus' blood and righteousness. Can you see how most of America's problems are all knit together? Various groups of people with restless weary souls are all seeking significance and purpose, power and love. "We were made for God and our souls are restless until we find rest in Him" St Augustine said.

SOLUTION:

Oh love, that will not let me go, I Rest my weary soul in thee: I give thee back the life I owe, That in thou ocean's depth its flow may richer, fuller be. O light that foll'west all my way, I yield my flick'ring torch to thee: My heart restores its borrowed ray, that in Thy sunshine's blaze its day May brighter, fairer, fairer be. (George Matheson)

Imagine:

A flickering torch into a blazing daylight for We Were Born to Shine . . . Because We Believe. Oh, restless souls find rest in Jesus.

LET MY PEOPLE GO (Metacognition)

It is not a travesty, but a tragedy. Let my people go. Once filled with pride and part of a tribe. Let my people go. Stolen, purchased from across the sea. Let my people be. Enslaved they labored, not given a fee. Let my people be. No heed to the cries, I want to be free. Let my people go. Then freedom rang. With Abe we sang. Let my people be. On easy street was a political retreat. Let my people seek. We tried it, obliged it. Let my people think. But spirits died, minds retired. Can my people think? Lost is the pride, betrayed the tribe. Let my people hope.

Sadly for us more than thirteen million Black babies have been killed as a result of the sickness of sin, hate and evil. I am sorrowful for the guilt one must carry for a life time for participating in such a horrible crime that was unbeknownst to them.

They (Blacks) orchestrated the dirge for the procession that carried these babies to their graves and did not realize they were playing the music. Have we been raped? Let thy people pray.—Florence Ames

REVELATION OF THE LOVE OF GOD: FROM SERMONS BY PASTOR ALLEN MCNAIR

Compiled by Dr. Alveda King

"Love never fails." I Corinthians 13: 8

Any and all problems of human suffering that we experience can be addressed with the Agape Love of God. Stumbling blocks become building blocks when we apply Agape Love to any situation. "Build your hope on things eternal, hold to God's unchanging hand," are the words of a popular Christian song. Our hopes for a better life become reality when we apply faith, which works by love.

Today we live in a fast paced world where material possessions are often more valuable to us than kind and loving relationships. Why? For some, it is easier to acquire material gain than it is to express genuine agape love.

Meanwhile, family relationships are starving to death. People try to feed each other by portraying Hollywood personas, with all the fancy hair, clothes, cars and such. Yet simple acts of compassion and human kindness can become a pretense that you show to the outside world, and drop on the doorstep when you get home.

People suffer enough at work, at school and out in the cold, cruel world. When we get home, we should be prepared to give kind words, actions and thoughts towards those who are closest to us. Notice that I say give, not get, and not receive from others.

How often do we say that "I will love him or her when he or she gives me some love? Yet, don't we love Jesus because He loved us first? It stands to reason that in order to get love, you have to give love. That's in line with the law of sowing and reaping. If you sow much, you reap much. If you sow little, you get little.

Oh how easy it is to put on public displays in public. At church, when it's time to greet our neighbor, we put on the biggest show of smiling and hugging. Yet, sometimes before we reach the parking lot after service, we are ready to give someone a piece of our mind; not realizing that a mind is a terrible thing to waste. We need to have our whole minds, and added to that, the mind of Christ and the love of God—For God is love; and love covers a multitude of sins. I Peter 4:8.

John, Love's Apostle

Often, when counseling people, I advise that they read the book of I John. This little book teaches us more about love than we could ever learn from love songs on the radio, and from popular books and movies.

The closest personality who was popular in the news and who also walked the "love walk" in our times was Dr. Martin Luther King, Jr. He preached many sermons on the love of God; and he didn't just talk the talk, he walked the love walk.

What is the love walk? It is living a life well developed and saturated with the love of God. John, often called "The Revelator", is also known as "The Apostle of Love". He wrote several books in the Bible, including The Gospel of John, I-III John, and the Book of Revelations. History reports that John was so well developed in a life of Agape, God Love, that he couldn't be killed. Reportedly, after surviving a sentence of being boiled in oil, he was exiled to the Island of Patmos, where he wrote the book of Revelations.

Using the words in I John, I counsel people to begin to do kind deeds for the people that they want to give them love. In other words, can we be kind and generous to someone who isn't being kind and generous to us? Of course we can, but we may not want to. In order to give love, without expecting love in return, we need a revelation.

The revelation of the love of God is wrapped up in the reality of the Lordship of Jesus Christ. It is not about being kind, although being kind comes along with God's love. It is not about being emotional. The Love of God was revealed to the Apostle John, and God will reveal His love to you! You will have to go deep to find it. The Bible says to seek the Lord with all your heart. The Word also says to love the Lord with all of your mind, your heart, your soul and your strength. Can you truly say that you are doing this today? Are you really after seeing the love of God manifested in your life?

Love God with all of your being. Love other people like you love yourself. Jesus said that these are the most important commandments. God is love. In the gospels of Matthew, Luke and John, we see where Jesus first met John. James and John were fishermen with Peter. John caught the greatest revelation of the love of God in his walk with Jesus. The life that Jesus lived, never changing no matter what anyone did or said to him, affected John. John made a decision to live with this reality in his own life. In the book of John, chapter one, John wrote: In the beginning, the word was with God, and the word was God.

Jesus brought knowledge into this life that darkness, unredeemed people could not understand. You know, we have never majored in the Word of God. Now, today, all these years after John wrote these things, this eternal Word is full of life for us today, this particular life from the beginning.

Let's picture ourselves in John's position as a young man. Young folks like to know and experience everything. Now, if we as Christians don't catch hold of what John was saying, that Jesus was the only begotten Son of God, the living Word, with God, was God, we come to see that the Word is the personality that speaks the Word. That makes Jesus and what He says the same. What He says will never pass away. He is still upholding all things by the Word of His Power. Jesus' relationship with God is so much more than just being born of a virgin. He dwelled among us.

The miracles, turning the water to wine . . . That must have been awesome. How would you feel having lived with someone who raised people from the dead? Someone who walked on water? Caused demons to depart? The demons recognized Jesus. And John had the awesome experience of knowing Jesus. Really knowing Jesus . . . Not a religious experience, a real experience. There is something in John's little book that will affect your life! In the life and testimony of John, God is giving us the revelation of Jesus. Here was a man, who was also God that defied the powers of that age. The Pharisees and the government couldn't contain Him. Yet, who can contain the Love of God? Only those who believe . . .

There was no question in John's mind that Heaven exists; that the devil was real. These issues are debated in the minds of people today, because they do not have the revelation that John had. John knew that when eternity said, "roll the stone away," a miracle would occur. John knew that He who set time into existence could call Lazarus forth. John left us the roadmap in his first letter: "That which was from the beginning, which we have heard, which we have seen with our eyes, which we have looked upon, and our hands have handled, of the Word of life."

Yes, John knew that he had handled the Love of God, the living Word of God, revealed: For the life was manifested, and we have seen it, and bear witness, and show unto you that eternal life, which was with the Father, and was manifested unto us.

Yes, the Love of God can be manifested if you have the heart to receive it! John did. Do you? That which we have seen and heard declare us unto you, that you also may have fellowship with us: and truly our fellowship is with the Father, and with His Son Jesus Christ. And these things write us unto you, that your joy may be full.

Is your joy full today? If so, glory be to God, pass it on. If not, keep pressing on. This love is available to you! This is not just a religious saying. This is not a storybook tale. You can know the love of God!

John had a face to face encounter with the Love of God! Jesus looked like a man, but He was so much more outstanding! John was allowed to go on the Mount of Transfiguration with Jesus. After that experience, John was even more convinced that Jesus could accomplish whatever He set out to do. John understood that Jesus controlled the armies of the world. John understood that all power belonged to Christ. John said he'd looked upon Him, handled the Words of Life! Get this, now.

Here is a being in a physical body, yet John knew that he'd had the occasion to touch He who had framed the worlds and all creation. John is speaking from experience. He is saying that I've had the occasion to witness the Son of God free a woman bent with infirmity for eighteen years. John saw Jesus speak to the circumstances and saw the woman's body completely restored. Would you say that that woman's joy was full after that?

This reality became such a part of John, that they couldn't kill him. The other disciples and apostles ran into some things, but not John. History has it that they even tried to boil him in oil, and it didn't hurt him. What a revelation of the power of the love of God!

Jesus said, "I am come that they may have life, and have it more abundantly." Man did not have abundant life. He'd lost it in the Garden of Eden. Jesus brought it all back to us. Think about it. God told Adam that once he'd partaken of that tree, he'd surely die. God meant a lot when He said that. Then, hundreds of years later, after witnessing all kinds of deaths and curses, John lived to see Love in Action. John saw Love alive! John touched and handled the Love of God! So can you! Can you handle it! More importantly, do you want to handle it? Do you want to touch and feel the Jesus that John knew?

You must be aware that you don't have to be denomination minded. You don't have to be church minded! You don't have to be church duty minded. When there is a revelation that you serve God with all of your heart, your mind, your soul, serving the eternal, everlasting Word of God—He is just as real today, then you are on the road to Love that John knew.

Think about this, now. We as Christians are about the only group who doesn't major in what we believe. Athletes major in sports. Singers major in singing. We can get to know mathematics, computers, and mechanics. Most of us are up on that because we have applied ourselves to coming to know these things. People even major in serving idols and the devil. Yes, we approach these kinds of things with an attitude of mastering them, so we succeed.

Yet, we Christians are just failing when it comes to spiritual things. In our knowledge and use of spiritual things, we don't even know two plus two equals four. If the Church were the learning institution it should be—most Christians would fail. We get after kids for playing hooky, yet we play spiritual hooky all the time. The professor is in class, the students don't show up. The things we should know most of all, we know least of all. The spiritual things that directly affect our lives, we don't know. We are not like John. We've not had that spiritual experience, of handling the Word of life. We want to treat the preacher's like doctors. We don't have to know what they know to get well. We don't want a teacher who will teach us how to live for ourselves. You don't have to know what the doctor knows, use what the doctor uses. We just expect the doctor to perform. Yet the Bible says: "People perish for lack of knowledge." You need to have this same experience, this same knowledge that the Word is giving you.

You need to know where your healing is, your prosperity is, and your right standing with God is. You need to know the assistance of angelic forces you have. But we don't have this, so life remains a mystery to us. We fail to comprehend spiritual things. Light will shine in a place of light, but light won't comprehend it because light won't do what needs to be done to comprehend, to handle the Word of Life. This is one of the most disheartening things for a minister of the gospel. You see that people are not equipped, and they won't try to get it. It's like never learning how to count, or what money is, then going to the grocery store and have the man ask you for twenty dollars. You don't know what it is. You never took the time to find out how to count. Or you have a car; you're driving and can't read. You'll be in a mess sooner or later.

How many Christians know how to cook better than they know God? God should be above everything else that we know. One day, you'll come face to face with the reality that you need this. It's almost like trying to get somebody to breathe for you, or to get his or her heart to beat for you. It won't work. You'll have to touch, to know to handle this reality for yourself. And you'll have to handle it with skill and experience. You must personally know your own God.

This is what John is talking about. We must have this same kind of experience. When you are living every day, the Word of God should be just as real in everything you do as when you open your Bible and read it. You need to pray and ask God to reveal His Word to you—not just from a book, but for real, everyday life. When you ask God to reveal His Word to you, allow Him to do it. Then, live the Word, do the Word! From Genesis One to the last page of Revelation, the Word of God should be real to you. The fall and redemption of man should be just as real to you as breathing. You need to know that God is involved in your life. You are a product of the plan and purpose of God! His Love is higher than anything else you can ever think of is. Your racial ties are not even important. You are a member of the family, the kingdom of God. You are of God, little children.

This is what is so sad about Christianity. We can have racial differences, social differences, and lack of associations. Yet, Christianity is supposed to bring us together. You know why it hasn't happened? There's no revelation of the Love of God in the Church. When you see yourself more than you can see God, you don't have a revelation of God. When you can see yourself and the difference in other people, you're not seeing God, the Father, Son and Holy Spirit. And to have a revelation of God is to have a revelation of the Love of God. This should be growing in your life every single day, hour, and year. There should be a depth of the reality and application of this love that wasn't here last year. You have to get your purpose, which is to be fulfilled in the love of God! You might want to start by majoring in First John. Once you get a handle on that, you can go on to learn the character of Love in First Corinthians 13. Don't jump ahead of yourself, thinking you know algebra when you don't have two plus two down. Touch, handle, and know the love of God for yourself.

Now abide faith, hope and love. Yet, the greatest of these is love. Keep yourselves in the love of God, dear ones. May your joy be full, complete and overflowing.

Allen McNair is the Senior Pastor of Believers' Bible Christian Church in Atlanta, GA. Amen.

NO GREATER LOVE

Dr. Alveda C. King

The ageless quest for the meaning and experiencing of true love burns steadily into the 21st century. People make love, take love and break love every day. Yet, we still wonder, "What is love?"

One day while reading my Bible, I came across a passage where in 2 Samuel 2:26, David writes of Saul's son Jonathan, his slain friend: "I am distressed for you my brother Jonathan; very pleasant have you been to me; your love to me was extraordinary, surpassing the love of women.

I couldn't help wondering if this is why some people get confused, and want to think that love between two men has to be homosexual. There is some confusion here between sex and love in such a case of thinking this way.

There are many kinds of love, with Agape (God's total and complete unconditional love, which by the way does not include sex,) Philos (the love between friends) and Eros (sexual expressions of affection and love) being the most commonly considered.

People get confused about love, and expressions that can be attributed to love. The greatest love is Agape love. God, after all, is love.

Below is a passage discovered during a morning meditation. It concludes with a passage from a work of Oswald Chambers, author of MY UTMOST FOR HIS HIGHEST which I read from almost every day. I hope you enjoy this reading as much as I did.

From www.gracedoctrine.org:

The Doctrine of Laying Down your Life for your Friends
2010

John 15:13, "Greater love has no one than this,
That one lay down his life for his friends
(PHILOS—loved ones = fellow believers)."

1 John 4:7-12, "Beloved, let us love one another, for love is from God; and everyone who loves is born of God and knows God. [8]The one who does not love does not know God, for God is love. [9]By this the love of God was manifested in us, that God has sent His only begotten Son into the world so that we might live through Him. [10]In this is love, not that we loved God, but that He loved us and sent His Son *to be* the propitiation for our sins. [11]Beloved, if God so loved us, we also ought to love one another. [12]No one has seen God at any time; if we love one another, God abides in us, and His love is perfected in us."

1 John 4:18-21, "There is no fear in love; but perfect love casts out fear, because fear involves punishment, and the one who fears is not perfected in love. [19]We love, because He first loved us. [20]If someone says, "I love God," and hates his brother, he is a liar; for the one who does not love his brother whom he has seen, cannot love God whom he has not seen. [21]And this commandment we have from Him, that the one who loves God should love his brother also."

1 John 5:1-3, "Whoever believes that Jesus is the [£]Christ is born of God, and whoever loves the Father loves the *child* born of Him. [2]By this we know that we love the children of God, when we love God and observe His commandments. [3]For this is the love of God, that we keep His commandments; and His commandments are not burdensome."

1. Definition:

In the command to love by "laying down our lives", Jesus is comparing all realms of love to the love that is self sacrificial for the benefit of our fellow believers, (whether they are current or future believers). There is not greater love in the entire universe than that AGAPE love that puts others first and ourselves second.

1 John 3:16, "We know love by this, that He laid down His life for us; and we ought to lay down our lives for the brethren."

   a. "Laying down your life" is in the Aorist tense which views the entirety of the action.
   b. Therefore, it does mean suffering martyrdom for the sake of fellow believers, but that is just one aspect of "laying down our lives", Rev 6:9; 20:4.
   c. "Laying down your life" is also the day to day carrying of your Cross for the benefit of others, Luke 9:23-24; Gal 5:24-25.

Our Lord said in Luke 9:23-24, "If anyone wishes to come after Me, he must deny himself, and take up his cross daily and follow Me. For whoever wishes to save his life will lose it, but whoever loses his life for My sake, he is the one who will save it."

Gal 5:24-25, "Now those who belong to Christ Jesus have crucified the flesh with its passions and desires. [25]If we live by the Spirit, let us also walk by the Spirit."

   d. "Laying down your life" is also the day to day self sacrificial AGAPE love for the benefit of loved ones (fellow believers current and future).
   e. Whether we are witnessing the gospel or serving our fellow believers, we are in fact laying down our lives for their spiritual benefit whatever it may be.

Gal 6:9, "Let us not lose heart in doing good, for in due time we will reap if we do not grow weary. [10]So then, while we have opportunity, <u>let us do good</u> to all people, and <u>especially to those who are of the household of the faith</u>."

2. As believers, we each have received at least one spiritual gift at the moment of our salvation, which we should be applying in the service of God each and every day. As you learn what your gift is and apply it on a consistent basis, you are fulfilling the command of John 15:12-14.

   a. How so? Because there are many other things you could be doing with your life each and every day, yet when you put those things aside to serve God in the application of your spiritual gift you are sacrificing those "other things" of your life, you are sacrificing your life. See 1 Cor. 12:4-7, 12-21; 13:1-7; Gal 5:22-23.

1 Cor. 12:4-7, "Now there are varieties of gifts, but the same Spirit. [5]And there are varieties of ministries, and the same Lord. [6]There are varieties of effects, but the same God who works all things in all *persons.* [7]But to each one is given the manifestation of the Spirit <u>for the common good</u>."

Gal 5:22, "But the fruit of the Spirit is love, joy, peace, patience, kindness, goodness, faithfulness, [23]gentleness, self-control; against such things there is no law.

3. Scripture provides detail as to what "laying down your life" entails. There are two aspects, a) your mental attitude, and b) your actions:

1 John 3:23, "This is His commandment, that we believe in the name of His Son Jesus Christ, and love one another, just as He commanded us."

1 John 3:18, "Little children, let us not love with word or with tongue, but in deed and truth (Bible doctrine resident in your soul)."

   a.   <u>The Appropriate Mental Attitude for "Laying Down Your Life", Rom 14:7-8; Phil 1:21-25</u>.

Rom 14:7, "For not one of us lives for himself, and not one dies for himself; [8]for if we live, we live for the Lord, or if we die, we die for the Lord; therefore whether we live or die, we are the Lord's."

   1)   Mentally put God's will for your life before your own will or anyone else's, Luke 22:42.

Our Lord prayed in Luke 22:42, "Father, if You are willing, remove this cup from Me; yet not My will, but Yours be done."

   2)   Mentally put aside worldly titles, credits, power and prosperity that are a hindrance to serving God and his children, Phil 3:7-8, 15-17.
   3)   Overcome the sinful desires of your Old Sin Nature with the Word of God resident in your soul, Gal 5:24. The precursor of mental attitude that leads to "carrying your cross daily."

Gal 5:24, "Now those who belong to Christ Jesus have crucified the flesh with its passions and desires."

    4) Do not judge your fellow believer, Rom 14:10, 13

Rom 14:10, "But you, why do you judge your brother? Or you again, why do you regard your brother with contempt? For we will all stand before the judgment seat of God."

Rom 14:13, "Therefore let us not judge one another anymore, but rather determine this—not to put an obstacle or a stumbling block in a brother's way."

    5) Have an absence of hatred, (for whatever reasons), toward fellow believers, 1 John 2:4-11
    6) Dwell on righteousness rather than the garbage of the world, (Satan's Cosmic System), Phil 4:8-9 with 1 John 3:7.

1 John 3:7, "Little children, make sure no one deceives you; the one who practices righteousness is righteous, just as He is righteous."

    7) Strive for peace with your fellow believer and the edification of their souls, Rom 12:18; 14:19.

Rom 12:18, "If possible, so far as it depends on you, be at peace with all men."

Rom 14:19, "So then let us pursue the things which make for peace and the building up of one another."

  b. Your Actions in "Laying Down Your Life".

    1) Behave according to God's mandates in society, Romans 13:8-14; Gal 5:24-26.
    2) Suffer and rejoice with others when they are suffering or honored, 1 Cor. 12:26.
    3) Give graciously to your fellow believer who is in need, 1 John 3:17.

1 John 3:17, "But whoever has the world's goods, and sees his brother in need and closes his heart against him, how does the love of God abide in him?"

> 4) You are not the 007 of Grace. Do not use Grace as a license to sin, Gal 5:13-14.
> 5) Do not gossip or malign in order to get ahead, Gal 5:15.

Gal 5:13-15, "For you were called to freedom, brethren; only do not turn your freedom into an opportunity for the flesh, but through love serve one another. For the whole Law is fulfilled in one word, in the statement, "You shall love your neighbor as yourself." But if you bite and devour one another, take care that you are not consumed by one another."

> 6) Have an absence of self righteous arrogance, Gal 5:26.

Gal 5:22, "But the fruit of the Spirit is love, joy, peace, patience, kindness, goodness, faithfulness, [23]gentleness, self-control; against such things there is no law. [24]Now those who belong to Christ Jesus have crucified the flesh with its passions and desires. [25]If we live by the Spirit, let us also walk by the Spirit. [26]Let us not become boastful, challenging one another, envying one another."

> 7) Forgive the sins of others and encourage them to go forward in the Plan of God, Gal 6:1-2; Eph 4:1-3; Col 3:12-17.

Gal 6:1-2, "Brethren, even if anyone is caught in any trespass, you who are spiritual, restore such a one in a spirit of gentleness; each one looking to yourself, so that you too will not be tempted. Bear one another's burdens, and thereby fulfill the law of Christ."

Eph 4:1, "Therefore I, the prisoner of the Lord, implore you to walk in a manner worthy of the calling with which you have been called, [2]with all humility and gentleness, with patience, showing tolerance for one another in love, [3]being diligent to preserve the unity of the Spirit in the bond of peace."

Col 3:12-17, "So, as those who have been chosen of God, holy and beloved, put on a heart of compassion, kindness, humility, gentleness and patience; [13]bearing with one another, and forgiving each other, whoever has a complaint against anyone; just as the Lord forgave you, so also should you. [14]Beyond all these things *put on* love, which is the perfect bond of unity. [15]Let the peace of Christ rule in your hearts, to which indeed you were called in one body; and be thankful. [16]Let the word of Christ richly dwell within you, with all wisdom teaching and admonishing one another with psalms *and* hymns *and* spiritual songs, singing with thankfulness in your hearts to God. [17]Whatever you do in word or deed, *do* all in the name of the Lord Jesus, giving thanks through Him to God the Father."

8) Strive for harmonious rapport inside the body of Christ, 1 Peter 3:8-12 with Gal 6:10.

1 Peter 3:8-12, "To sum up (what AGAPE love is), all of you be harmonious, sympathetic, brotherly, kindhearted, and humble in spirit; [9]not returning evil for evil or insult for insult, but giving a blessing instead; for you were called for the very purpose that you might inherit a blessing. [10]For, 'THE ONE WHO DESIRES LIFE, TO LOVE (AGAPE) AND SEE GOOD DAYS, MUST KEEP HIS TONGUE FROM EVIL AND HIS LIPS FROM SPEAKING DECEIT. [11]HE MUST TURN AWAY FROM EVIL AND DO GOOD; HE MUST SEEK PEACE AND PURSUE IT. [12]FOR THE EYES OF THE LORD ARE TOWARD THE RIGHTEOUS, AND HIS EARS ATTEND TO THEIR PRAYER, BUT THE FACE OF THE LORD IS AGAINST THOSE WHO DO EVIL'."

9) Have harmonious rapport inside your marriage and family, Eph 5:22-6:4; Col 3:18-21.
10) Apply authority orientation to human institutions, governments, bosses, Pastors, etc., Rom 13:1-7; Col 3:22-25; 1 Thess. 5:12-13; 1 Tim 5:17-18; 6:1-2; Titus 2:9-10; 3:1-2.
4. Conclusion: "Laying down your life", means living righteously with confident expectation in the Plan of God, Titus 2:11-14.

Titus 2:11-14, "For the grace of God has appeared, bringing salvation to all men, [12]instructing us to deny ungodliness and worldly desires and to live sensibly, righteously and godly in the present age, [13]looking for the blessed hope and the appearing of the glory of our great God and Savior, Christ Jesus, [14]who gave Himself for us (*laid down His life*) to redeem us from every lawless deed, and to purify for Himself a people for His own possession, <u>zealous for good deeds</u>."

In John 15 verses 13-17 we have the friendship of Jesus Christ, and in verses 18-27 we have the hostility of the world. So that leads us to . . .

"Will You Lay Down Your Life?"
By Oswald Chambers, My Utmost for His Highest.

"Greater love has no one than this, than
to lay down one's life for his friends . . .
I have called you friends . . ." (John 15:13, 15)

Jesus does not ask me to die for Him, but to lay down my life for Him. Peter said to the Lord, "I will lay down my life for Your sake," and he meant it (John 13:37). He had a magnificent sense of the heroic. For us to be incapable of making this same statement Peter made would be a bad thing—our sense of duty is only fully realized through our sense of heroism. Has the Lord ever asked you, "Will you lay down your life for My sake?" (John 13:38). It is much easier to die than to lay down your life day in and day out with the sense of the high calling of God. We are not made for the bright-shining moments of life, but we have to walk in the light of them in our everyday ways. There was only one bright-shining moment in the life of Jesus, and that was on the Mount of Transfiguration. It was there that He emptied Himself of His glory for the second time, and then came down into the demon-possessed valley (see Mark 9:1-29). For thirty-three years Jesus laid down His life to do the will of His Father. "By this we know love, because He laid down His life for us. And we also ought to lay down our lives for the brethren" (1 John 3:16). Yet it is contrary to our human nature to do so.

If I am a friend of Jesus, I must deliberately and carefully lay down my life for Him. It is a difficult thing to do, and thank God that it is. Salvation is easy for us, because it cost God so much. But the exhibiting of salvation in my life is difficult. God saves a person, fills him with the Holy Spirit, and then says, in effect, "Now you work it out in your life, and be faithful to Me, even though the nature of everything around you is to cause you to be unfaithful." And Jesus says to us, ". . . I have called you friends" . . . Remain faithful to your Friend, and remember that His honor is at stake in your bodily life.

LIFE

HOW CAN THE DREAM SURVIVE IF WE MURDER OUR CHILDREN?

Dr. Alveda King
www.priestsforlife.org

In this great country of ours, no one should be forced to pray or read any religious documents, and a woman should have the right to decide what to do with her own body. Thank God for the Constitution. That Constitution, though, guarantees freedom of religion, not freedom from religion. The so-called doctrine of "separation of church and state" is not in our Constitution. Nothing in our Constitution forbids the free exercise of religion in the public square. Inherent in our Constitutional right to life, liberty and the pursuit of happiness, is the right to know the serious consequences of making a decision to deny religious freedom, or to abort our children.

Oh, God, what would Martin Luther King, Jr., who dreamed of having his four children judged by the content of their characters, not just the color of their skin, do if he'd lived to see the contents of thousands of children's skulls emptied into the bottomless caverns of the abortionists pits?

What would he say about the rivers of blood of the children cut down in gang wars and other dark deeds?

It is time for America, perhaps the most blessed nation on earth, to lead the world in repentance, and in restoration of life! If only we can carry the freedom of repentance to its fullest potential. If only America can repent and turn away from the sins of our nation. We must allow light and life back into our lives!

Today, I live with a repentant, heavy heart, and I pray each day for the Lord's forgiveness and blessing. I am a mother of six living children and a grandmother. Regretfully, I am also a post-abortive mother. I offer a tearful prayer that my sharing the tragedy of my life-altering experiences will help save the life of a child yet unborn.

In the early 1970's, even though some Black voices were protesting against forced sterilization, artificial chemical birth control methods and abortion, there were many who were fooled and misled by propaganda that promoted such strategies. I was among those who were duped. As a result, I suffered one involuntary and one voluntary "legal" abortion.

My involuntary abortion was performed just prior to the passage of Roe v. Wade by my private pro-abortion physician without my consent. I had gone to the doctor to ask why my cycle had not resumed after the birth of my son. I did not ask for and did not want an abortion. The doctor said, "You don't need to be pregnant, let's see." He proceeded to perform a painful examination which resulted in a gush of blood and tissue emanating from my womb. He explained that he had performed an abortion called a "local D and C."

Soon after the Roe v. Wade decision, I became pregnant again. There was adverse pressure and threat of violence from the baby's father. The ease and convenience provided through Roe v. Wade made it too easy for me to make the fateful and fatal decision to abort our child. I went to a Planned Parenthood sanctioned doctor and was advised that the procedure would hurt no more than "having a tooth removed."

The next day, I was admitted to the hospital, and our baby was aborted. My medical insurance paid for the procedure. As soon as I woke up, I knew that something was very wrong. I felt very ill, and very empty. I tried to talk to the doctor and nurses about it. They assured me that "it will all go away in a few days. You will be fine." They lied.

Over the next few years, I experienced medical problems. I had trouble bonding with my son, and his five siblings who were born after the abortions. I began to suffer from eating disorders, depression, nightmares, sexual dysfunctions and a host of other issues related to the abortion that I chose to have. I felt angry about both the involuntary and voluntary abortions, and very guilty about the abortion I chose to have. The guilt made me very ill. Like my uncle, Dr. Martin Luther King, Jr. who had received the Margaret Sanger Planned Parenthood Award in 1968, I became a victim to the lies of Planned Parenthood. They told my uncle, they told me and millions of mothers and fathers that their agenda was to help our people. They lied. Their agenda is deadly!

I pray often for deliverance from the pain caused by my decision to abort my baby. I suffered the threat of cervical and breast cancer, and experienced the pain of empty arms after the baby was gone. Truly, for me, and countless abortive mothers, nothing on earth can fully restore what has been lost—only Jesus can.

My children have all suffered from knowing that they have a brother or sister that their mother chose to abort. Often they ask if I ever thought about aborting them, and they have said, "You killed our baby."

This is very painful for all of us. My mother and grandparents were very sad to know about the loss of the baby. The aborted child's father also regrets the abortions. If it had not been for Roe v. Wade, I would never have had that second abortion.

My birthday is January 22, and each year this special day is marred by the fact that it is also the anniversary of Roe v. Wade—and the anniversary of death for millions of babies. I and my deceased children are victims of abortion. The Roe v. Wade decision has adversely affected the lives of my entire family.

My grandfather, Dr. Martin Luther King, Sr., twice said, "No one is going to kill a child of mine." The first time Daddy King said this was to my mother, who was facing an "inconvenient pregnancy" with me. The next time, I was facing a pregnancy, and told him about it. In both instances, Daddy King said no, and saved his seed.

Tragically, two of his grandchildren had already been aborted when he saved the life of his next great-grandson with this statement. His son, Dr. Martin Luther King, Jr. once said, "The Negro cannot win as long as he is willing to sacrifice the lives of his children for immediate personal comfort and safety. Injustice anywhere is a threat to justice everywhere."

In light of Uncle Martin's prolife stance, I find it extremely troubling that Planned Parenthood uses a ploy of publishing a speech Dr. King didn't write or deliver to pretend that Dr. King would have supported their agenda of death.

Dr. Martin Luther King, Jr. was prolife. His wife Coretta was pro-choice. Mrs. King attended the Planned Parenthood Award Ceremony in 1966, read a speech written by someone other than her husband and accepted the Margaret Sanger Award in his name. Dr. Martin Luther King, Jr. did not attend the ceremony. He did not write the speech!

Like Mrs. Barbara Bush, and also Mrs. Laura Bush who in interviews and her book admits she is pro-abortion, while both of their husbands are prolife; Mrs. Coretta Scott King was at odds with her husband's ideology regarding life and human sexuality. These women chose platforms that were not reconciled to the reality of the blessings of procreative reproductive health leading to monogamous healthy marriages between husbands and wives; the births of healthy babies; and the continuation of God's plan for families nurtured in love and righteousness.

It is ludicrous to suggest that Martin Luther King, Jr. would have endorsed any acts that chemically or surgically dismember and kill babies in the womb; butcher women under falsehood of providing "safe abortions"; and hide the truth that many hysterectomies, breast cancer surgeries and other "female reproductive illnesses" are the result of abortion. They promote death over life in the name of abortion, and call it civil rights.

My uncle, Dr. Martin Luther King, Jr. could never have endorsed such tactics! This understanding leads me to ask this question:

How can the "Dream" survive if we murder our children? Every aborted baby is like a slave in the womb of his or her mother. In the hands of the mother is the fate of that child—whether the child lives or dies—a decision given to the mother by Roe v. Wade. That choice, the final choice of whether the child lives or dies, should be left to God, Who ultimately says "choose life!"

I join the voices of thousands across America, who are SILENT NO MORE. We can no longer sit idly by and allow this horrible spirit of murder to cut down, yes cut out and cut away, our unborn and destroy the lives of our mothers. Our babies and our mothers must live!

I am very grateful to God for the Spirit of Repentance that is sweeping our land. In repentance there is healing. In the name of Jesus, we must humble ourselves and pray, and turn from our wicked ways, so that God will hear from Heaven and Heal Our Land.

I, like my uncle, Martin Luther King, Jr., have a dream. I still have a dream that someday the men and women of our nation, the boys and girls of America will come to our senses, humble ourselves before God Almighty and receive His healing grace. I pray that this is the day and the hour of our deliverance. I pray that we will regain a covenant of life and finally obtain the promised liberty, justice and pursuit of happiness for all.

Let us end injustice anywhere by championing justice everywhere, including in the womb. May God, by His grace, have mercy on us all.

HE SAVED ME

By Sonya Howard
www.almostwasnt.com

"For God so loved the world, that He gave His only begotten Son, that whosoever believes on Him, should not perish, but should have everlasting life." John 3:16

If only I knew. Lying there staring into the bright light above my head, I was anxious to get it all over with. Finally, my life would 'go back to normal' and I would forget the mistake I made. No one would know my secret because they would take care of it.

As I left the clinic cramping, drowsy, and starving, I was temporarily relieved. His mom dropped me off at home; my mom was still at work and I was left alone with my conscience. As I laid there a sharp pain pierce through my heart—it felt like it was broken in half. A deep dark hole filled my stomach. And that's when I knew I had done something horrible.

'What have I done? I screamed inside. 'I just killed my baby!' what is wrong with me? God will never forgive me. Immediately I screamed to the top of my voice and began crying as if I were a two-year-old.

Satan tricked me that day. He made me believe killing my baby was a good thing. But thank God, because He was right holding me. He already knew I would abort my baby and all the consequences that would follow. It would take 20 years before I confessed my sin to God, but He was waiting on me and ready to forgive and restore me.

I was always alone. Why was that? All of that crying, worrying, and skipping meals, reduced me to head-turning hour-glass. I was young and all the men noticed. I wore the tightest, shortest shorts to show off my long brown sugar thighs.

I loved attention; from any male. Young boys did not appeal to me; I wanted a mature guy. He would tell me I was beautiful. I just hadn't found him yet; so I looked.

I didn't even mind if I had to sleep with him; every girl had to do that. He would see how special I was and he would be my boyfriend, and even married me some day.

Once I joined the Navy, I thought 'surely I will find the one, with such an array of choices, how could I not'. I had the true 'bad sailor' reputation of sleeping around. Even through the sexual transmitted diseases, I couldn't find him. All I was left with was loneliness. Why couldn't I be loved? Didn't I deserve to be loved?

Finally, a guy asked me to marry him. I didn't really love him, but that didn't matter. He promised he would always be there. He loved me; at least that's what he said. So I married him. After two years, he left me; even after all those promises. I thought my heart would crack again. I even thought I would lose my mind. I felt so betrayed.

'What is wrong with me? Why am I not lovable? Why does everyone leave me?'

I married again five years later. This guy, I really liked; we actually grew up together. But he didn't love me either. He knew my mom died and left me some money and only wanted to use me. I re-marrying him three times and dealt with his drug addiction. I had to keep trying; I already had one failed marriage.

Maybe I didn't do enough. After all, I am a Christian and I'should stick with him through it all. Finally, I had enough; I couldn't make him love me or chose. I was always at the bottom of his priorities. By the way, neither husbands wanted to take care of their child—how unlucky can one girl get?

But God! He knew my father would abandon me at age two and I would cling to every guy except Him. God was so sweet that He flushed out all those bad self-esteem issues and took His time to build me back up again. Now I know who I am and who I belong to. He loved on me, comforted me, and encouraged me through it all. He is keeping my body, mind, and soul pure until the husband He has for me, finds me.

"Girl, you're going to die; just like your mother. So what, if you don't drink, smoke, or curse? You love to eat and I'm going to fatten you up for the kill"—signed satan.

I laid there grasping for each breathe. It felt like I was under water and could not make it to the surface. My eyes bucked and my heart raced as I was aware that God was in charge of every breath that He allowed me to have.

My job didn't matter, my bills didn't matter, and my full schedule of activities definitely were nowhere on my mind. Every second I was aware that I could die. I had plenty of time to think about if I truly believe God's word and promises.

Satan tormented me that week in the hospital. He reminded me of all the times my doctor had pleaded with me to lose weight so that I could drop my medication. As I slowly dragged to the rest room with the oxygen tube in my nose, he flashed a picture in the mirror of my mother when she too lived with an oxygen tank, until Cancer wiped her out.

'You are fat. Nobody loves you. Nobody even cares you are about to die. You can't lose this weight and now I have you right where I want you', satan bragged.

But guess who else never left my side, my Lord and Savior, Jesus Christ. He told me 'this will not take you out. You will live past this. I love you and have given you a vision to help millions of your girls and you will do just that. I don't lie. Keep your mind and heart on me and trust me to pull you through this; even while you are struggling for each breath.'

I knew then that I had to choose who I would believe. I chose God and he rescued me. With God's help, I will conquer this battle to lose weight and I trust him to help me.

God has saved me through so many trials. I have only mentioned a few. Whether you are struggling with abortion, self-esteem, sickness, or anything else, He can save you too.

Reach out to him.

BILL BENNETT, BLACKS ABORTION AND CRIME

Day Gardner
www.blackprolifeunion.com

It seems everyone is talking about the recent statement made by talk show host Bill Bennett about abortion and Black babies.

It is my understanding that Bennett is pro-life and opposes abortion. However, what everyone is so upset about is the fact that, as an example on his radio show, he stated that the crime rate would drop if all Black babies were aborted.

With that remark, Bennett opened up a can of worms that I believe we should not try to seal back up. We must admit that there are those who think the world would be safer with fewer Black teenagers. And it is important to know that Bennett is not the first person to discuss a link between African-Americans, crime and abortion.

On August 9, 1999, the Associated Press ran a story headlined, "Study Suggests Link Between Crime Drop, Legal Abortion." Its sub-headline read, "Researchers Conclude That Unwanted Children are the Most Likely to Break the Law." The authors concluded, in part, that those most likely to give birth to "unwanted" children are minorities and the poor.

In fact, the co-author of that 1999 study, Steven D. Levitt, is the author of the recent bestseller Freakonomics. This is the book Bennett referenced when he made his controversial comment. While Levitt's book did not tie race and abortion, his 1999 study makes it obvious that he must have had that notion in mind as he was writing the book.

It's telling about the agenda of Bennett's critics that they are focusing their rage on him rather than the source of such an abominable theory.

Black Americans must wake up to the ugly truth that there are many who think the answer to fixing our society's problems is to reduce the number of Black Americans through abortion. The fact is that there are those who think Blacks who reside in our inner cities are nothing more than poor welfare recipients who just sit around selling drugs and committing crimes all day.

These people believe that our children will only grow up to be worthless criminals, so they place abortion facilities at our doors. "We'll convince them that we are helping their race and making it affordable to kill their children," they must think. "And the big plus is that we can lower the crime rate!"

If what I am saying is not true, then why is it that abortion providers pick our neighborhoods to set up shop?

According to the Alan Guttmacher Institute, the research arm of Planned Parenthood of America, more than 90 percent of all abortion facilities are placed in minority and poor areas—mostly in the inner cities. The Cybercast News Service similarly compared the location of abortion facilities with population data from the U.S. Census in 2000, with the results bolstering the charge that the abortion industry targets Black communities. Black people need to know this and see it for what it really is.

Therefore, in my opinion, Bill Bennett just brought to light a fact that has been well hidden since the 1973 Supreme Court decision in Roe v. Wade. To date, more than 14 million Black babies have been targeted and killed by abortion. This makes abortion the leading killer of African-Americans.

Bill Bennett only spoke aloud about what some people have been thinking all along.

Though the media may try to divert our focus to chastising the messenger, I am praying that Black America will look deeper in to the message and stand firmly against the notion that our Black children are criminals even before they are born.

'DANGEROUS UNCONSTITUTIONAL HHS ABORTIFACIENT/ CONTRACEPTIVE/STERILIZATION MANDATE HURTS WOMEN—NOT HEALTHCARE'

ATLANTA, March 19, 2012 /Christian Newswire/—The following is submitted by Dr. Alveda King:

There are eight law suits addressing the unconstitutionality of the HHS ACS MANDATE. Added to their legal argument is the fact that abortion and it's "cousins" are not health care. Many in the pro-life movement versus anti-life debate are reluctant to make a connection between contraception and abortion. They insist that these are two very different acts—that there is all the difference in the world between contraception, which prevents a life from coming to be and abortion, which takes a life that has already begun.

To the contrary, with some contraceptives there is not only a link with abortion, there is a relationship. Some contraceptives are abortifacients; they work by causing early term abortions. The IUD likely prevents a fertilized egg—a young human being—from implanting in the uterine wall. The pill does not always stop ovulation, but sometimes prevents implantation of the growing embryo. And, of course, the new RU-486 pill works altogether by aborting a new fetus/baby.

Few talk about how abortions and artificial birth control not only kill and/or prevent the birth of babies, they are also very bad for women's health. Both, for instance, are linked to controversial breast cancer discussions.

A gray area—forced or coerced sterilization. The most visible and classic case of forced sterilization is noted in the testimony of Elaine Riddick. Her case, and those of other women who were sterilized in North Carolina is currently being considered for new litigation.

Dr. Chris Kahlenborn's book: Breast Cancer, Its Link to Abortion and the Birth Control Pill brings seven years the research, review and analysis of more than 500 studies and related works. It is very timely because of the breast cancer epidemic, which currently threatens every woman. Both abortion and artificial birth control are linked to breast cancer.

Research shows that induced abortion increases the risk of breast cancer for all women with Black women and other minorities having higher rates. Black women number higher and also tend to develop more aggressive cancers. There is also a greater risk in women who have had abortions if they were under age 18 at the time; if they do not have any more children after aborting; or if they have a family history of breast cancer. Family history of breast cancer sometimes also shows family history of abortions.

In 2009, in a study of more than 50,000 African-American women, Boston University epidemiologist Lynn Rosenberg found a 65 percent increase in a particularly aggressive form of breast cancer among those who had ever taken the birth-control pill. The risk doubles for those who had used the contraceptive within the past five years and had taken it for longer than 10 years.

Rosenberg studies black women because they have been underserved in cancer research so far, even though they suffer from higher rates of "triple negative" breast cancer. Rosenberg's findings linked these cases to the "pill." A number of other studies of women of multiple ethnic groups support her research linking the pill to breast cancer, including research done in New England; South Carolina; Long Island, N.Y.; and Scandinavia.

Breast cancer in the U.S. is more prevalent in young black women than in white women of equivalent age, and is the second leading cause of cancer death (after lung cancer) among black women. This may be a consequence of more common hormonal contraceptive use and/or a greater frequency of abortion among young black women. Black women who develop breast cancer generally have more aggressive cancers resulting in a shortened life expectancy.

It has been noted that while Black American's make up approximately 13% or less of America's population, nearly 33% of abortions reported since the passage of Roe v Wade in 1973 have occurred on Black Women. Planned Parenthood, the nation's largest abortion provider, who also distributes free or low cost artificial abortion drugs has a highly targeted market to Black Women. So, Black women are at a higher risk for abortions and breast cancer and other health related problems as a consequence of being marketed for the causes.

How does abortion impact breast cancer?

At the beginning of pregnancy there are great increases in certain hormone levels (eg. estrogen, progesterone, and HCG) that support pregnancy. In response to these changes, breast cells divide and mature into cells able to produce milk. Abortion causes an abrupt fall in hormone levels, leaving the breast cells in an immature state. These immature cells can more easily become cancer cells. Read more HERE.

As of January 1999, 11 out of 12 studies in the United States, and 25 out of 31 studies worldwide, showed that women who experienced an induced abortion had an increased risk of breast cancer. In 1996 Joel Brind, PhD [1], assembled the results of all the studies up to that time. Brind concluded that women who have an abortion before their first full-term pregnancy have a 50% increased risk of developing breast cancer while those who have an abortion after their first full-term pregnancy have a 30% increased risk.

A 50% increased risk means a 50% higher risk than someone would have otherwise. For example, if a person already had a 10% risk of developing breast cancer, then a 50% increase would bring the risk up to 15%.

ABC Breast Cancer Link

Breast cancer is the worldwide leading cancer in women and is the most common cause of cancer death for U.S. women age 20-59. In the U.S. every year about 175,000 women are diagnosed with breast cancer and more than 43,000 women die from this disease. This means that about one U.S. woman out of eight will develop breast cancer at some time in her life and about one fourth of such women will die from this disease. Induced abortion, especially at a young age, markedly increases a woman's risk for developing breast cancer. This risk is increased even further by other breast cancer risk factors such as synthetic hormones (including hormonal contraceptives like the Birth Control Pill, Norplant and Depo-Provera), family history of breast cancer, and others.

Abortion and Fibromyalgia

Psychiatrist and researcher Dr. Philip Ney relates the story of a patient of his who developed fibromyalgia, which causes chronic pain without any apparent cause. He found that she had undergone an abortion just before this pain began, and since then, has developed a theory that in some cases, the pain of fibromyalgia may in fact be caused by chemicals released by the aborted baby's flesh when it is torn apart. These chemicals cross the placenta, and lodge in the mother's nervous system. In reality, she is feeling not her own pain, but that of her aborted child. We have not yet begun to understand all the implications of abortion, and of how destroying a child in the womb destroys the rest of us. Let's pray that our society may forsake abortion and find healing.

Physical Effects and Psychological Effects of Abortion (WEBA)

— Sterility—Guilt
— Miscarriages—Suicidal impulses
— Ectopic pregnancies—Mourning/Withdrawal
— Stillbirths—Regret/Remorse
— Bleeding and infections—Loss of confidence
— Shock and comas—Low self-esteem
— Perforated uterus—Preoccupation with death
— Peritonitis—Hostility/Rage
— Fever/Cold sweat—Despair/Helplessness
— Intense pain—Desire to remember birth date
— Loss of body organs—Intense interest in babies
— Crying/Sighing—Thwarted maternal instincts
— Insomnia—Hatred for persons connected with abortion
— Loss of appetite—Desire to end relationship with partner
— Exhaustion—Loss of sexual interest/Frigidity
— Weight loss—Inability to forgive self
— Nervousness—Nightmares
— Decreased work capacity—Seizures and tremors
— Vomiting—Feeling of being exploited
— Gastro-intestinal disturbances—Horror of child abuse

Additional Effects of Harm Caused by certain "reproductive health care" procedures

— Premature Labor and Births due to weakened cervix, scarred and/
or perforated uterine walls, etc. (Note: the IUD and surgical
abortion procedures have been known to cut or scar the woman's
reproductive organs)
— Trauma to Mammary System
— Trauma to Reproductive System
— Exposure to STD germs where failure to properly sterilize
instruments occur
— Permanent Sterility (leaving the woman no option to changing her
mind later)

Conclusion

It may not be immediately obvious that there is any connection between
contraception and abortion, but on further examination, a relationship
between the two becomes apparent. Ignoring the issue of contraception
leads to a lost opportunity to respect life to the fullest degree. Neither
abortion nor artificial contraception are health care. There are at least three
connections between contraception and abortion to consider:

1. Many contraceptives can directly cause early abortions.
2. Contraceptive use creates a perceived need for abortion as a
"back-up."
3. Contraceptive use causes a devaluation of human life.
4. Both abortions and artificial contraceptives are bad for women's
health.

End Notes:

*Somehow, for political reasons, selfish gain, lack of knowledge and other
variables, there are very obvious solutions that are not on the general or public
radar.*

BREAKING NEWS!

1. *Women do not have to have unplanned or undesirable pregnancies in
most cases. It is a scientific and medical fact that a woman can't become
pregnant if she is not ovulating. There are inexpensive ovulation kits
on the market that women can obtain and exercise power and control*

over their right to get pregnant or not. A woman should have the right to say when she will and will not have sex. She should have the right and knowledge to control her reproductive rights.

2. *There are natural and relatively inexpensive solutions for women who have irregular cycles and ovulation schedules. There is generally no need for invasive measures such as artificial drugs and such in these cases.*

3. *The $365 million a year, $1 million per day that our government tax dollars pay to Planned Parenthood who is the nation's largest abortion provider does not provide information and resources regarding reproductive freedom regarding ovulation and pregnancy choices to women.*

4. *If women do not have sex when they ovulate, there is no reason for them to take harmful chemical and surgical birth control measures, many of which are known to cause heart attacks, strokes, exposure to possibility of cancer and other illnesses.*

So the question is why is it so hard to break through the information barriers surrounding women's health and reproductive rights? Could it be that people on each side of the isle, each side of the arguments have so much vested in their own interests that everyone has forgotten the women and the babies in the midst of the melee?

TRAYVON MARTIN: ANOTHER LIFE CUT SHORT

Saddened by the "Senseless Killing" of Trayvon Martin, Black Prolife Leaders call for Nonviolent Action

Atlanta, GA—March 26, 2012: "Trayvon Martin's death is senseless, and we are deeply grieved that a young man's future has been aborted and hidden under a cloak of Florida's "Stand Your Ground law," says Dr. Alveda King, daughter of slain civil rights strategist Rev. A. D. King, and his widow, Mrs. Naomi King.

King whose father was also a victim of a violent death in 1969, says that she is "praying for the family of young Trayvon." The youth was killed in Florida by George Zimmerman, a man who has sidestepped arrest so far by citing the Stand Your Ground law in Florida. This law gives citizens license to claim self defense in wielding a firearm. King, who recognizes the constitutional provision to bear firearms for protection of individuals and their families, is admittedly concerned about "motives of those who shoot at will. After all, my uncle, Dr. Martin Luther King, Jr. and my grandmother, Mrs. Alberta King were shot to death by firearms."

Florida is only one of 21 states with such laws, which have since come under intense scrutiny even by previous supporters. Prior to that law being passed in Florida, there were 13 "justified" killings in the state in previous years. Since then, there have been 36 such killings, as reported by the Associated Press.

Trayvon's case has sparked controversy across America. Some have gone so far as to suggest that that Trayvon may have opened himself up as a target by wearing a hooded sweatshirt. For others, this argument touches on gang war violence, where youths are slain because of the colors they wear or where they choose to walk in their neighborhoods.

"To place the blame on a youth for wearing a "hoodie" is to play over into potential racial profiling if we aren't careful," says King.

Other members of the Black Prolife Community are also concerned about the death of the Florida youth. "All too often, people say that the Black Prolife Community is only concerned about the issue of abortion. Nothing could be further from the truth. We mourn Trayvon's death because his life has been cut off."

Day Gardner, founder of the National Black Prolife Union added: "Our hearts go out to the family of Trayvon, his young life cut so short. As we pray for other lives lost, including those in the womb, it is important for us to remember that every life is sacred, from conception and fertilization until natural death. There was nothing natural about the killing of Trayvon, and we are saddened."

The leaders are calling for soul searching nonviolent peaceful conflict resolution as justice is sought for Trayvon Martin, "a young Black man who is now denied his freedom to experience life, liberty and the pursuit of happiness."

OPEN LETTER: THE BELOVED COMMUNITY AND THE UNBORN

As our nation pauses to recommit itself to fulfilling the dream of Dr. Martin Luther King, Jr., we invite our fellow citizens to reflect on how that dream touches every human life. Dr. King taught that justice and equality need to be as wide-reaching as humanity itself. Nobody can be excluded from the Beloved Community. He taught that "injustice anywhere is a threat to justice everywhere."

In his 1967 Christmas sermon, he pointed out the foundation of this vision: *"The next thing we must be concerned about if we are to have peace on earth and good will toward men is the nonviolent affirmation of the sacredness of all human life. . . . Man is a child of God, made in His image, and therefore must be respected as such . . . . And when we truly believe in the sacredness of human personality, we won't exploit people, we won't trample over people with the iron feet of oppression, we won't kill anybody."*

Scripture teaches, "Seek first God's Kingdom and His righteousness and all else shall be yours as well" (Matthew 6:33). Dr. King humbled himself before God and became increasingly dependent on Him. Dr. King's search for the "Beloved Community" was really part of his search for the Kingdom of God. Because "God is Love" (1 John 4:16), His Kingdom is founded on love (*agape*). That is why, in his search for the Beloved Community, Dr. King discovered God's love.

The work of building the Beloved Community is far from finished. In each age, it calls us to fight against poverty, discrimination, and violence in every form. And as human history unfolds, the forms that discrimination and violence take will evolve and change. Yet our commitment to overcome them must not change, and we must not shrink from the work of justice, no matter how unpopular it may become.

In our day, therefore, we cannot ignore the discrimination, injustice, and violence that are being inflicted on the youngest and smallest members of the human family, the children in the womb. Thousands of these children are killed every day in America by abortion, throughout all nine months of pregnancy.

We declare today that these children too are members of the Beloved Community, that our destiny is linked with theirs, and that therefore they deserve justice, equality, and protection.

And we can pursue that goal, no matter what ethnic, religious, or political affiliation we have. None of that has to change in order for us to embrace Dr. King's affirmation of the sacredness of *all* human life. It simply means that in our efforts to set free the oppressed, we include the children in the womb.

We invite all people of good will to join us in the affirmation that children in the womb have equal rights and human dignity.

Dr. Alveda King, Director of African American Outreach, Priests for Life

Father Frank Pavone, National Director, Priests for Life

Mrs. Naomi King, Widow of Rev. A. D. King

Rev. Derek King, Professor of Nonviolent Conflict Resolution

Dr. Lynne Jackson, Great-great granddaughter of Dred Scott

Dr. Gloria Jackson, Great granddaughter of Booker T. Washington

LIBERTY

NO MORE STUMBLING BLOCKS: LET OUR CHILDREN GO!

By Jennifer Beal
www.urbanmothersonthemove.org

A quality education system is essential for the success of a nation. In the past, America prided itself on providing the necessary tools not only to compete, but also to lead the world in technology, industry and space exploration. That is no longer the case.

Compared to the rest of the world, the state of education in America is disappointing and embarrassing. After World War II, the United States' had the number 1 high school graduation rate. Today, we have dropped to number 21 among industrialized nations. American students rank 25th in math and 21st in science compared to students in 30 industrialized countries. Even America's top math students rank 25th out of 30 when compared with the best students across the globe. While America spends more money each year on education, we are losing more and more American students. While we agree that no American student should be left out, written off or ignored, far too many of our poorest and minority students today still lack adequate resources to learn.

The children of today are our hope for tomorrow! They are the future leaders that will help solve many of the social ills such as violence, drug abuse and poverty. They must be equipped with the necessary tools and, more importantly, they must possess the hunger for knowledge and service. Adults have an obligation to help children—all children—learn and be prepared for life. Quality education is an American "right," and our children deserve nothing less.[1]

Education is an American issue that affects us all. Jobs are leaving this country and American employers say that students today lack the basic skills to do even the simplest jobs. Without dramatic changes, the U.S. economy will continue to suffer, crime will go up and our children won't be able to find a job or afford a house. Educated people make better neighbors, colleagues, parents and responsible citizens. If we do not create dramatically new opportunities to educate our youth, our standard of living will decline, our democracy will be at risk and we will continue to fall behind as other countries surpass us.

The basic concept of choice has become the cry of many citizens. School choice—which involves vouchers, tax credits, public, private, and charter schools, along with home schooling—is a solution for all America. Not just for white or black, rich or poor, but for everyone. For everyone can benefit from having the opportunity to choose the best learning environment to help each student achieve his or her greatest potential.

This article seeks to outline and in the process enlighten as to why school choice is imperative for the survival of the United States as a super power. Educational choice is not about the welfare of just some cities, counties or states: It will touch us all, whether we are parents, students or educators. An improved educational standard will benefit everyone.

History of formal education in America

Education in its broadest, general sense is the means through which the aims and habits of a group of people lives on from one generation to the next.[2] Hundreds of years ago, most learning happened at home. Parents taught their children or, if their families could afford it, private tutors did the job. The Puritans were the first in this country to point out the need for some kind of public education. They established schools to teach not just the essentials-reading, writing and math—but also to reinforce their core values.

After the American Revolution, Thomas Jefferson argued that the newly independent nation needed an educational system, and he suggested that

---

[1]   http://broadeducation.org/about/crisis.html

[2]   Dewey, John (1916/1944). Democracy and Education. The Free Press. pp. 1-4.

tax dollars be used to fund it. His pleas were ignored, however, and the idea for a public school system languished for nearly a century. By the 1840s, a few public schools had popped up around the country in the communities that could afford them. However, that smattering of schools wasn't good enough for education crusaders Horace Mann of Massachusetts and Henry Barnard of Connecticut. They began calling for free, compulsory school for every child in the nation.

Massachusetts passed the first compulsory school laws in 1852. New York followed the next year, and by 1918, all American children were required to attend at least elementary school.

Next came the movement to create equal schooling for all American children, no matter what their race. At the turn of the 20th century, schools in the South, and many in the North, were segregated. The 1896 Supreme Court ruling, Plessy v. Ferguson upheld the legality of segregation. Finally, in 1954, the Supreme Court overturned its ruling with the landmark case, Brown v. Board of Education, and public schools became open to people of all races.

Although segregation was outlawed in the late fifties, most public schools remained separate and unequal. In many parts of the United States, after the 1954 decision in the landmark court case Brown v. Board of Education of Topeka that demanded US schools desegregate "with all deliberate speed", local families organized a wave of private "Christian academies". In much of the US South, many white students migrated to the academies, while public schools became in turn more heavily concentrated with African American students. The academic content of the academies was usually College Preparatory. Since the 1970s, many of these "segregation academies" have shut down, although some continue to operate.

The Supreme Court decision in Miliken v. Bradley in 1974-that desegregation cannot take place across school districts-creates practical limits to desegregation efforts in urban districts as well as those in wealthy suburbs. Also in 1974, District 4-the Harlem District of New York City Schools-creates an intra-district school choice program.

In the 1980s, the first charter schools are set up in Minnesota. In 1990-91, the first voucher legislation that allows a choice of public or private secular schools is passed by the Wisconsin legislature. Also in 1991, Minnesota creates a statewide, inter-district choice system, which has spread to sixteen more states in the next decade.

In 1994, Proposition 187, which says that it is illegal for children of illegal immigrants to attend public school is passed in California. It is declared unconstitutional in Federal court. In 1995, religious schools become an accepted alternative in Wisconsin's school choice program, and the following year, Ohio allows vouchers to be used for religious schools.

By the 1999-2000 school year, a quarter of K-12 students are no longer attending their local neighborhood school, according to a survey conducted by the National Center for Educational Statistics (NCES).[3]

Public Education in America

As President John Adams said "The whole people must take upon themselves the education of the whole people and be willing to bear the expenses of it. There should not be a district of one mile square, without a school in it, not founded by a charitable individual, but maintained at the public expense of the people themselves."

To understand the impact that school choice will have on America, one must first examine the status of public education in America. We are losing a generation of American minds. American students are not learning the skills and knowledge they need to succeed in today's world. Today, 70 percent of our eighth graders can't read proficiently and most of them will never catch up. Some 1.1 million American high school students drop out every year. [4]

As of fall 2011, population increases and high enrollment rates led to America's schools welcoming back record numbers of students. In particular, more prekindergarten and kindergarten students entered U.S. public school systems than ever before.

As of Fall 2011, over 49.4 million students attend public elementary and secondary schools.

Public schools have become more interested in passing children on to the next grade level without mastering necessary requirements. Grading systems are rewarding effort more than achievement. Self-esteem is what matters instead of skills. Across America, public schools are giving grades of pass/fail, or circles and squares instead of the traditional numerical systems. Students are also receiving inflated grades which do not reflect their true academic level.

---

3   http://www.educationbug.org/a/history-of-public-schools.html
4   http://broadeducation.org/about/crisis.html

The most often stated reasons of public schools shortcomings: large classroom size and unqualified educators. Because of educators who do not understand this culture, our children fail to matriculate. If all inner city and rural public school systems truly wanted to educate these children, they would have already made the necessary changes to increase low test scores, decrease school violence and motivate higher learning. Students are assigned to public schools based on their home address. Schools are funded based on the taxes of the school area. No wonder so many schools are failing. It is clear that it is not always the amount of money spent, but how the money is allocated. Public schools spend the bulk of their money on administrative costs. A small percentage of pupil allocations actually gets to the classroom.

Where do professional educators send their own children to learn? According to a report published by the Fordham Institute, urban public school teachers are more likely than either urban households or the general public to send their children to private schools. Across the states, 12.2 percent of all families (urban, rural, and suburban) send their children to private schools—a figure that roughly corresponds to perennial and well-known data on the proportion of U.S. children enrolled in private schools. But urban public school teachers send their children to private schools at a rate of 21.5 percent; nearly double the national rate of private-school attendance. Urban public school teachers are also more likely to send their children to private school than are urban families in general (21.5 vs. 17.5 percent).[5] This report reveals that teachers are don't trust the public school system with their own children's education. This is a serious dichotomy. How can society trust public schools if the teachers don't?

With theses startling statistics, it is obvious that public schooling must elevate itself and welcome educational choice, in order to prepare our children and to survive in the new millennium.

Educational choice will force public schools to develop successful curriculums and safe learning environments in order to keep their doors open. Competition in the educational field for primary through secondary levels will only enhance children's learning opportunities.

---

[5]   http://www.wispolitics.com/1006/_fordham_study.pdf

Private Education in America

The idea of private school is often viewed as a superior alternative to public education. In the United States, the term "private school" can be correctly applied to any school for which the facilities and funding are not provided by the federal, state or local government; as opposed to a "public school", which is operated by the government or in the case of charter schools, independently with government funding and regulation.

Religious institutions and organizations operate the majority of private schools in the United States. Funding for private schools is generally provided through student tuition, endowments, scholarship/voucher funds, and donations and grants from religious organizations or private individuals. Government funding for religious schools is either subject to restrictions or possibly forbidden, according to the courts' interpretation of the Establishment Clause of the First Amendment.

The average tuition for a private school in the United States is approximately $8,500 a year.

The National Center for Education Statistics reported that private school students scored higher on standardized tests, had more demanding graduation requirements, and sent more graduates to college than public schools. The report said that students who had completed at least the eighth grade in a private school were twice as likely as other students to graduate from college as a young adult. NCES statistics also showed that students in private schools are much more likely than others to take advanced-level high school courses.[6]

Gaps between minority students and majority students are narrowed in private schools. According to NCES, minority students in private schools are more than twice as likely to enter four-year colleges than their counterparts in public schools, making private schools the nation's greatest hope for boosting minority participation in society from boardroom to classroom.[7]

---

[6] U.S. Department of Education, National Center for Education Statistics, Private Schools: A Brief Portrait (NCES 2002-013) (Washington, D.C., 2002) tables 11 and 12, figures 9 and 10.

[7] College-going rates were provided to CAPE by the National Center for Education Statistics using data from the National Education Longitudinal

University of Chicago economist, Derek Nea has found in his research that many minorities who are not Catholic choose Catholic education. In urban areas, this parochial schooling increased the probability of high school and college graduation rates, with the probability of graduating from high school rising from 62 to 88 percent. New York City Mayor Rudolph Giuliani, taking notice of this data, has asked New York City to use the Roman Catholic schools as an educational blueprint. He has also pointed out that although in New York the Catholic and public schools enroll about the same percentages of children with risk factors for failure; Catholic schools have a dropout rate of 0.1 percent while public schools have an 18 percent dropout rate. In addition, Catholic schools only have an expulsion factor of 2%.

Middle and lower income families have always wanted the same opportunities that affluent children are granted. Most important of all, they want equality and freedom for their children. High standards, safe environments, caring and knowledgeable teachers, with a strong concentration in reading, writing and mathematics are many of the cited reasons as to why parents choose private schools.

A Developing Educational Force: The Charter School

The charter school is another alternative to public schools which fail to educate all children. Charter schools offer educationally sound curriculums, smaller classrooms, educated and committed teachers, and a safe environment for learning. Because a vast number of students who graduate from public schools are functionally illiterate, the charter school has become an appealing solution, especially to minority and low income children.

According to the U.S. Department of Education, in 1997 there were 50 million children in public schools. In 1995, there were 45 million students in public schools. Of that 45 million, 2.5 million graduated from high school. Shockingly, of that 2.5 million, over 1 million were functionally illiterate! If that is not enough to open one's eyes, here is some more data about public education in America. From 40 to 45% of seniors graduating from teaching colleges and universities are incompetent to teach. With the

---

Study of 1988 (NELS: 88). Details are available in the September 2001 issue of CAPE Outlook

bottom of the barrel of teaching applicants being employed at inner city schools, it is no mystery why there is a problem. It is clear: the need for charter schools is growing each year.

In April of 1996, T. Willard Fair, the president and chief executive officer of the liberal Urban League of Miami, Fl., teamed up with the Reverend R.B. Holmes of Tallahassee and became key advocates of a charter school law. With the name The Florida Plan, this law allows any innovative individual to establish a school. These schools are unique because they are free of the red tape that binds most public schools. Charter schools are free to operate without state imposed standards.

Willard Fair worked with Jeb Bush, the 1994 Republican candidate for governor, to get the legislation passed. Fair, who created Florida's first charter school, whose student body is largely black and low income, views public schools as "too regulated, entrenched in bureaucracy, with overcrowded classrooms, out of control children, and teacher who are not held accountable due to too much union interference."

Following in Fair's footsteps, R.B. Holmes opened the C.K. Steele—Leroy Collins charter School. Its population is 75% black. This school is similar to a Christian school that the also established. He describes his school as a place that "all people (whether) black, white, rich or poor want to send their kids too."

Many people like Holmes see charter schools as upholding the standards of excellence, parental involvement, and discipline. It's a place where children won't be lost in the cracks and academic achievement is top priority.

Another argument in support of charter schools comes from the Hudson Institute's Educational Excellence Network. This report revealed that there is a high level of satisfaction among most students attending charter schools. These schools have clearly defined academic expectations, committed educators, individualized instruction, plus a safe and familiar learning environment. Of all the students attending these schools nationwide, 63% belong to a racial minority.

It is quite clear that charter schools are a positive alternative to inner city and other unsuccessful public schools. Charter schools have done an excellent job in recognizing and fulfilling the needs of the poor. With parents wanting their voices heard and understood regarding the education crisis, the charter school is an emerging and powerful force to be reckoned with.

Home-based Education

Once upon a time in America, people were educated at homes by parents, relatives or neighbors. Each family knew what subjects and life skills that were needed for adulthood and the world of work. Even in those early days, there was educational choice. Choice existed because parents, who are children's first teachers, were not bound by state laws and regulations. In essence, every child had an individualized education plan.

With prayer being outlawed in the public school system, many families have looked for an alternative learning environment that would emphasize morals, values, and religious beliefs, in addition to academics. A private education was not an option for some families because of the extra economic cost. So many mothers and fathers decided to teach their children at home, as in days gone by.

At first, this seemed like a radical, far-fetched idea, but look at the facts. Parents know their children better than anyone else. They know how to motivate them and what learning styles and environments fit their needs. In the nineties, the first major "reported groups" of home schooling have been graduating and entering college. Home-schoolers have been scoring just as well or higher on standardized tests, and—most importantly—they have not been compromising their families' values and morals.

For many parents, a key reason for home schooling is safety. At home, they do not have to worry about weapons, gangs, drugs and bullies. As public schools have become more and more unsuccessful and dangerous, home schooling has become more and more acceptable.

Home schooling should be a party of educational choice and families who make this sacrifice should receive some type of compensation. When a family decides to educate their child at home, they should receive a tax credit. While some people argue, this is somehow unfair; it is unfair not to give them this credit! When children don't attend public schools communities still collect the same amount of tax dollars. Why not help families who, on most occasions, must sacrifice one income in the family in order to educate their children?

Home schooling has withstood hundreds of years and various forms of educational change. It has remained a viable force in the educational process. With computers entering into more homes, home-based education is becoming increasingly popular. If we are the great nation that we were created to be, then we should seriously look for ways to help families succeed. With education being the most crucial aspect of a civilized nation, we must accept home-based education as a part of school choice, and give tax credits to families using this choice.

A Quality education is Not Only a Necessity but a Civil Right!

As the world approaches a new and exciting time in history, there is a new civil rights struggle that will determine if the United States remains as great as her founding father hoped. In the 60's, Dr. Martin Luther King, Jr. had a dream that was rooted in the American Dream. That dream was for blacks and minorities to have the same opportunities as whites.

In education, separate but equal was a myth created to keep minorities in their place. Dr. King knew that the success of this nation rested upon quality education for all Americans, and that meant equality in education.

Now there is a powerful wake-up call, 30 years after the racial civil rights struggle, Dr. King talked about America's "promissory note" to deliver to all of its people the unalienable right to life, liberty and the pursuit of happiness. He dreamed of an America where all children, regardless of their color, religion or other circumstances, would enjoy the full exercise of those rights.

For our children, an education that equips its students with the necessary tools for excellence is an integral part of this pursuit. The King family believed in educational choice, and so do many people across America. Dr. King along with his brother the Rev. A.D. King, and their sister, Christine King Farris attended both public and private educational institutions.

Alveda's father, A.D. King continued in this family tradition by sending Alveda to public and private school. Even though a divorced single mother, Alveda managed to maintain this family tradition by educating her six children in both public and private settings. If Dr. Martin Luther King, Jr. was alive Jr. was alive today, he would join us in this fight for this essential civil right, as would Alveda's father who was assassinated less than a year after his brother Martin.

There are only a small percentage of families who can afford to pay taxes to support public school while at the same time sending their children to private schools. Even more critical, there are fewer families who can live in neighborhoods where the public schools are excellent, because the majority of successful public schools are in areas where the revenue is plentiful from property taxes.

It is a travesty that this country has allowed families suffering from economic deprivation and inequality to be trapped in failing school systems. This is the worst possible violation of one's civil right; for a quality education is a necessity, not a privilege. There are many hard working families who pay taxes who are trying to rescue their children from the nightmare of failing schools and bleak futures. They have been told that they do not have the "right" to use their tax dollars to provide the best possible education for their children.

In other words, the message has been simply this: If you are not privileged and blessed with the economic power to live in an upper income neighborhood, your child doesn't deserve the best education.

Wake up America! We are not talking about whether a child wears designer jeans or discount jeans. This is about something of substance: an investment in our future. Education has been and will always be the main factor that can unhook the shackles of poverty. All children born are a part of this future. Children come into this world with an innocence and hope that will be meaningful and filled with success. All children are created equal. Why should we not do everything possible to give them equal educational opportunity? The poor child that is placed in a failing school could be the one that discovers a cure for AIDS with the right education. The little brown-skinned boy from the inner city without a father at home may be blessed by God and given a drive so intense that he cures cancer.

We can't afford to pick and choose which children will be successful, based on their parents' achievements. There must be no more hesitation: we must have sincere acceptance—and provision—of quality education for all. For this nation, our children are precious pots of gold at the end of the rainbow. Unlike most rainbows, however, the gold can be claimed, for the nation's continued economic growth and cultural enrichment.

School choice will fulfill this promise and help this world move even closer to the day when all God's children will not be judged by the color of their skin but by the content of their character. Education builds character and destroys ignorance, fear and poverty. We are all one America—red and yellow, black and white—all of us are precious in God's sight. We must admit that our children are in trouble. We must act now to rescue our children first, and in so doing, rescue our schools. Without educational choice, there is a similarity to the bondage of slavery. Choice of education will finally free us from this powerful and deadly evil.

Be a part of the freedom train! Join the thousands of mothers, fathers, educators, concerned citizens, and even children: fight for this important freedom. Let's allow school choice to build a better a more productive and a safer nation for us all. May the Lord help us to turn those stumbling blocks into building blocks for a happier and truly free America! Let's finally remove these stumbling blocks of low standards, violence and illiteracy, and be proud to say that all of America's children are ready to lead this nation to a bright and productive future.

BULLYING: LEGISLATION AND LOVE

By Eddie Beal, Esq.

(The following is, in part, excerpted from Overcoming Bullying and Harassment in the U.S. Educational System: Building a foundation of Nonviolent Conflict Resolution, an analysis of the legal approach to solving the problem of bullying in American schools.)

INTRODUCTION

Access to a quality education is one of the key ingredients that a child must have in order to obtain success in the future. Without a quality education, children are prevented from obtaining the tools that allow them to make valuable contributions to society. In the United States, the U.S. Department of Education has the goals of promoting student achievement and providing students with equal access to education.[8] School districts that fail to comply with these goals undoubtedly open themselves up to liability.

Currently, one of the greatest threats posed to access to a quality education comes from bullying and harassment that occurs in schools. The 1999 Columbine High School massacre in Colorado led to a nationwide

---

[8]   Lee, Mark. "How Important is Education?" uas education article directory : http://www.uaseducation.com/articles/355/1/How-Important-is-Education/ Page1.html

effort to prevent bullying and harassment in schools.[9] The Columbine tragedy demonstrated to a nationwide audience what the end result of bullying and harassment in school could be. As a result of this, states throughout the country have passed Anti-Bullying statues to address the threat posed by bullying and harassment in schools. However, even with this increased nationwide legislative focus on the problem, the current body of law throughout the United States is insufficient to adequately address bullying and harassment in the educational system.

This paper is an attempt to review and discuss many of the complicated issues surrounding bullying and harassment in schools. I will begin by discussing the state of bullying and harassment as they exist in schools today, and the effects that it imposes on the overall educational system. I will then discuss the state of the law as it attempts to prevent bullying and harassment through the use of legislative means.

THE STATE OF BULLYING

Bullying and harassment are clearly major problems that are occurring throughout educational systems nationwide. The prevalence of bullying and harassing conduct in schools cannot be understated. By some estimates, approximately 15% of children either bully or are bullied regularly.[10] Both males and females engage in bullying conduct as both victims and bullies. However, females are more likely to engage in indirect bullying conduct such as socially rejecting the victim or spreading rumors.[11] While such conduct is less likely to be noticed by school officials than more direct means such as making physical threats, it nevertheless causes harm to the victim.

One of the greatest difficulties in addressing this problem comes from accurately identifying the types of conduct that is bullying and harassment.

---

[9]   "Seven Years after Columbine, States continue to push for Anti-Bullying Legislation" newswise : http://www.newswise.com/articles/seven-years-after-columbine-states-continue-to-push-for-anti-bullying-legislation?ret=/articles/list&category=&page=13&search%5Bstatus%5D=3&search%5Bsort%5D=date+desc&search%5Bchannel_id%5D=67

[10]   "Bullying: a major barrier to student learning" UCLA Center for Mental Health in schools : http://smhp.psych.ucla.edu/hottopic/hottopic(bullying).htm

[11]   Id.

Most children will most likely be picked on at some point by their peers while in school. However, such conduct does not necessarily equate to bullying and harassment. Mental health experts have identified bullying and harassment as conduct that repeatedly takes such forms as teasing, threatening, taunting, socially rejecting, stealing, or hitting.[12] Traditionally victims of bullying and harassment were safe from such conduct once they reached the confines of their own homes. However, technological advances have expanded the reach of bullying and harassing conduct. The prevalence of so-called cyber-bullying has left bullying and harassment targets with virtually no place to hide.

Types of bullying

Cyber-bullying has been defined as a condition where a child has been tormented, threatened, harassed, humiliated, embarrassed, or otherwise targeted by another child through use of such technology as the internet or cell phones.[13] Cyber-bullying generally comes in two forms. The first form is a direct cyber-bullying attack that involves messages sent directly to the victim by another child.[14] The other form is cyber-bullying by proxy, which is where third parties assist in bullying the victim.[15] An example of cyber-bullying by proxy is where third parties are asked to rate a victims physical attractiveness on a public website poll.

It is difficult to identify a direct cause for why cyber-bullying occurs. Some of the various motives for cyber-bullying include revenge, entertainment value, or the boosting of the bullies social standing.[16] No matter how difficult it is to identify the causes of cyber-bullying, the behavior is clearly as harmful as more traditional forms of bullying and

---

[12] Id.

[13] "What is cyberbullying, exactly?" STOP cyberbullying : http://www.stopcyberbullying.org/what_is_cyberbullying_exactly.html

[14] "How cyberbullying works" STOP cyberbullying : http://www.stopcyberbullying.org/how_it_works/index.html

[15] Id.

[16] "Why do kids cyberbully each other?" STOP cyberbullying : http://www.stopcyberbullying.org/why_do_kids_cyberbully_each_other.html

harassment.[17] In fact, cyber-bullying is possibly more dangerous given the fact it has the ability to follow its victims home from the schoolhouse.

Emotional bullying uses such tactics as spreading rumors and excluding victims from social activities.[18] To outsiders, it may not seem as serious as serious as other forms of bullying, and many observers will simply chalk it up as kids being kids.[19] However, emotional bullying and harassment is a widespread and extreme problem for the education system. In fact, it's estimated that as many as 160,000 children skip school every day in order to avoid emotional bullying and harassment.[20]

The most easily identifiable form of bullying is physical bullying, and as a result is the form most likely to be punished.[21] It occurs when a bully uses a physical act such as kicking, punching, or hitting to gain physical power over another child.[22] Physical bullying is more likely to occur between males, and the bullies are often physically stronger than victims.[23]

Effects of bullying

Bullying and harassment cause a number of harmful effects with which victims must deal. In addition, bullying and harassment also cause harmful effects for the bullies and third parties who witness the bullying and harassment. While harm caused from physical attack will usually subside over time, many of the emotional harms caused by bullying and harassment

17 FitzGerald, Eileen. "Mom of bullied teen who committed suicide shares her chilling story in Brookfield" newstimes.com : http://www.newstimes.com/local/article/Mom-of-bullied-teen-who-committed-suicide-shares-1337893.php

18 "What is emotional bullying?" Answers.com : http://wiki.answers.com/Q/What_is_emotional_bullying

19 "Emotional Bullying Scars Grades Schoolers" ABSNEWS : http://abcnews.go.com/GMA/AmericanFamily/story?id=128025&page=1

20 Id.

21 Fraser-Thill, Rebecca. "Definition of Physical Bullying" About.comTweens : http://tweenparenting.about.com/od/socialdevelopment/a/physical-bullying.htm

22 Id.

23 "Physical Bullying" Bullying Statistics : http://www.bullyingstatistics.org/content/physical-bullying.html

are often long-lasting for its victims.[24] Bullying and harassment lower a victim's self-esteem because it damages their ability to view themselves as a desirable, capable, and effective person.[25] As a result of being repeatedly bullied, victims are likely to develop a type of defeated attitude that leads to a sense of hopelessness. This sense of hopelessness then increases the likelihood that the victim will have to battle depression in the future.[26] This in turn leads to victims of bullying and harassment having higher rates of suicide. Bullying and harassment also harm the academic performance of their victims.

Bullying and harassment also have a harmful impact on the bullies themselves. Bullies are more likely than other children to frequently get into physical fights.[27] Bullies are also likely to engage in other anti-social behaviors that lower the overall learning environment in the school. In addition, bullies are more likely than other students to carry weapons into school, which has the effect of endangering the safety of both themselves and other children.[28] As the lesson of the Columbine massacre has taught us, weapons have no place in our schools.

The effect that bullying and harassment have on other third party observers often goes unnoticed at the time of the harmful conduct.[29] However, third party observers suffer harmful effects similar to those experienced by victims and bullies. They are likely to feel unsafe in the school environment and may in fact be tempted to participate in the bullying and harassment or retaliate against the bully.[30]

Clearly, bullying and harassment create a number of harmful effects that must be addressed in some fashion. This in turn creates pressure on school and state officials to prevent bullying and harassment. Attempts to prevent bullying and harassment are complicated by the fact that children

---

[24]   Dombeck, Mark. "The Long Term Effects of Bullying" MentalHelp.net : http://www.mentalhelp.net/poc/view_doc.php?type=doc&id=13057

[25]   Id.

[26]   Id.

[27]   "What is Bullying" OLWEUS : http://www.olweus.org/public/bullying.page

[28]   Id.

[29]   Id.

[30]   Id.

still possess some free speech rights within the schoolhouse. [31] This fact raises the ultimate question of what is the most effective means of addressing bullying and harassment in schools.

There have been and are before the U.S. courts as well as state courts. Legislation and legal actions to curtail bullying serve as a method for curtailing bullying.

Anti-Bullying Statues

In an attempt to combat the harms caused by bullying and harassment in schools, a number of state legislatures across the country have passed anti-bullying statues. Currently, 45 states have such a statue. [32] Yet, the lack of nationwide uniformity in anti-bullying statues has the effect of not adequately protecting numerous schoolchildren throughout the country from bullying and harassment.

How anti-bullying laws are evaluated

It is important that state anti-bullying laws be evaluated for their effectiveness at combating bullying and harassment. An evaluation of anti-bullying laws throughout the country reveals that many states fail to fully protect schoolchildren from the harms caused by bullying and harassment. [33] Several key points must be covered in a state's anti-bullying law for it to effectively protect schoolchildren from the harms caused by bullying and harassment. [34] A key evaluating criteria that is used to grade anti-bullying laws is whether the law itself actually contains the word bullying within it. [35] Not all anti-bullying laws across the country contain the word bullying within them. [36] They may instead choose to contain language

---

[31]   "Free Speech Rights of Students" : http://law2.umkc.edu/faculty/projects/ ftrials/conlaw/studentspeech.htm

[32]   http://www.bullypolice.org/

[33]   Id.

[34]   High, Brenda. "How states are Graded on their Anti Bullying Laws." Bully Police USA : http://www.bullypolice.org/grade.html

[35]   Id.

[36]   Id.

such as hate crime, harassment, discrimination, or intimidation.[37] The use of such language is not as effective as using the word bullying because the definition of such words is often outside of common knowledge, while everyone knows what a bully is.[38]

Another factor that is used to evaluate anti-bullying laws is whether the law is clearly identified as an anti-bullying law.[39] Some anti-bullying laws ineffectively describe themselves as school safety laws.[40] However, an effective anti-bullying law should describe the rights of individual students instead of focusing on the overall safety of the school.[41] In addition, an effective anti-bullying law must contain definitions for bullying and harassment.[42] By specifically defining what conduct is prohibited, the anti-bullying law provides offenders with sufficient notice that conduct that constitutes bullying and harassment is prohibited.

An additional factor that determines if an anti-bullying law is effective is whether it contains recommendations about how to make policy and what needs to be in the model policy.[43] School districts clearly require guidance in terms of how they should implement their anti-bullying policies. An effective anti-bullying law should also require anti-bullying training and education for both students and teachers.[44] By doing so, the law would enable all stakeholders within the classroom to become more aware of the harms caused by bullying and harassment.

An anti-bullying law will also be evaluated based upon whether it requires for schools to have anti-bullying program in place.[45] The use of the word "shall" will indicate that the law requires for an anti-bullying program to be in place.[46] Another point used to evaluate an anti-bullying law is whether the law states a time deadline for school districts to

---

[37]   Id.
[38]   Id.
[39]   Id.
[40]   Id.
[41]   Id.
[42]   Id.
[43]   Id.
[44]   Id.
[45]   Id.
[46]   Id.

have anti-bullying policies in place, and whether it states a deadline for anti-bullying programs to be in effect in schools.[47]

An effective anti-bullying law must also protect against reprisal, retaliation, or false accusation.[48] Doing so will ensure that a bully is placed on notice that they will be severely punished if they retaliate after the bullying has been reported to school officials. The requirement will also guard against the risk that a student will be falsely accused of bullying in order to bring down punishment on them. An additional requirement of an effective anti-bullying law is that it provides protection from lawsuit to school districts that follow anti-bullying policies.[49] The law should also place parents of bullies on notice that they can be sued if they fail to prevent their child from bullying.[50]

In addition, an effective anti-bullying law will protect victims of bullying by providing for counseling for victims of severe bullying.[51] As has been previously discussed, bullying can have a severe impact on a victim's life. These include such harmful outcomes as increased risk of depression and suicide. Another point that an effective anti-bullying law will be evaluated on is whether it requires school districts to file an accountability report on their compliance with anti-bullying policies to a state level monitor.[52] Such a requirement will ensure that school districts are held accountable for actually complying with the anti-bullying law. A final point used to evaluate an effective anti-bullying law is whether the law contains a provision prohibiting cyber-bullying.[53] As has previously been discussed, cyber-bullying is a growing threat that causes harm to victims even when they are not physically located in the schoolhouse.

UPCOMING TRENDS

The state of student free speech rights in schools is in constant flux. New cases emerge from time to time that threaten to redefine the

---

[47]   Id.
[48]   Id.
[49]   Id.
[50]   Id.
[51]   Id.
[52]   Id.
[53]   Id.

existing constitutional framework. One such case was *Saxe,* in which an Appellate Court pushed back an attempt to limit student speech rights in schools.[54] In *Saxe,* the school district had a statue in place that prohibited the harassment of students for a number of reasons, some of which could include the sexual orientation of the victim.[55] The plaintiff filed suit because he felt this requirement went against his Christian faith, which he felt required him to speak against immoral acts such as homosexuality. The Court in this case found that merely because speech is harassing does not mean that it's not entitled to First Amendment protection, and as a result the statue was unconstitutional. Other cases will also likely emerge as threats to student free speech rights in schools. It's important that student free speech rights continue to be protected. Schools should remain places where even unpopular ideas may safely be expressed. In particular, religious opinions are a type of pure speech that is most deserving of Constitutional protection. People often learn from opinions expressed by their peers in the classroom. If certain types of beliefs are forbidden from being expressed, the only views expressed in the classroom will be those of the school district. This poses the risk that the next generation of voting citizens will become unable to think for themselves. As a result, future attempts to redefine student speech rights in schools should be resisted.

NONVIOLENCE CONFLICT RESOLUTION CURRICULUMS:

While anti-bullying measures seem to be the current focus in preventing the harmful and negative effects of bullying, there is another school of thought that supports nonviolence conflict resolution. Dr. Martin Luther King, Jr. and his contemporaries effectively implemented this strategy in the 1950's and l960's in the American Civil Rights Movement of the 20th Century. Dr. King's strategies were inspired by the Agape Love of God. His methods were inspired by Gandhi's peaceful non-violent movement.

The Martin Luther King, Jr. Center for Nonviolent Social Change is at the forefront in providing nonviolent leadership training and curriculum for schools, governments, corporations, community groups and other

---

[54]   *Saxe v. State College School District.* 240 F.3d 200. (2001)

[55]   Id. at 202

venues in need of preventing human interaction that can lead to violence rather than peaceful conflict resolution.

CONCLUSION

Existing anti-bullying laws alone are ineffective in terms of protecting students from the harms posed by bullying and harassment. The reason for this is that each individual state has its own anti-bullying law. Unfortunately, some state anti-bullying laws are weakly drafted, and as a result fail to fully protect students. The existing Constitutional framework for student free speech rights in schools allows for anti-bullying laws to be drafted in a way that fully protects students from the harms caused by bullying and harassment in schools.

It would seem that a reasonable solution that would protect students from being bullied while also protecting the students rights to free speech would be to implement strategies that would encourage the students to adopt less violent means of speech and expression that would result in reducing the bullying behavior while allowing students to express ideas that would contribute to creating a stable community environment by building on blocks that are formed from intelligent nonviolent reasoning, with Agape Love being a foundational building block used to cement the process.

THE FIERCE URGENCY OF NOW: REFORMING THE CONSCIOUSNESS OF THE BLACK MAN IN AMERICA

By Rev. Derek King, Sr.
http://www.phumc.org/DerekKing

Dr. Martin Luther King, Jr. wrote a book titled "Why We Can't Wait." In the book he coined a phrase, "the fierce urgency of now." President Obama enjoined Dr. King's sentiments during his campaign to occupy the White House; on more than one occasion the President challenged America to embrace the necessity for change in the spirit of urgency. I contend that the Black man in America is in urgent need of reformation. There are measurable percentages of Black men, who are victimized by what I call internal elemental maladies; namely, low self-esteem, character deficiency and spiritual disconnection. These conditions have caused some men to abandon their pursuit of living a life of meaning and purpose. This despair is not acceptable; we must reform the Black man in America, for the urgency is upon us.

Webster defines esteem as, "to regard with respect; prize." There is an adage that says, "If you can't stand the heat, get out of the kitchen." There is a Black man in America who would say in response to this adage, "every room is hot." There was a time in America when Black men stayed in the hot kitchen. Their determination and focus was clear. Their attitude was clearly understood; they were not torn between "fight or flight."

In April of 1968, Black men who collected garbage as city employees for Memphis, Tennessee became outraged over the disrespect they experienced form the city of Memphis with regard to fair wages. The Black garbage collectors certainly had no complaint about the job they were employed to perform. They were challenging the perspective and consciousness of their employer. Consequently, the garbage collectors said to the city government of Memphis, "I AM A MAN."

The spirit of the battle cry, "I AM A MAN" announced to all whom would hear, said, I am not what you perceive me to be, I am a man. I am not a garbage collector, I am a MAN. There is another adage that states, "if you don't stand for something, you will fall for anything." Those men in Memphis chose to take a stand for who they were in their consciousness. They chose to fight the systemic prejudices that were attempting to degrade them. They respected themselves, they had positive self-esteem.

Forty five years later, in the 21st century we have a crisis, the self-esteem of the Black man in America is in decline. There is a way we can redirect the decline. We have to help them elevate their consciousness. We have to assist them in reaffirming themselves. They have to understand that they have worth and purpose. They have to realize that they are not what they do, they must focus on who they are.

With regard to character deficiency, some Black men have made some decisions that have resulted in consequences that affect their ability to be systemically productive. There are some men who have histories that they feel is an impediment to being able to do it right, so they use the past as a justification to do what is comfortable to them.

A colleague of mine at Martin University, Professor John Mize, states, "the content of a person's character is usually defined by their behaviors." Black men must be challenged to behave morally and ethically. The Nike corporation has a brand slogan that says, "just do it." Some Black men have taken that slogan to heart and they just do it. They have to be challenged to do it right.

There is a moral high ground that must be embraced and cemented into the character consciousness. There is a prevalence of thought in the American mindset that focuses on survival and not success. The mindset that suggests that it is hard for a Black man to survive in America is defeatist. Their consciousness should be focused on success and not survival. A mentality of survival can lead one to becoming debase and animalistic.

The Black man in America must not become disconnected from nor despaired in the responsibility of doing justly and walking humbly before God.

In conclusion, I must speak to the spiritual disconnection that exists in the lives of some Black men in America. Men are empirical in their thinking, to the point of being victimized by what I call, the Missouri mindset, "I am from Missouri, before I believe it, show me." Many Black men in America have been challenged to believe in God, a God who is not visible to the human eye. Some went to church and they did not see God there.

For many Black men in America, they want to change their destinies. How we can help them reform is to help them walk in the wisdom of this proverb: "Trust in the Lord, and, lean not to thy own understanding, in all thy ways acknowledge Him, and, He will direct thy path."

THE GENOCIDE/SUICIDE OF BLACK AMERICA

Dr. Loretto Grier Cudjoe Smith

An aborted education kills the dreams of our youth. A prison sentence aborts the dreams of a young person. Our children, who are not lost/killed in the wash (abortion), are finished in the rinse (school drop outs and incarceration).

Since the legalization of abortion in 1973, Black America has lost 35% of its population with an estimate that over 20+ million Black children have been killed by the abortionists. Of the reported 12% of the population in 1973, some numbers reveal that today Black Americans now constitute only 9% of America's population, with numbers still declining.

The incarceration of Black males at younger and younger ages, often before they have the opportunity finish school or to reproduce; and often remaining incarcerated for longer periods beyond their natural abilities to reproduce and function as healthy parents, is an integral part of the plan to control the birth rate of Blacks in America.

This explains why the liberal white racist, who has strongly contributed to promoting harmful social behaviors, releasing social constraints and instigating the overall moral deterioration in our communities leading to the criminalization of young Blacks (who are the victims and scavengers for every human experiment promoted by these social architects), is also the same racist who is strongly pro-abortion and who most recently is first in line to promote the "two strikes you're out" (locking up Black males en masse) and the expansion of the death penalty.

The social sympathizers of the 60's and 70's are part of the lynch mob in the 90's and into the 21st century. In essence, they gave us the rope to hang ourselves.

Criminal Justice and Welfare Reform

More insidious means of implementing these policies have been through criminal justice and welfare reform. This will eventually give way to a more violent means of eradicating these "human pests" for the survival of the "master race". Utilizing the death penalty, abortion, infanticide (becoming a reality with late term and post-birth abortion) euthanasia, fetal tissue research, melanin extraction, human experimentation, and organ removal from healthy individuals particularly prisoners and aborted babies; human lives are being exploited and eliminated.

How can Blacks expect to survive this onslaught by those who wish to annihilate all nonwhites via contraception, abortion, sterilization, imprisonment and poor medical care? Black ministers have been virtually silent to this holocaust as more unborn Black children are painfully executed. While these_innocents (victims of unplanned and or undesired pregnancies) are blamed for a multitude of social problems, the greed of the rich continues to absorb a greater and more unequal share of God's kingdom which was created for all of his children, regardless of man's standard for poverty or wealth.

Sanger's Negro Project and Planned Parenthood mandates have been so successful in indoctrinating Black leaders that today, Blacks politicians are the most consistent promoters of exterminating future generations of our children through abortion. They also are often the major supporters of harsh mandatory sentencing for young Black men and supporters of the death penalty (Anti-Terrorism and Effective Death Penalty Act 1995) which are all part two of the plan for peaceful genocide of Black Americans proposed by Margaret Sanger and other racist eugenicists.

While our leadership attacks our youth in response to Black-on-Black crime, they are willing to tolerate abortion's human sacrifice, a more violent form of Black on Black crime, to appease white political allies. Like the unwillingness to speak for the innocent unborn, there is a similar unwillingness to speak for the thousands of innocent Black men and women and children who are unjustly incarcerated.

The 21st Century

Now, in the 21st century, America is on the brink of overly unleashing Margaret Sanger's genocide plan against Blacks, the poor, minorities, the handicapped, the elderly and all who are perceived as burdens on the elite. It's no wonder that the perceived differences in the political parties have become fewer and fewer.

Though pseudo-liberals have a plan to get you in the wash (abortion and choice) and the conservatives have a plan to get you in the rinse (criminal just-us and welfare reform), the agenda is the same—the extermination of nonwhites. Most recently, Democrats have become increasingly pro-incarceration and pro-death penalty and Republicans are becoming more and more pro-abortion, and both promoting the Sangerian philosophy of "the cruelty of charity."

By promoting and advancing the payment of over $365 million federal tax dollars a year to Planned Parenthood, our nation's political leaders are sending us a message. In essence, they are telling us that they will pay abortion supporters over a million dollars a day to control the population.

We should rise up and demand that Planned Parenthood be defunded and that the tax dollars go to education and prison reform that will regenerate and affirm the lives of those who are currently deemed "useless eaters" and burdens on society.

We must urge Caucasian prolife advocates to stand firm under attacks that would label them "racist" for telling the truth about Black Genocide. These Caucasian allies against Black Genocide are not racists, they are 21st Century Abolitionists, and the Pregnancy Care Centers are the Underground Railroads, rescuing womb babies from the womb lynchers.

As Jesus Christ stated, even Beelzebub (Satan) knows that a kingdom divided against itself cannot stand. Therefore in coming days we can expect to see greater unity amongst these men of evil. In urgency, God's people must unite, mindful of the fact that the destruction of all mankind is the ambition of Satan!

Faithfulness to the laws of God, the Master Creator of all life, and willingness to protect the innocent could avert this impending doom. "All that it takes for evil to conquer is for the good to do nothing." My people shall perish for the lack of knowledge. Those who can't remember history are bound to repeat it.

Dr. Loretto Grier Cudjoe Smith is past President of the Coalition for Equal Justice Project Truth Representative, L.E.A.R.N.

BURDEN OTHERS ONLY AS YOU'D HAVE THEM BURDEN YOU

By Chaplain Ayesha Kreutz
http://moveonup.ning.com/profile/
ChaplainAyeshaKreutz

Part of being a good Christian, a good citizen and a good neighbor is taking individual responsibility. I have the responsibility to my neighbor to take care of myself to the best of my ability so that my neighbor does not have to. I say "to the best of my ability" because everyone's abilities are different. Some of us need help, while others have the ability to help their immediate family, their extended family and even their neighbors so that the government does not have to. 1 Timothy 5:8 (KJV)—"But if any provide not for his own, and especially for those of his own house, he hath denied the faith, and is worse than an infidel."

Government is supposed to be the last line of defense for those in need. It should not by any means be the first source of help. Too often, in today's world, I hear people say things like: "Well it's okay. The government will take care of that for me."

But truth be told, it used to be that we took pride uncaring for ourselves so that our families did not have to take on the extra burden of taking care of us. The government wasn't even part of the equation. Throughout time, when our families could not help, our neighbors could not help, our churches could not help and every other possible source of help for those in need was exhausted; only then would we even consider the government.

And when taking aid, we did it reluctantly and with a sense of urgency. We'd feel self pressure: "I have to fix my situation quickly so my sister or brother can stop bringing me food or paying my rent." Today things are so convoluted, and we have become so numb and misled about individual responsibility that many do not even take responsibility for their bodies and sexual behavior—so much so that much of society finds it easy to justify killing children in the womb.

We, as a people, had enough pride to take care of ourselves and our own. However, with the breakdown of the family—due to do-gooder government programs that for all intents and purposes destroy that which is good so as to become the source of food, healthcare, housing and money—our society has slowly given up the stigma of shame that used to be attached to the seeking of government help.

When you think about it, the money and help that come from the government actually comes from your neighbor and your family. This help is paid for with tax money taken through government coercion rather than money and help willingly given by those who'd be willing to give it. The more one does not work and care for oneself, the more one's neighbor and family has to work in order to support those who cannot and will not work.

This is true whether those neighbors even have enough to fully support themselves and their family. 2Thessalonians 3:10 (KJV)—"For even when we were with you, this we commanded you, that if any would not work, neither should he eat."

We wind up taking from those who are too often in need themselves in order to give to others in need via tax money, BUT if the able-bodied would work, then the burden on our neighbors would lessen. I think this basic and beautiful principle has been lost somewhere along the way. Essentially, it is the golden rule. Burden others only as you'd have them burden you. But for many (not all of course) who willingly refuse to take care of themselves, it's as though "work" is somehow a bad word. But Genesis 2:15says "The LORD God took the man and put him in the Garden of Eden to work it and take care of it." Who are we to ignore that duty?

When we think on God's design for us and use the skills and creativity HE purposed for us, we are happier. People are happier as individuals when they have purpose, as they are able to transform the world around them for the good. Those without purpose, who too often find their lives meaningless, often get lost in the shuffle of government programs. Government benefits become an addictive drug that perpetuates living a meaningless life because the cost of getting to a point where one no longer needs the benefits means giving up those benefits.

That seems simple, but when the benefits coming from the taxpayer are so good that one needs a pretty good job to keep up financially with living on the benefits (especially with the extra costs of travel and childcare), it becomes a harder decision than those on the outside might think. For that reason, society needs to bring back the added cost of shame to those taking the benefits. Fear of shame will lead to the development of pride, and when one has something to legitimately be proud of, it's normally because they've overcome their deficiencies through effort and diligence.

I believe God gave us individual responsibility. God includes individual responsibility for salvation, work, charity and caring for others in the profile of being Good Samaritan; these same characteristics are necessary for all forms of servant leadership.

It is the fool, who says in his heart that there is no God, who also tells us that it is the government that is good and is to provide for us all things. This is not a new concept as we can see all the way back in Isaiah they were talking about it.

> (Isaiah 32:5-8) "The vile person shall be no more called liberal,
> nor the churl said to be bountiful. For the vile person will
> speak villainy, and his heart will work iniquity, to practice
> hypocrisy, and to utter error against the LORD, to make
> empty the soul of the hungry, and he will cause the drink of
> the thirsty to fail. The instruments also of the churl are evil: he
> devises wicked devices to destroy the poor with lying words,
> even when the needy speaks truth. But the liberal devises liberal
> things; and by liberal things shall he stand."

And that's not just some Republican talking point. It's the Word of God.

When God is replaced by the government, the food that comes from the government leaves one hungry, the drink leaves one thirsty, and the soul is left untended. That is the cost of having no regard for burdening others unlike you'd allow them to burden you. Yet, when government is replaced by Jesus Christ, helping others is a choice and a blessing—never a burden.

LIBERTY AND FREE SPEECH IN 21ST CENTURY AMERICA

Doc Ed Holliday
http://webtalkradio.net/tag/doc-ed-holliday/

Liberty and free speech are weaved into the very fabric of what it means to be an American. From our colonial days when the "Father of the American Revolution," Samuel Adams risked his life to speak freely for independence, Americans know the price and the value of free speech. On December 16, 1773, Samuel Adams stood before both foes and friends alike at the Old South Meeting House in Boston, Massachusetts. In the crowded chamber British redcoats listened to every word. They wanted to find a reason to arrest Adams, but he used coded words that the Sons of Liberty understood. And that night the Boston Tea Party tipped the colonies on their journey toward being free.

Our founders like Thomas Jefferson knew the cause of liberty rested on the foundation to speak freely. Today anyone can look up into the dome of the Jefferson Memorial in Washington, D.C. and read these words from Jefferson,

> "I have sworn upon the altar of God eternal hostility
> against every form of tyranny over the mind of man."

Just as Jefferson wrote in the Declaration of Independence that we are endowed by our Creator with certain unalienable rights we Americans have been given liberty by our very birth into the land of freedom. The costs of these freedoms have been high; paid for by the blood of patriots, the continuing outpouring of free speech and the wrestling of ideas on the stages of American life. I know of no better example of the price of freedom than that my father told me.

My father spoke to me about the price of liberty by telling me about two his boyhood friends. There are no monuments for their service or great poems of their deeds. They were simply American boys who were called to duty. American soldiers were called upon on June 6, 1944 to gain a foothold in what was Hitler's fortress Europe. Many men went in and some were just boys.

My father can remember the names of two boys just over 18 who were from his community. But by the setting of the sun, their life on earth was done. My father can even to this day remember their names, Harvey Moffat and Harris Jennings. Harvey Moffat had an old "Model A" car and the farm boys in the community would put their change together to buy enough gas for Harvey to take them into town to see a picture show.

Harris Jennings had a son growing in the womb of his wife when he hit the beach on D-Day. His son still lives today, never knowing his father who gave everything he had for freedom—so that his son and others could live in liberty. And in communities all over America people can still remember names of American sons and fathers who never came home after D-Day.

It is good that we remember their names, because all gave some and some gave all. We can never forget those who gave all they had so that we can be free today. I once spoke to a soldier who went on shore in Normandy two days after D-Day. He told me about one of the most amazing experiences that any human throughout the history of time could have experienced.

He had a vial or small jar of sand from that day on that beach. He told me that ever since that day he could count on one hand how many times that he had opened that container. Every time that he opened it he could not stop his tears from flowing nor hold back the overwhelming feelings that turned his stomach, stirred his heart, and troubled his soul. In that jar was his experience of the day that he marched on the sand as all the world was in the midst of war.

This soldier had scooped up the sand because he knew as he was marching through that stretch of beach he was witnessing an event that was unfolding unlike any other in history. He told me about the hundreds of planes roaring over head and the sight of huge ships unloading cargo as far as the eye could see down the beach. Three years of massive shipments from America that had been stored in Great Britain were now being unloaded. Jeeps, tanks, trucks, cannons, and every type of military hardware imaginable filled into crates that were being transferred from ship to shore.

He told me of the sounds of trucks and tanks and the smells of fuel burning mixed with the aftermath of a horrible battle just two days before left a unique aroma that quickened the spirit but sickened the stomach. As the direction of the wind changed whiffs of burnt flesh emerged from the Blackened parts of the white sand beach. The smell of death was still everywhere on that battle field and the makeshift morgue was hidden but every soldier knew what was in those tents. He told me how the aftermath left an untold story of the ferocity and the intensity of the battle that had taken place—how it made him want to weep for those who gave their all.

The military brass were busy trying to sanitize the battlefield so as not to unnerve the new troops unloading by the thousands but it didn't work. His nerves were too numb to be unnerved anyway.

He was scared stiff like every other country boy from Mississippi or Alabama or Nebraska or California or New York. And he remembered marching by the bullet pocked Nazi pill boxes with their burned interiors thanks to the American flamethrowers. The burnt flesh smell fresh as smoldering debris caused trails of smoke to rise.

He said that he knew what he was marching through was a part of the largest military invasion in all human history. Mind-boggling could not even describe the scene as he told me he could look in any direction as see more supplies, more soldiers, more planes, more tanks, more trucks, and always more scenes of the horrific battle that had just taken place.

That's why he rarely opened that small vial of sand because it would make him cry and feel those feelings and smell those smells from so long ago just like it was yesterday. My father's friends were his friends—he was from the same small community. I often wondered if he thought that Harvey Moffat's or Harris Jennings' blood was in that vial of sand. They were there to him and so many others. The sand was tattooed to his soul.

Just as this soldier could not open that vial of sand without weeping so do Americans everywhere have stories about the price of freedom. Whether it is family and friends of Medgar Evers or Dr. Martin Luther King, Jr., or if it is the family of a slain soldier from Iraq or Afghanistan we Americans do know the price of freedom. We know that the principles of free speech are paid for and must be protected. And all living Americans have within us the vials of contained memories that make liberty worth fighting for. Whether on the battlefield, or the campaign trail, or in the town squares across America freedom of speech is the song America sings that keeps us free and strong.

In the 21st century we are witnessing policies and trends that are threatening to free speech. The Judeo-Christian traditions that have been the foundation on which this nation was founded must be protected and preserved for future generations. We are seeing forces that want to restrict speech, prevent free thinking and seeking to silence what all Americans at one time took for granted. We can see these things in the gay activist movements that seek to control and silence groups that speak out about biblical views on homosexuality. The Muslims are guaranteed freedom of religion but they are not guaranteed that others cannot challenge the words found in the Quran. In many instances we are seeing international laws and world rulings challenging the U.S. Constitution.

Life, liberty and the pursuit of happiness which we are given by our Creator cannot be taken away by our government unless we refuse to defend our liberties. That is the essence of the freedom of speech. Being able to speak freely even though we may make some mistakes is paramount in keeping our experiment in self government a journey that we will pass to the next generation. Liberty is a gift that came to the shores of America by Christians who wanted to live free and wanted a land where there was freedom of speech and religion. No other country has been as blessed as the United States. We have great challenges and great potential. But our freedom to speak without fear of tyrannical laws or tyrants is what will make America's future brighter and better.

Now is the time to assemble the stumbling blocks of our generation and transform them into building blocks today for the hope of tomorrow. Our Creator has given us life, liberty, and the pursuit of happiness. We have within our grasp the freedom to move mountains with our God given talents. Pursue excellence, promote freedom, praise God. "Lift every voice and sing"—sing a new song for a new day standing on the promises of God.

MASSACHUSETTS FAMILY INSTITUTE STRENGTHENING THE FAMILY JARRETT ELLIS TESTIMONY

April 28, 2003
TO THE HONORABLE MEMBERS
OF THE MASSACHUSETTS GENERAL ASSEMBLY

Thirty-nine years ago, my great-uncle, Reverend Dr. Martin Luther King Jr., delivered to mindful citizens of America a prophetic dream which envisaged all of this great nation's people living in the full exercise of all rights granted to them by the Constitution of the United States. My forebear's dream was deeply rooted in the American dream wherein the Founders of this Union saw every lawful citizen standing in dignity outfitted by unalienable rights from God to life, liberty and the pursuit of happiness free from the threat of tyranny posed by kings, dictators, oligarchies, and yes, institutions of some representative forms of government.

Even though Dr. King was taken from us, the dream lived on. In fact, it did more. Through the efforts of wonderful people like A.D. King, Martin's brother, my grandfather also taken from us, through the continued efforts of my great-grandfather, Dr. Martin Luther King Sr., who helped raise me and shape my values, and through the efforts of so many others of like mind and faith in the intervening years across this nation, people across the world began to see Dr. King's dream and the American dream merge.

Today, progress toward a full actualization of civil rights in America continues through the efforts of brave men and women who trace their philosophical lineage to Dr. King. True civil rights advocacy is carried on as well by others who may claim no formal association with Kingian philosophy but are nevertheless members of the true household of keepers of the American Dream descended from the founding fathers, of which Dr. King was a rightful heir. True sons and daughters of America have certainly helped her and continue to help her to live out the true meaning of her creed, that all people are created equal.

Yet, inherent in this ongoing responsibility to hold America's promises true to all citizens is a corresponding responsibility to protect the integrity of the American way as defined by free public and private exercise of liberty within the ambits of our nation's charter. Thus, while our forefathers certainly saw the need to equip America to protect the weakest amongst its citizens, they also saw an equal need to protect the American system from the <u>weaknesses</u> of its citizens. Any civic exercise or campaign must therefore square with the constitution or serve as destructive a measure as the denial of the rights America extends to all.

Certainly Dr. King saw the centrality of this need to subscribe to and protect the integrity of the Constitution in any civil campaign. Dr. King, in fact, began all efforts for social change with an examination of all attending facts to determine whether or not there existed an injustice that necessitated any civil action at all. Following this examination, in his mind, was a necessary period of self-purification to ensure that aberrant motives were not at the heart of the impetus toward social change. Drawing from the axiom that not all change is good change, or "if it is not broken, don't fix it", Dr. King and others true to his philosophy sought and seek only to heal discrepancies between constitutional philosophy and institutional grant. All other civil exercise must be scrutinized and ultimately resisted vigorously if found to be incongruent with this principle.

After careful consideration of the facts at hand, I have decided to stand with the Massachusetts Family Institute in favor of a constitutional amendment to protect the traditional structure of marriage in this state. This constitutional action has become necessary as groups, in my opinion, have recently attempted to subvert the edicts of our nation's constitution in order to obtain privileged dispensation that would be granted if the tenets of the Constitution's integrity were preserved.

I gratefully acknowledge that within our federal system of governance, each state may independently establish laws and policies which regulate the activities of citizens within that state so long as the provisions of the Constitution are not violated. Same-sex marriage advocates in Massachusetts have recently claimed that their state has historically violated Fourteenth Amendment provisions by denying marriage licenses to couples of the same sex. Thus, they claim that the civil rights of those seeking same-sex marriages have been denied. This is truly an explosive assertion, for civil rights are a proxy for the inalienable rights the founding fathers identified as the touchstone of the American constitutional system. Civil rights endow all American citizens with the guarantee of equal treatment in all matters of law and policy and thus civil rights must be fiercely defended without prejudice at all times.

In light of a perceived breach of their civil rights, rights, same-sex advocates sued the State Department of Public Health in Massachusetts in 2002. Yet given the transcendent importance of civil rights to our national identity, should we not rightfully ask whether or not this action was correct? Was this striking effort for social change necessary and proper, as Dr. King would have asked?

Same sex marriage advocates in Massachusetts claim that civil rights were violated because the state historically treated seekers of same sex marriages differently from those seeking traditional marriages. Those reasonably conversant with civil rights law and policy understand that the purpose of civil rights is not to destroy the government's ability to treat people differently under the law. Anyone who receives tax benefits for dependent children will appreciate the government's ability to make decisions which affect different people in different ways. Instead, civil rights provision with U.S. governance seeks to make sure that different effects of public policy upon different people are not to be found unreasonable or the product of suspect motives.

Accordingly, through the years, American courts have developed guidelines for defining legitimate civil rights issues. The purpose is twofold: one, to establish a clear system of judgment that helps ensure that civil rights provisions are applied equitably despite the passions of those who may stand opposed to civil rights advancement, and two, to ensure that the laws for which my family shed blood, and for which America paid so dearly, are not taken, hijacked in effect, to advance questionable causes for questionable purposes, thereby threatening the system of governance that protects all American citizens.

So immediately, the question arises, does the cause for the legalization of same-sex in marriage meet civil rights criteria as it claims to? In order to answer that question, we recognize that under the laws of this nation, any person seeking relief for the denial of civil rights must specifically show:

a history of economic disenfranchisement;

a history of political disenfranchisement; or

discrimination based upon an immutable, intrinsic trait or characteristic.

Thus, in order to legitimately claim that a denial of same-sex marriages equates to a denial of civil rights, same-sex marriage advocates must prove that marriage licenses to same sex couples were denied for one of the above reasons. Let's weigh the facts accordingly.

As to the issue of economic disenfranchisement, though the poverty and unemployment rates among blacks in America remains roughly two times the national average, economic performance in the gay community is roughly 1.5 times greater than the general population. Complaints against gay discrimination in the workforce barely register against the backdrop of minority and gender based discrimination complaints. Gay people in this nation have never been able to claim economic disenfranchisement or oppression.

As to the issue of political disenfranchisement, gay people have always enjoyed free access to America's voting system and show increasing access to, and exercise of, political representation absent civil rights initiatives. So again, where lies the cause of action?

As to the issue of unfair discrimination based on an immutable intrinsic trait or characteristic, the gay rights agenda again short of a legitimate cause of action. Science can offer no proof of intrinsic homosexual orientation. Yet, the many who have willingly left the gay lifestyle to practice celibacy or heterosexuality lend support to the position that homosexual action is a matter of choice and is therefore not an immutable or intrinsic trait.

To be fair, I acknowledge that there is growing evidence that many human impulses have some impetus in genetics. Some people are more disposed to substance abuse than others, some people are more responsive to heterosexual pleasure than others, and some are more sensitive to food consumption than others, all by virtue, as the evidence suggests, of some measure of genetic programming. Homosexuality falls into this category according to the research of many respected scientists such as Angier, Bailey and Pillard, Levay, et al.

Yet, there is a larger body of evidence, acknowledged even by the above scientists, that agrees that mature behavior patterns rely much more on social shaping and choices than genetic predisposition, such that most human behaviors may be successfully modified by a variety of means. The food addict may eat responsibly, and the alcoholic may avoid drinking. All people may live according to a wide range of sexual choices as well. Certainly, mutable behaviors may be practiced freely and are granted substantial constitutional protection under the Fourth Amendment, but those who choose certain lifestyles may not claim political asylum under the aegis of civil rights.

Again, to the extent that any aspect of personhood may be altered, then such aspect may not claim protection by virtue of civil rights. Homosexual practice clearly falls into this category. As my mother, Alveda C. King has said, "I have met many ex-gay people just as I have met many ex-husbands, ex-wives, ex-drug addicts and ex-lawyers. Yet I have never met an ex-Negro, ex-Caucasian or ex-Native American." The politics of preference does not jibe with the principle of civil rights.

So, we have established that same-sex marriage is not a civil right because, simply, homosexuality is not a civil right. The argument is direct and powerful. Yet, does the issue stop there? Unfortunately, no. Because same-sex marriage advocates have sued the Massachusetts Public Health Department for dispensation, a huge threat has been unleashed.

The U.S Constitution gives each citizen the right to set public policy for the good of the commonwealth within its borders. As long as the Fourteenth Amendment is not violated, a state may set policy to protect the interests of the general populace. Marriage between a male and female has historically been held and has been statistically shown to best provide the cohesion and stability necessary to sustain societies. A state may therefore encourage heterosexual marriage by sanctioning that form only and providing benefits to participants as a means of promoting the welfare of the commonwealth. All adult males and females in this country may marry an adult of the opposite sex, so no one is excluded on the basis of immutable or intrinsic characteristics. All states are thus well within constitutional purview in setting policy accordingly.

It is therefore wrong for any court to in effect legislate from the bench to force same-sex marriage. There is no constitutional imperative for such action. The creation of law based on social policy is the domain of legislators, not adjudicators. Given the facts, it is clear that an amendment to the Massachusetts constitution is necessary to prevent the usurpation of the Massachusetts legislative system by the judiciary.

In the name of those who fought to establish a true legacy of civil rights in this nation, in the name of all citizens everywhere, ladies and gentlemen of the Massachusetts General Court, please protect the legislative system in Massachusetts so that the system may work to protect the interests of all through the rightful actions of those participating in the system. Please pass the Marriage and Family Protection Amendment. Thank you.

Respectfully,
J. R. Ellis

A FATHERLESS CHILD

Nicholas Alexander

A child is born to a Mother and a Father
not knowing if they are together,

Innocent and fragile,

With no knowledge of whom he is, whining and crying trying to fit in,

Time goes by and he gets older just to find out all he has is his Mother!

Not understanding why his father came and went
but later tries to understand his intent,

He asks why?

But his mother tries, tries to keep things together,
to over compensate for his father,

When a father leaves his child with his mother, or as they call it
"Baby's Mama"! How does he feel? Like he wants to holler and pop his
collar, telling his friends, partners, hommies, compadre's I did it? But,
I can't handle it as of now.

They'll be ok, there are people who will take up the space,
I need to go and find my place.

My place you ask? You know in the streets where
I can move my feet and be me.

I'll be back one day to look up and see that he has grown up, grown up
to be a strong young black man that so happens to look like me!

Wondering how did she do it? His mother you see.
Keeping him straight even with all the extra's on her plate.

Lot's of tears and fears ponders her mind asking the lord why oh why?

And he says let not your heart be troubled, keep your head up
there are people or should I say men

That went through the same, time and again,

Seeking and trusting that they too will find a strong mentor in mind.

Possibly someone he can look up and see that positive
things can happen to me.

A poet named Saddiq Mo stated that" when you ask for oranges
and get lemons, make lemonade", and don't be afraid.

It's ok!

Just don't make the same mistake, live right take care of
your responsibilities, and think of all the possibilities.

Of how much joy a child can bring if you take time to stop and think,

You can be a boy having a baby but it takes real man to be a father!

As I close I look around and see that there is a strong possibility that
there are people just like me. Seeking and searching for the unknown
question of WHY?

Why did this happen?

Why does it hurt?

Why is it me?

My name is Nicholas Alexander and I am a fatherless child!

FATHERLESS CHILDREN

By LaVerne Tolbert. P.H.D.
www.teachinglikejesus.org

Fatherlessness has become a common reality for many children growing up without a dad means living without what God originally ordained when he established the covenant relationship of husband and wife. What strategies can teachers employ to teach fatherless children, and what can the Church do to help strengthen the family?

UNDERSTANDING FATHERLESSNESS

Causes of fatherlessness are death, divorce, separation, or non-marital childbearing. Today, only 55 percent of U.S. adults are married and living together, which is the lowest figure in history. For too many, the covenant relationship of marriage is replaced with the transitory commitment of "shacking up." Unfortunately, some unmarried women who hear their biological clocks ticking away simply decide to become single parents—yes . . . even the Church. The result is that more than one-third of the nation's 71 million children don't live with their biological fathers. And research indicates that 40 percent of children haven't seen their fathers in a year.

How possible is it for fatherless children to truly believe in and relate to God as Father while coping with emotional issues such as abandonment and rejection by their earthly fathers? If it's true that having a relationship with an earthly father who is a real daddy, helps understand the value and importance of having a relationship with our heavenly Father, then how difficult is it for fatherless children to grasp the compassionate, caring nature of a God who is available and ever present?

As a Christian nation, we are raising children many of whom have no idea what it is to have a relationship with their biological dad. These children sit in our children's church, Sunday schools and youth groups where teachers are faced with the challenge of assuring them that their heavenly Father will never leave them or forsake them. (Hebrews 13:5)

EFFECTS OF FATHERLESSNESS

While single parenting is commonly accepted among adults, it is difficult for children to cope with the effects of fatherlessness. More than half—59.4% of families with a single mother live near poverty; 48.9% live in poverty; 27.9% live in extreme poverty. (Payne, R K., revised2003 a Framework for understanding poverty. Highlands, TX aha! Process, Inc). Economic disparity is not always, but often, the breeding ground for drug abuse, gang warfare, and at its worst extreme, homelessness. Children from fatherless homes are:

5 times more likely to commit suicide
32 times more likely to run away
20 times more likely to have behavioral problems
14 times more likely to commit rape
10 more times more likely to abuse chemical substances
9 times more likely to end up in a state-operated institution
20 times more likely to end up in prison

Source: childrensjustice.org

Obviously, absent fathers can't appropriately discipline their children. When they don't do their jobs, correction is left in the hands of authority figures in blue uniforms. Absent fathers give boys a model of parenting that says it's okay for dad not to be around the home. Without fathers boys and girls are more likely to be sexually promiscuous. Homosexual orientation may also have its roots in fatherlessness. And, since children learn that they are loveable by experiencing the love of their earthly fathers, the fatherless suffer from poor self-esteem. They may reason that they must be undesirable or else their fathers would want to see them.

THE FATHER GOD CONCEPT

The scars from being raised without dad leave an indelible mark on the soul. Fathers are crucial to the spiritual development of their children. The concept of God is formed by watching mothers and fathers acknowledge, pray to and rely upon our Heavenly Father. Here, parents in the covenant relationship serve as role models, and role models help shape behavior. Unfortunately, there are milli9ons of fatherless children who have never seen or heard their fathers pray.

RESTORING THE FAITH

Restoring the faith so that children believe in and perceive of God as father must begin with educating men about the vital role they play as role models. What happens to a child who doesn't have a father's faith to embrace? Fatherless, a child's imagination may lead him to picture God the Father as detached from his life, like an amputated arm. The fatherless child may come to the conclusion that since survival in the future does not necessitate God the Father.

It's reasonable to see why some adults who raised in fatherless homes struggle in their relationship w3ith God as Father. They may have difficulty developing an intimate relationship because their real-life experience with their own dad was one of disappointment, abandonment, and rejection.

God designed the family as a training ground. He intended that children be taught about life and relationships-including their covenant relationship with God and the covenant relationship between husband and wife-within the context of the family.

WHAT THE CHURCH CAN DO

When fathers are not in the home, the Church must assume the responsibility of doing as Christ commands. "Pure religion and undefiled before God and the Father is this, to visit the fatherless and widows in their affliction." (James 1:27)

The Church is the principle institution capable of reaching those who have abandoned by their fathers. These children, "tweens", and teens are on our campuses, in our classrooms and often show up in our counseling sessions.

What opportunities for teachable moments! Modeling family, teaching about faithfulness and responsibility, and drawing real examples from scripture will build a new foundation of rock to replace the crumbling fatherless foundations.

The church might also focus on developing meaningful ministries to fathers. Bible study and fellowship groups could be utilized to teach men who are not actively involved with their children or who are struggling with demands of fatherhood.

For wives and mothers, female-only ministry settings such as Dr. Betty Price's "Women Who Care" may be beneficial in addressing the day-to-day concerns and frustrations that some women face. Here is a safe place to discuss with divorced women the necessity that children spend time with their dads.

Ministry to single parents is key as well, especially if addressed within the context of parenting seminars that teach women how to live holy.

WE'RE ALL FAMILY

The good news is that God did not plan for children to live in isolation, apart from the community of the Church. We're all family! Here is a reservoir of mature adult men to serve as mentors' to fatherless boys! A Rites of Passage program, for example, tailored after the African model, will assist young men in manhood development. As the mentor works with the youth, he in turn helps re-form the view of father.

In you youth ministries, teenagers need to see husband and wives ministering together, modeling what it means to be family. Lessons about dating and abstinence and loving God with all our heart will break the generational curse of fatherlessness. A ministry for girls that teaches them how to respect themselves, how to dress appropriately, and how to conduct themselves in different social situations gives females confidence and builds self-esteem.

At Crenshaw Christian Center in Los Angeles where Dr. Frederick K.C. Price is the founder-Pastor, we have a special place specifically designed for teenagers in the community. On Friday nights, kids are welcome to play basketball and "hang out" in the Billy Blanks Youth Activity Center—a $5 million, 28,000 square-foot state-of-the-art gymnasium fashioned after the downtown Staples Center.

In such surroundings, teenagers learn what it means to belong in a family. They watch mentors who are living out the example of true fatherhood and find in these role models someone who is giving them guidance, love, and correction. In this way, the spiritual family truly becomes the extended family that is so desperately needed for children living in fatherless homes.

Christian educators have such a limited access to reshaping the minds of impressionable children—approximately two hours a week on Sunday plus two hours of Bible study during the week. This is simply not enough time.

It takes the family—both mom and dad—plus the community of believers together. It takes mom . . . and dad.

Footnote: on the statistics, the website: childrensjustice.org is not a valid web address.

COMMENTARY ON SLAVERY AND THE EIGHT VEILS

By Dr. Alveda C. King

At the turn of the 21st Century, I read the article below. The author is since deceased. It was a great conversational piece back then, and still is today. Don's concept of the seventh and eighth veils differs from mine a bit. I don't necessarily believe that the seventh dimension is reserved for martyrs, but that "mere mortals" can dare to approach that veil.

As to the realms beyond the eighth veil, I firmly believe those places to be where God abides. Of course, for Christians, we also believe that God abides in our hearts, in the core of our "earthen vessels."

I do believe in God, the Creator of all things. I believe that through the sin cleansing shed blood of my Master Jesus Christ, I will live with Abba God forever. I also firmly believe in accepting the power of God's Holy Spirit in my life.

Do I believe in angels? Yes. Do I believe that satan and his fallen angels are enemies? Yes. As to dragons, they appear in the Bible. So, yes, I believe that they have existed too.

Why include this article in this anthology? It is part of the collection of research in the annals of King for America. Is that reason enough for you to read it?

From the December 2001 Idaho Observer:
(Excerpt from) Slavery and the eight veils

By Don Harkins

Over the last several years I have evolved and discarded several theories in an attempt to explain why it is that most people cannot see truth—even when it smacks them in the face. Those of us who can see "the conspiracy" have participated in countless conversations amongst ourselves that address the frustration of most peoples' inability to comprehend the extremely well-documented arguments which we use to describe the process of our collective enslavement and exploitation. The most common explanation to be arrived at is that most people just "don't want to see" what is really going on.

Extremely evil men and women who make up the world's power-elite have cleverly cultivated a virtual pasture so grass green that few people seldom, if ever, bother to look up from where they are grazing long enough to notice the brightly colored tags stapled to their ears.

The same people who cannot see their enslavement for the pasture grass have a tendency to view as insane "conspiracy theorists" those of us who can see the past the farm and into the parlor of his feudal lordship's castle.

Finally, I understand why.

It's not that those who don't see that their freedom is vanishing under the leadership of the power-elite "don't want to see it"—they simply can't see what is happening to them because of the un-pierced veils that block their view.

All human endeavors are a filtration process. Sports is one of the best examples. We play specific sports until we get kicked off the playground. The pro athletes we pay big bucks to watch just never got kicked off the playground. Where millions of kids play little league each spring, they are filtered out until there are about 50 guys who go to the World Series in October.

Behind the first veil: There are over six billion people on the planet. Most of them live and die without having seriously contemplated anything other than what it takes to keep their lives together. Ninety percent of all humanity will live and die without having pierced the first veil.

The first veil: Ten percent of us will pierce the first veil and find the world of politics. We will vote, be active and have an opinion. Our opinions are shaped by the physical world around us; we have a tendency to accept that government officials, network media personalities and other "experts" are voices of authority. Ninety percent of the people in this group will live and die without having pierced the second veil.

The second veil: Ten percent of us will pierce the second veil to explore the world of history, the relationship between man and government and the meaning of self-government through constitutional and common law. Ninety percent of the people in this group will live and die without having pierced the third veil.

The third veil: Ten percent of us will pierce the third veil to find that the resources of the world, including people, are controlled by extremely wealthy and powerful families whose incorporated old world assets have, with modern extortion strategies, become the foundation upon which the world's economy is currently indebted. Ninety percent of the people in this group will live and die without having pierced the fourth veil.

The fourth veil: Ten percent of us will pierce the fourth veil to discover the Illuminati, Freemasonry and the other secret societies. These societies use symbols and perform ceremonies that perpetuate the generational transfers of arcane knowledge that is used to keep the ordinary people in political, economic and spiritual bondage to the oldest bloodlines on earth. Ninety percent of the people in this group will live and die without having pierced the fifth veil.

The fifth veil: Ten percent of us will pierce the fifth veil to learn that the secret societies are so far advanced technologically that time travel and interstellar communications have no boundaries and controlling the actions of people is what their members do as offhandedly as we tell our children when they must go to bed. Ninety percent of the people in this group will live and die without having pierced the sixth veil.

The sixth veil: Ten percent of us will pierce the sixth veil where the dragons and lizards and aliens we thought were the fictional monsters of childhood literature are real and are the controlling forces behind the secret societies. Ninety percent of the people in this group will live and die without piercing the seventh veil.

The seventh veil: I do not know what is behind the seventh veil. I think it is where your soul is evolved to the point you can exist on earth and be the man Gandhi was, or the woman Peace Pilgrim was-people so enlightened they brighten the world around them no matter what.

The eighth veil? Piercing the eighth veil probably reveals God and the pure energy that is the life force in all living things-which are, I think, one and the same.

Conclusions:

And so now we know that it's not that our countrymen are so committed to their lives that, "they don't want to see," the mechanisms of their enslavement and exploitation. They simply "can't see" it as surely as I cannot see what's on the other side of a closed curtain.

The purpose of this essay is threefold: To help the handful of people in the latter veils to understand why the masses have little choice but to interpret their clarity as insanity; 2. To help people behind the first two veils understand that living, breathing and thinking are just the beginning and; 3. Show people that the greatest adventure of our life is behind the next veil because that is just one less veil between ourselves and God.

OF ONE BLOOD—ONE RACE: HUMAN

By Dr. Alveda King

**Galatians 4:16: Have I now become your enemy
by telling you the truth?**

**John 8:32: Then you will know the truth,
and the truth will set you free.**

Only God knows everything. My lack of knowledge has led me to write this book. Several themes are approached several times in various ways, thus seeming to be redundant. Restatement is an excellent tool for learning. Alveda is the foremost student in this project, with The Holy Spirit being the expert teacher. The Bible says that if we lack wisdom, we must ask God for instruction, and receive His insight in faith. In my seeking truth, the information, passages and messages in this book have come before me. In the sharing of these words, it is my sincere desire that you may also find reason to continue on in your quest for truth.

For many years, I looked upon the Euro-icon-portraits and faces of "Jesus" Christ, wondering if He remotely favored the modern portrayals. When I was a young girl watching the movie "Cleopatra," I often wondered how could the ancient Egyptians, who lived in a remote blazing hot region in Africa, look like the Euro—actresses or actors cast in Hollywood movies. Of course, in recent years, casting directors have begun to cast actors who are more ethnically aligned to their roles.

In the historical chapel of our family church, there is a stained glass rendering of the Lord Jesus Christ. In the portrait, He is viewed as the traditional westernized image, with fair skin, fine hair, and slender body. I remember wondering as a little girl why a carpenter didn't have more muscles. I also wondered how He and His parents were able to hide in Egypt, which is in Africa, and not be the center of attention as a white family in a predominantly brown culture. When I would address these questions to the Christian community, I was quickly "shushed" for fear of "blasphemy."

I accepted the deity of the Lord Jesus Christ, and was water baptized when I was five years old. I believed even then, in spite of my questions about His ethnicity, that He was born of His virgin mother, Mary. I fully accepted that He ministered here in the earth, died on Calvary and rose again.

Many years later, I accepted Him as my personal Savior. I understood then, that not only had He been born of the Virgin Mary, crucified and raised from the dead, but that between death and resurrection, He went into hell and defeated the devil. Thus, as He told Peter, "the gates of hell will not prevail!" And He died for my sins. His blood redeemed me. And right now, He is in Heaven, as my High Priest, praying for me and for all who receive Him! He sent God's Holy Spirit to comfort us and teach us! What good news, the Gospel truth!

In the dawn of this reality, race and color seem to have ceased to be an issue for me. Due to my understanding of Acts 17, there is only one race, human, created of one blood. We must look to "Star Trek" for other races and species. We are born into ethnic groups, but the demonic deception of race and racism are lies and trickery from hell!

While the years rolled on, I began to realize that many of my Black brothers and sisters remain in bondage, due to myths and evil influences, which prevent us from discerning and accepting the true word of God.

As the decades continued to pass, I saw the race battles engaged among not only whites against blacks and Native Americans, but blacks and whites against Asians and Hispanics. Added to all of this, the class and caste battles of Blacks against Blacks in the Motherland, whites against whites in Europe, Asians and Indians against their own kind, all boiled down to people against people due to the deceptions of a common unseen enemy.

Such realizations made me even more aware that many of our White brothers and sisters are also victims of their own misconceptions, thus bringing me to question my own heart concerning; what is a man, who is the Black man, and why were we born?

For thousands of years, since the distinguishing of the nations, with the beginnings of the family of Noah, and subsequently the nations of Shem, Ham, and Japheth, race has been an issue. Remember, God did not create "races" of humans. Although at the dawn of history there appear to have been various species and races of "man," God created only one "human race," a race of people of variously colored ethnic groups.

"Of one blood and one man has God made all nations of men for to dwell on the face of the earth; determining the times before appointed, and the bounds of their habitation; that they should seek the Lord, if by chance they might search after Him, and find Him, though He be not far from being found: For in Him we live, and move, and have our being, For we are also His offspring. (Acts 17:25-26).

> In his book ONE BLOOD, Ken Ham discusses racism.
> "One of the biggest justifications for racial discrimination in modern times is the belief that people groups have evolved separately. Thus, different groups are at allegedly different stages of evolution, and so some people groups are more backward than others. Therefore, the other person may not be as fully human as you. This sort of thinking inspired Hitler in his quest to eliminate Jews and Gypsies and to establish the "master race."

Sadly, some Christians have been infected with racist thinking through evolutionary indoctrination that people of a different "color" are inferior because they are supposedly closer to the animals. Such attitudes are completely unbiblical (e.g., Acts 17:26, Colossians 3:11), although out-of-context Bible verses are often conscripted in attempts to justify racist views."

Since, as was stressed earlier, all other races or species of man have either disappeared off the planet, or are in a serious minority, it is evident that the human race is intended to be a family. Because this is a fact that has been established and ordained by God, and since Satan has done everything that he could do to eradicate the family of man, it is no surprise that the wicked old Devil came up with the plan of racism to divide and alienate the populations housed on Planet Earth.

Satan remains crafty enough to know that as long as he can keep man looking at issues of skin color and "race," his nefarious tactics of hate and division can work. Tragically, throughout the generations, people have continued to be used as tools to propagate racism. Primarily, this weakness has sprung from insecurities rooted in a fear of admitting that one's roots are in an ethnic group that has fought to dominate other ethnic groups for thousands of years.

The concept of "race" is a tool of the Devil designed to separate and uproot God's family tree. The White man nor the Black man is the Devil, but Satan seeks to spread the lie of racism to divide the world; a wicked method used to inspire extreme emotional responses and racial conflicts, in the social and intellectual realms of man's reality. Violence, hatred, fear, confusion, deceit, distortion and ignorance are all part of this diabolical plan of Satan to divide God's family.

Fear and denial have sometimes driven people to oppress all who are not like them; under what could be called a "superiority complex". In America, The African-American tribe has been Satan's most recent target, but is not by any means the world's only victim of racism. Even people of the same color and ethnic origins oppress their own kind!

White supremacy or supremacy of any kind is a product of fear! The "White" ethnic family became the last human tribe to emerge on earth, and some have desperately tried to make up for this position by oppressing everyone in their path. This insecurity has made the Caucasian family a very vulnerable entity in the human family structure.

An example of this insecurity is noted in the work of the Afrikaner writer André Brink, who writes of his people, "the White tribe of Africa.

"This group is symbolic of the massive European colonization of the 16th century colonization of Africa by Whites. This radical Afrikaner people have refused to leave the area, or blend with the indigenous cultures, as other Europeans sometimes have. Such classic example of denial, insecurity, and supremacy is just one of the many examples of a racial process that has plagued nations for centuries."

The aim of racism is to conduct self-destruction; a process of killing an individual's roots without killing the person. The Devil must continue to deceive the White man into thinking that the people of color are the enemy. On the contrary, people of color are deceived into thinking that the White man is the enemy, lacking the understanding that "racist people" are controlled by Lucifer. Other tools of Satan's diabolical trade are white privilege, race baiting, and even using Blacks to play the "race card" against White people of good intent.

This is Satan's plot, playing one camp against the other; and has been used by Satan as an instrument to instigate confusion, whereas God is

not the author of confusion (I Corinthians. 14:33)! There are millions
of White people who serve God, who are redeemed, and blessed to be
members of God's family. Remember, racism is just one of Satan's tools used
to destroy God's family. We must not over look that often communities
of people of the same ethnicity are used by Satan to destroy themselves.
people. Some harmful factors are Drugs, crime, sickness, venereal disease,
homosexuality, and abortion: All of these factors have a destructive impact
on the reproduction of all nations. No single people group can be blamed
for these weapons of mass destruction.

White people, Black people, Brown people, Red people, Yellow
people . . . . All human people spring from one human race (Acts 17). The
White people are not the enemy. The Devil is the enemy. Martin Luther
King, Jr., and Malcolm X both reached this revelation before they were
assassinated. Both men preached that the people of color should never
despise or hate our White "brothers." Both men preached the message of
love that is advocated or heavily stressed in the Bible.

Interestingly enough, just as both men were reaching a point of
influencing thousands of "Black" Americans to turn their hearts to love,
rather than hate; or to stress the unity of the nations, rather than the
division of God's children, both men were unfortunately slain. Satan could
not afford to have man to understand the power of unity and love among
the "nations" or "families" of man. *Matt. 5:43-44; Mark 12:33; I John 2:9;
4:20-21.

We cannot love God and hate our brother, no matter what color he
or she is. God ordained the various complexions. God did not ordain
racism. God is not the author of racism (I Corinthians. 14:33). Neither
the Caucasian man nor the Black man is the author of racism. The Devil
is the author of racism.

As human beings of every color, nations and tribes continue to discover
that all people are part of the same family; racism can be confronted and
finally eradicated, with the forces of love and wisdom. Wisdom, knowledge
and understanding go hand in hand. It is wise to consider the teachings of
the Bible, which show that God desires a family, which includes people of
all colors.

AND THE PURSUIT
OF HAPPINESS

King for America
Where Jesus Christ is Lord

Defund Planned Parenthood Campaign

Regret My Abortion

Alveda with Day Gardner on the set of THE VISION

Rev. A. D. King
Brother
to the Dream

Fond Memories

Georgia State
Legislator
1982

THE ECONOMIES (OR POVERTY) OF SIN

Dr. Alveda C. King

"For all have sinned and fallen short of the glory of God."
Romans 3:23

Okay. I'm using the "s" word. Sin. Believe me, I have no fear of being called a Holy Roller for telling you this. I've sinned enough in my lifetime, and been rescued from a life of sin by Jesus, which has given me the courage to "tell the truth and shame the devil."

By definition, sin is:

1. transgression of divine law: *the sin of Adam.*
2. any act regarded as such a transgression, especially a willful or deliberate violation of some religious or moral principle.
3. any reprehensible or regrettable action, behavior, lapse, etc.; great fault or offense: *It's a sin to waste time.*
4. Here are some more examples:

   1. Missing of a mark or aim
   2. Over-passing or trespassing of a line
   3. Disobedience to a voice
   4. Falling where one should have stood upright
   5. Ignorance of what one ought to have known
   6. Diminishing of that which should have been rendered in full measure

7. Non-observance of a Law—sins of omission
    James 4:17
8. Lawlessness or anarchy—utter disregard for the law
9. Debt, failure in duty, or not meeting one's obligations to God

A few years ago, scientist found the remains of an ancient woman. Her DNA thread is found in all women who have lived since her time. The scientists determined that she was the "Eve" of the Bible, the wife of Adam. The Bible teaches that as a couple, Adam and Even disobeyed God in an act resulting from the manipulations of an alien enemy some call satan.

As a result of their disobedience which can be termed as sin, they were separated from God. They lost contact with that loving and intimate relationship with our Creator. The same thing happens with us today. If we are not close to God through our obedience to His Word, we forfeit His blessing. There's no fun in that, is there?

Sin is also expensive. After all, the Bible teaches us that "the wages of sin is death." Think about it. We do something that we know we will regret later—like having unprotected sex outside of marriage. Then we catch something, and end up having to spend money for the "cure." Or we get drunk and end up with a hangover, and have to buy pain relievers. Or we get hooked on drugs and spend fortunes on "rehab." Yes, the "r" word.

Our actions, all of them, good or not so good, mistakes count too . . . They all have consequences. Yes, I said the "c" word.

How about the "a" word? Yes, abortion. Some people think it's cheaper to have an abortion than to birth and raise a baby. Yet, too many women find out that there are certain very costly consequences related to the "choice" (okay, "c" word) to abort a child.

So why do people sin? We were all born with a "sin nature." Okay, and "s" and "n" word together. You don't have to believe this, but your unbelief won't change the fact that sin exists. Also, the forces of evil trick people into believe that sin is actually fun. Can you believe that?

I was once hooked on so many things, that I was an expert in explaining why I wasn't really sinning. Then, I was led to repentance (by the Holy Spirit), and was set free.

By the way, I'm only writing this little message because maybe someone reading this may have the same testimony.

Listen, sin isn't fun. Sin is expensive. Sinning can make you poor, even if you seem to become rich by doing things like stealing someone else's money (I never did that one, by the way).

And we don't have to live in sin. Jesus died to set us free. Even though the wages of sin is death, there is another part to that Bible verse: "The gift of God is eternal life." We can have eternal life by repenting and turning to Jesus.

Here's a little prayer I have prayed for myself, and now invited you to pray and share with your family, neighbors, friends and co-workers:

Heavenly Father, in the name of The Lord Jesus, I come. I confess my sins before your today and ask for your forgiveness. I do believe that Jesus is Your Son, born of the Virgin Mary, lived and ministered in this earth for 33 years, died on the cross at Calvary and shed His blood for my sins. He went into Hell and defeated my enemy Satan, and took the keys of Hell and death. He rose again and came to Heaven to sit on His throne on Your right hand, and serve as my High Priest. He is coming back again soon, as He promised. He has given me the Keys of Your Kingdom, and granted me Your authority to trample on snakes and scorpions and to overcome all the power of my enemy. I believe this Father, and ask You to take me as Your child, to deliver me from all my sickness, disease, and every evil curse and thing that has and could come against me. Break every yoke Father. Fill me with your Holy Spirit and release your ministering angels to take charge over me. Teach me, and lead me into my inheritance according to your promise. Thank you Father, Praise You Lord Jesus, Bless You Holy Spirit. I thank you, and praise you and worship you right now! In Jesus' Name. Amen

I hope you will share this little testimony with someone along the way.

I SING BECAUSE I'M HAPPY

Vernessa Mitchell
www.vernessa.com

As a little girl, I would sing in my father's church. I still sing gospel music today. Along the sometimes rocky, sometimes lofty road to what some would call success as a recording artist, I have never abandoned my gospel roots. I was born into a family of ten where there was no shortage of gifting and talent. Yet, I maintained a steadfast determination to make my mark.

I hit what the world calls stardom at a young age with my sister Barbara and two other teenage girls. We called ourselves High Energy. Berry Gordy of Motown spotted our talent and signed us to a recording contract during the late '70s. Our first album went gold and produced the hit single "You Can't Turn Me Off (In The Middle Of Turning Me On)."

Our fame was affirmed by invitations to appear on American Bandstand, Soul Train and television shows hosted by Merv Griffin, Dina Shore, and Mike Douglas. However, in mid-success I decided to leave the group and Motown. The Lord spoke to me and said "It's time to leave all of this"."

I loved the people at Motown but I was concerned about the message my music gave young people. You have to be so careful about the things you put out there . . . our young people are so influenced by music. I felt a burning need to meet head-on the negative messages that are portrayed through music and contribute to the violent destruction of our youth.

After leaving Motown, I joined Dr. Wayne Davis' World Won for Christ Ministries in California. There, I gained a solid foundation in the Word. God told me I couldn't sing about a man I didn't know about. I soon found the real star in life is Jesus Christ. I became a staff member and served with Dr. Davis' ministry for ten years.

Meanwhile, Kent Washburn, who'd produced me during my Motown days, had given his life to Jesus Christ. He found me, told me about his change of heart and convinced me to sign with his label Command Records. I released two critically-acclaimed albums with Command, the Grammy and Dove Award-nominated "This Is My Story: and "Higher Ground." I praise God that He sent me the same level of professional people and expertise I had experienced at Motown; only now, we are all serving the Lord!

Later, I recorded with the Nicholas Family and co-wrote and sang the lead on the hit song "I Gotta Tell Somebody." My other hits include "Stand Up and Be Counted," "Trust in The Lord," "When I'm Weak I'm Strong" and "He'll Find A Way." My next album was entitled "On A Mission". Released on the Benson label, it featured a stirring song called "Soldier" set to a militaristic beat. This song was nominated for a Stellar award.

Just as I was compelled to leave Motown because of the influence on youth, I am continuing to fight the spiritual warfare against the forces that attempt to destroy our youth. There's such an outcry. Our youth are searching for something more than the world has to offer. Someone needs to challenge them, share the gospel with them, and say, 'You don't have to hurt or settle for less.'"

I issue challenges through special events such as Youth Crisis Awareness Week, a marathon week of youth evangelism spearheaded in the Midwest by Cheryl Hurley, director of the High School Ministry network. Top national Christian youth speakers were paired with well-known musicians to enter 73 high schools in four days and give motivational assemblies.

I teamed up with friend Joseph Jennings, who is a former Black Nationalist who is known for cutting to the heart of gang members. The week culminated in a stadium filled with 15,000-20,000 kids, set against a backdrop of one of the most troubled neighborhoods in Wichita, Kansas. Governor Joan Finney heard about the event and invited us to come to Topeka, Kansas to present our message. Governor Finney was so moved by our outreach that she gave us a letter of recommendation, endorsing our work as we go into other high schools.

My album "Destiny" is geared toward youth and focuses on urban outreach. It's more contemporary than my other releases, and appeals to secular audiences. "It has a nice R&B urban tone; it's the gospel without compromise." Dick Clark Productions took notice of "Destiny", so did top NBA and NFL athletes. I have plans to work alongside athletes associated with a Christian athletic association whose aim is to capture the attention of youth and point them toward higher ground.

My new album "Let Your Presence Fall" takes me back to my roots of Gospel, Inspirational, and Praise & Worship. It is a blend of different styles that once again highlight my God given versatility as a singer. The project is on my new label Priority Sound.

As I tour Italy, France, Germany, Mexico, Puerto Rico, and Trinidad and speak at youth conferences, women's lectures, and before single groups, my God given gifts and talents are heard in my music and are delivered in my preaching.

As an ordained minister working to finish a Master's in Biblical Studies, my focus is to carry the gospel to those who need it most, including inmates behind prison walls. It's important to take the gospel to those who are hurting, who never go inside a church. I also desire to counsel young people. And one day, I hope to open a home for abused children and pregnant teens.

Along life's journey, I have discovered many truths. I have seen music seduce the innocent, weaken the strong and mislead the masses. I have also heard music heal the hopeless and bring joy to the souls of nations. Thankfully, God has used my music to heal and uplift. All I have had to do is to obey His call and use the talents He blesses me with.

As much as I enjoy singing, and I truly sing because I'm happy, I am most blessed to give the gift back to God for his glory. I pray that my music blesses those who God allows me to minister to in song.

SUCCESS IS NOW!

By William Owens, Jr.
Entrepreneur / Author / Minister

Far away is the horizon to which the vision you have deep within your heart beckons you. It calls to you in the wee hours of the morning. It speaks to you at the dinner table. Vision is clearer than it has ever been, and until you hold this vision with your bare hands, success seems to elude you—or so you think. At times, and more often than you care to admit, trouble surrounds you. Even debt has a vice grip on your resources, constraining you emotionally and mentally.

ENOUGH!

"This is not success," declares voices that often arrive during the most troubling times. "What are you thinking?" this voice further utters.

Ignore it. It's part of the process to weed out those who just do not want success badly enough, or rather, cannot grasp the fact that success is NOW!

Success is where you live; it is the reward for staying in the game. Success is not the culmination of your vision but instead the actual living of that vision day in and day out. Living the vision should not be equated with the end of the event in and of itself. It is the beginning of the event as well.

Take Thomas Edison for example. Of the 10,000 failures he had, he found 1,093 patents. So for every patent, he merely had to process 10 events to discover it.

Many times, how we view our experiences defeat us. If you had a, ironclad guarantee from Michael Jordon that you'd get a check from him for $100,000 if you made 100 shots in ONE day from a free-throw line, you would get to it! The only thing that would matter at that point is to start shooting the ball! You wouldn't care how many shots you would miss, because the only thing that would matter to you would be to make those 100 shots within 24 hours.

God has given you more than 24 hours. If you are reasonably healthy, you have a good 80 plus years of life on this earth. If you don't count the beginning 30 years of learning and becoming acclimated to life in general, that leaves you 50 years to live your purpose.

A good example of true, successful living regards a man whose epitaph on his grave reads:

"He could have added fortune to fame, but caring for neither, he found happiness and honor in being helpful to the world."

That man was George Washington Carver. Carver, and agricultural chemist, had only three patents even though he discovered three hundred uses for peanuts aside from the hundreds of other ways that pecans, soybeans, and sweet potatoes could be used. Carver also supported southern farmers by sharing his recipes and ideas for a long list of items such as adhesives, axle grease, bleach, buttermilk, chili sauce, ink, instant coffee, linoleum, mayonnaise, meat tenderizer, metal polish, paper, plastic, pavement, shaving cream, shoe polish, synthetic rubber, talcum powder and wood stain.

"God gave them to me" he would say about his ideas, "How can I sell them to someone else?" In 1940, Carver donated his life savings to the establishment of the Carver Research Foundation at Tuskegee, for continuing research in agriculture. On July 14, 1943, U.S. President Franklin Delano Roosevelt honored Carver with a national monument dedicated to his accomplishments.

For Carver, success was NOW!

George Washington Carver is a tremendous example of why we must never allow success to be defined by what we have in terms of ownership, but what we leave behind for others in terms of benefits.

As we grapple to define success—as many of us do—we simply need to understand and enjoy the process of success and realize that our Success is NOW!

You are making a profound impact on the earth by your presence, and God is your ultimate judge, not the world, not the American way of thinking, and not even your own ideas about yourself. Your success can be enjoyed today, right this minute, when you accept that for every effort towards the end, for every free-throw shot made towards 100, you are winning, you are living, and you are experiencing Success right NOW!

GLOBALLY REGENERATING OPPORTUNITIES WORLDWIDE (G.R.O.W.)

By Michelle Uchiyama,
President, Charitable Connections, Inc.
www.charitableconnections.org

God says, "Rebuild the road! Clear away the rocks and stones
so my people can return from captivity." Isaiah 62:10

The United States healthcare system has failed. Violence is on the increase. Our mental health systems have collapsed and our prisons have replaced our mental health hospitals. The rate of deterioration of our housing, street, bridge and community infrastructure is moving faster than our existing financial systems can support its rehabilitation. Our distribution systems have become so oil dependent that our food costs have impacted our poverty rates and created food deserts, famine in our urban communities and obesity among our children. Our crumbling systems have produced high rates of diabetes, high blood pressure and heart disease. These disturbing epidemics are symptomatic of the failures in our economic, political, and social systems and have caused a tidal wave of dissent around the globe.

In 2004, Charitable Connections, Inc. gathered people from a variety of industries, from the philanthropic community and from around the globe to pray and discuss how we could come together and impact these issues. From three sessions held in Portland Oregon, Oklahoma City, Oklahoma and Nashville, Tennessee, Charitable Connections, Inc. determined that it would take a comprehensive approach on a community by community basis to transcend the barriers that have deteriorated the quality of life for a large number of American families and restore the respect, love and care for each other that made our nation great. So in 2007, Charitable Connections, Inc. set on a journey to begin building collaborations of "generals" (leaders) to regenerate people and places along the second largest industrial corridor in the nation that borders a street named after civil rights leader Martin Luther King Jr. in his hometown of Atlanta, Georgia and begin what is now called the Campaign to G.R.O.W.

Charitable Connections, Inc. started its work with a neighborhood planning unit in Atlanta called NPU-H/Adamsville. We started our work by listening to the community and understanding the issues at hand. The community was 94% African American. It housed the oldest, largest and most criminally active apartments in the country. Over 3,000 people lived in dire poverty in this community, isolated from grocery stores, relegated to poor public transportation, yet accessible to the largest industrial corridor in the southeast. In 2009, these 3,000 people were moved out of this property/community and given housing choice vouchers.

In addition to this government owned multi-family property becoming vacant, NPU-H also housed a very large number of low-income multi-family units of which over 700 had been abandoned because of mortgage fraud and the collapsing sub-prime financial markets.

The declining physical health of the community was also becoming more evident. Seventeen percent of the community was made up of seniors who had very high rates of asthma, diabetes, high blood pressure and heart disease. According to the Fulton County Department of Health and Wellness and the Atlanta Public School system, this area had the highest rates of asthma and high blood pressure in the state.

It was the combination of these housing and health issues that led Charitable Connections, Inc. to begin its focus on developing what is called, The Campaign to G.R.O.W.

What is the vision of the Campaign to G.R.O.W.?

To create a world focused on the love that connects people to a new vision for health, safety, security and peace of mind through its mission of:

- facilitating the development of healthy vibrant leaders;

- creating access to resources that support the health and well being of people, families, neighborhoods, workplaces, communities and the world;
- transforming minds/behavior by promoting healthy living and lifestyle choices;
- transcending the political, economic, and social barriers that keep individuals, families, neighborhoods and communities from achieving their God given destiny.

What are the goals of the Campaign to G.R.O.W. in Atlanta?

Rebuild, restore and replenish over 700 housing units in the next 10 years.

Rebuild, restore and replenish over 10,000 families in the next 10 years.

Improve the health outcomes of residents in the community by improving care and empowering residents to take ownership of their health.

Divert 1,000,000 pounds of waste per year

Increase the number of young families in the area by 50% in the next 10 years.

Re-establish respect and dignity as the basis for a value system among community members.

Improve the educational attainment and economic opportunity of residents in the community by alleviating illiteracy, improving educational outcomes and providing economic options with upward mobility.

How are people getting involved?

Charitable Connections, Inc. is facilitating connections of leaders across sectors. Charitable Connections Inc. is implementing and encouraging the leaders to establish learning communities. Charitable Connections, Inc. is linking these learning communities with mentors and subject matter experts and we are engaging the community to impact their own destiny.

An example of Charitable Connections work was to facilitate volunteers from the Centers for Disease Control to empower the NPU-H

Health Committee to implement a PACE-EH study. This study led to 1,000 residents giving their input to what health issues they thought were important for their community to address. This health study led to the community going after leadership grants, grants for better pedestrian access to their community, community beautification projects, advocacy in Washington on air quality, advocacy for a new public health facility addressing mental and physical health and community health and wellness classes.

Another example is in the area of funding housing initiatives by converting one man's trash to another man's treasure. Economic issues in the NPU-H community and along the Fulton Industrial corridor have led to over 1.4 million square feet of industrial space being available. In addition, the vacant housing market has led to a need for building materials. Finally, the lack of landfills for the material waste that is being generated in Atlanta has led to an innovative approach to reducing waste going to landfills. To bring these issues together and solve several problems at once, Charitable Connections, Inc. worked side by side with the Fuller Center for Housing of Greater Atlanta, the National Association of Remodeling Industry/Atlanta, the National Kitchen and Bath Association, the City of Atlanta Office of Sustainability, Clarion Partners, Fulton County and the Fulton Industrial Community Improvement District and created a market based approach to solve the social problems of affordable housing and waste diversion called Reclaim It Atlanta.

Reclaim It Atlanta started in 3,600 square feet of space off of the Fulton Industrial corridor and bordering NPU-H in April of 2010. In December of 2011, Reclaim It Atlanta expanded to 18,800 square feet of space and has created over 9 jobs and an income stream to support the Campaign to G.R.O.W. and the affordable housing work of the Fuller Center for Housing of Greater Atlanta. This next 18 months Charitable Connections anticipates over 1,000 volunteers to help with diverting one million pounds of waste and the restoration of over 150 housing units in NPU-H.

Charitable Connections, Inc. is looking at other market based approaches to social issues and facilitating the development of many more learning communities as an outgrowth of the Campaign to G.R.O.W. For more information on connecting with the Campaign to G.R.O.W you can contact Michelle Uchiyama at michelle@campaign2grow.net.

Remember, train up the generals in "HIS" army, for he is getting ready to set the captives free.

LORD REMOVE THESE STUMBLING BLOCKS LEST I FALL

By Fred V-Man Watson
http://www.victoryoverviolence.webuda. com/V-story.html

Regardless of political or religious affiliation voices cry out for divine intervention from a wilderness of broken hopes and dying dreams crying out "Lord Remove my stumbling blocks least I fall thus fail to meet the fulfillment of my purpose". Beyond theological reference or conceptual context, the practical reality of 'Stumbling Blocks' can be defined as conditions which impede physical, mental, social, emotional, environmental progress. Negative subliminal re-enforcement through music, entertainment, media and social media can be attributed to stumbling blocks which lead to sub-standard life performances which negatively impacts potential for reasonable economical sustainability.

The spirit of war and corruption among leaderships across our Globe has created such a paralysis in the spirit the common man that the call for healing, non-violence and education are no longer defined by culture, age, gender, political or economic groupings. The call is for Non-Violence & Educational tools for all children for mothers and fathers emotionally paralyzed and ill equip to alter the stumbling blocks that have left offspring victims enslaved by cages or caskets. Today all children are at risk. For most it's not the matter of if but rather when! Thus the growing need for specialist and tools related to Prevention, Intervention or Recovery are equally needed.

For over 15 years. through many collaborations and partnerships including King For America©, A.D. King Foundation© and Charitable

Connection© among many others Victory over Violence as a Non-Violence© Marketing Campaign fostering information, education and training linked to Entertainment Industry and events was able to create and test market a number of such tools in-house. V-Advantage©, HUYOE© and JUST SAY WAIT© are among the 'Contemporary Popular Culture Sensitive Tools' now available to individuals or services providers.

They can be used as a program supplement, stand alone or even permitted to co-brand using their own logo to best serve their constituencies without compromise of their autonomy, creativity, resources or funding bases a 'Stumbling Block' to 'Unity In Community' & Coalition Building.

V-Advantage© is an educational support tool that enables any parent, child or group regardless of language, educational or technological barriers the ability to insure that no child or adult does not have the ability to tutor themselves or their loved ones in terms of math, science, reading, social studies and foreign languages. 'HUYOE'© is a behavioral development support tool for home or institutional usage K-12 Non-Violence a science based Training guide with animated characters. It combines the ancient with the contemporary wisdom around the central moral theme of 'Do Unto Others as You Wish Done Unto You'. Children and Adults are made up of both positive and negative behaviors that characterize perceptions of what we and or others think we are. HUYOE exercises shared between parent and child contains antidotes to the poisons of self doubt and low esteem.

Like children's medicine, cognitive exercises strengthening skill sets needed for success in higher education today are emotionally tasty, entertaining and fun. Supporting the effort are well constructed mobilization instruments available for use under the name brands Dads to be on Duty© & Moms on Mission©.

They are joined as one reminiscent of Great Campaign/ Movements passed set forth to eliminate America's Stumbling Blocks of injustice driven by race or gender. To stumble and error is to be human. To fall and not fail is 'Devine but only possible though spirits of faith, love, hope and charity . . . . Fred Vman Watson, Victory over Violence Advocate: fredvman@bellsouth.net (404) 505-7918

MOTHERS' DAY MESSAGE 2012

By Dr. Alveda C. King

Isaiah 54: **5** "For your Maker is your husband—the LORD
Almighty is his name—the Holy One of Israel is your
Redeemer; he is called the God of all the earth."

The night before Mother's Day in 1963, our family home was bombed in Birmingham, Alabama. You can learn all about it at www.adkingfoundation.com. Little did I know that almost fifty years later, I would be standing here in the 21st century sharing about mothers and Mothers' Day with my church family at Believers' Bible Christian Church in Atlanta.

I was raised in a Christian home, with Christian parents and grandparents. My mother tells me that when I was five years old, I would tell her and my Daddy that I would have six children when I grew up. I was the youngest of five children, and my memories of my parents, and my grandparents and my aunts and uncles are very special, because as a child, I was loved and protected.

It is very important for children to know and to love and to be loved by their parents, by their family, no matter what is going on in the lives of the adults of their families, and in the world around them.

In Psalm 127, the Bible says:

A song for pilgrims ascending to Jerusalem. A psalm of Solomon.

¹ Unless the LORD builds a house, the work of the builders is wasted.
Unless the LORD protects a city, guarding it with sentries will do no
good.

² It is useless for you to work so hard from early morning until late at
night, anxiously working for food to eat; for God gives rest to
his loved ones.
³ Children are a gift from the LORD; they are a reward from him.
⁴ Children born to a young man are like arrows in a warrior's hands.
⁵ How joyful is the man whose quiver is full of them!
He will not be put to shame when he confronts his accusers at the
city gates.

Yes, children are a gift from God, and God has allowed me to have
six beautiful gifts in my life to live and grow up under me, and call me
their Mother; as well as nine precious grandchildren. I haven't been a
perfect mother, and I guess there is no such thing. What I have been is a
grateful mother. I am blessed by the smiles and the tears of my children
and grandchildren, and there is only one greater blessing in my life, and
that is my personal relationship with Abba Father, My Lord Jesus Christ
and Precious Holy Spirit.

I thank God for the gift of my children. I am also grateful for the lessons
on parenting and raising my children that I have experienced during my
years at BBCC. Pastor McNair has taught many lessons on how to be a
good mother and a good parent. They have made a big difference in our
lives over the years.

When I came to Believers' Bible Christian Church in 1989, I was
expecting my sixth child of my nine children; my last child to be born
alive. I came to BBCC expecting to receive something in my life. I knew
I wanted to be a better person, and a better mother. I remember enrolling
in the Believers' School of Ministry and taking my first class when my last
baby was still nursing. It was an amazing time.

Over the next few years, as the children grew older and three of them
were registered in Believers' Bible Christian Academy, I finally began to more
fully realize my responsibilities as a Christian mother. By the mid-nineties I
had been married and divorced two times, and was raising my children as
what would be called a "single mother" these days. This meant that there
was no father in the home.

One of my biggest challenges was to make sure that my children knew
and had genuine relationships with their fathers even though I was no
longer married. That meant learning not to say unkind things about their
fathers, teaching them to honor their fathers and their mother. It was hard
sometimes, because there were bad feelings among us as adult divorced

parents. But at BBCC, under the teaching of Pastor Allen McNair, I began to understand how important love and support would always be to my children.

One of the biggest highlights of my life was to have my daughter participate in the BBCA Coronation. Her father attended and escorted her to present her as a young lady. I remember during those days, she would tell me her favorite scripture was about how Moses picked up a serpent and as he lifted it up it became his rod and the people were healed. She also told me years later how my playing scripture music songs everyday helped her to learn the Bible.

People seem to marvel that all of my adult children enjoy spending time with me. We go to movies, cook together, talk about God together, and pray together. The Bible teaches us that we should not provoke our children to anger. When I was a little girl, most of my friends were raised by parents who taught that children should be seen and not heard. My Daddy and Mother and my grandparents were different. We were encouraged to talk to our parents as long s we were respectful. The thing is, my parents and "grandparents listened to us, and then, they corrected our foolish thinking. Oh yes, I remember discipline, whippings and things like that. But my parents took time to talk to us and to teach us.

My mother used to tell us that we could say anything to her, tell her anything as long as we were respectful. As a result, I told my mother many things that other young girls would never tell their mothers. I have raised my children the same way. They tell me just about everything. People don't believe that, but they do.

Mama used to say some of the things I would tell her made her hold her breath until she could get to her room and pray "help me Jesus." When she came out of her prayer closet, she always had some good advice for me. She still does. And that's the way I still talk to my children. Sometimes they bring me a very heavy load, and then they will say, "I know where you're going now Mom. And away to my prayer closet I go. They don't mind waiting for their answers until after God gives me His Word.

My friends, we live in some troubled times. The Bible says that we are to expect and beware evil in the last days . . . Just last Wednesday, when the President of the United States endorsed homosexual marriage, my children had a lot to say. They were not happy to hear this decision at all.

When the news came, they watched me go out the door for a long walk, to pray. I told them I was sad and needed to talk with God. Over the next few hours, we talked about praying for those in authority, and about what God did to Sodom and Gomorrah. They said that some of their friends didn't see anything wrong with what the President has done. I told them that they shouldn't pretend to go along with their friends' way of thinking because they know it is wrong. I told them not to be afraid to share their beliefs; to speak of God's Plan for sexuality; one man and one woman experiencing loving sex together in the marriage bed. The result? The birth of special gifts from God, children.

Yes, we must teach our children, whether they are little children or grown up. We must teach them what is right. We must tell them about how God changed our lives, how having Jesus as our Lord and Savior, and how Holy Spirit is our teacher, we must tell them that this is how we know what to say and to do in good times and in times of trouble. They must see us repent when we are wrong. They must see that God forgives us because we are not perfect. Then they will have an example to follow.

They must see us walk in love and forgiveness, so that they too can learn to love and forgive. When they make mistakes, they need our advice, not our scorn; our love and not our mean spirits. We should never say to them that they are ugly or stupid or worthless. We must never tell them that they should know better if we have not taught them better or shown them better. We must teach them the way, just as someone had to teach us the way. Our children are gifts from God.

Ladies, we are mothers for a reason. Our children need for us to encourage and teach them to obey authority—in the home, at school, at work, in church, and yes in the fullness of their lives; from conception until natural death. They need Jesus.

With a loving touch and a firm yet loving communication, we must make our lives an example of trusting and obeying God, an example of faith, hope and love. Our children are our blessings, our gifts. Let us pray.

> Dear Heavenly Father, we thank you for mothers, thank you for children. Help us today to value the gifts you have given us in our children. Help our children to honor and respect us as mothers, and to receive you as their Lord. Forgive us for all of our sins that we have committed against ourselves, our children and others. We bind every force of darkness that would prevent us from accomplishing our purpose in this gift of life that you have given to all of us. Help us from this day forward to know and appreciate more and more how to be good mothers, and grandmothers, good aunts, good sisters, and cousins, good

friends, good neighbors, good co-workers, good Christians,
so that our Children will know and fulfill their God given
destinies and have bright and shining lights of examples of your
love, grace and goodness as patterns for their lives, and bless us
all with the blessing of Abraham. In Jesus Name we pray. Amen

SINGLE, HAPPY, CELIBATE & FOCUSED YOU'RE WORTH THE WAIT

By LaKisha Chapman
www.mommyletmelive.com

In today's society where sex is strongly encouraged and women and men are pressured into sexual intercourse it is hard to remain pure and stay celibate—but it can be accomplished. You may ask yourself, "How does she know it can be successfully accomplished?" Well because I am doing it. I have been single and celibate for 6 years. Now there is a process we all must go through, a path we all must walk and a journey we all must take. This was part of my process and the way God took me along the journey to celibacy.

I was dealing with a lot of hurt six years ago from my childhood into adulthood and didn't know what to do with the pain. I had so much anger built up inside of me. It was if I was a bubbling volcano waiting to erupt and finally I did. I went through so much drama in my life.

I was searching and searching for love but in all the wrong places, yet I never found it. I was looking for love in all the wrong people but didn't see it. All the time I was looking for love and all the while, love was inside of me; and when you're looking and searching high and low for something you want so badly you will do anything to get it.

Love is powerful and sometimes blind. The search can become very addictive. It can make you seemingly fall in love with people you shouldn't even associate with; do things you don't want to do and it can make you do things you've never done before. When you don't love yourself that is when you will allow people to come into your life and commit love abuse and you think it's okay because you feel that their abuse is a strange kind of love.

In the process, you're not able to make sound decisions because your mind is not clear. Somehow, along the way, I gradually begin to love me andi discovered that I was the answer to a lot of my pain and that's why I didn't allow myself to let love abuse reoccur. It's just like when a mother has a child; because of the love she has for her child a person can do all they want to her but don't touch her child because when you do, you get a reaction you don't want to see. That's how it should be with you; when you love yourself, you will not let anyone harm, disrespect or hurt you.

God being God at the right moment in time grabbed my attention and I had no choice but to listen because He was my last alternative. Once He had my attention, I attended a church and started getting full off of His word. I was stunned by His unconditional Agape Love He had for me. Nobody has loved me like that ever.

When you experience the Love of Jesus you want to tell the whole world about it. I was drawn to Him like a moth to a flame. I couldn't get enough. You wouldn't understand where I'm coming from if you never tried God. Why not try him for He is so good. One real encounter with the Lord and you'll never be the same.

Once I fell in love with Him, sex was a wrap and I was a new woman. Just like that. It happened suddenly. I didn't have any thoughts of desires of sex for about the first three years and that's because God was doing His work in me. I didn't know it then but He was getting me ready to be an example for other women to follow.

Living Happy & Single

I started building my relationship with God and then I fell in love with myself and I started dating me. I mean, I learned to go places by myself, treat myself to dinner and a move, that type of thing. After all, I had to get to know this new person God had transformed me into. When you begin to love yourself, date and spend time with yourself, you start to get your mind right. I loved me like never before. I put me on my calendar, and enjoyed the quiet moments! A relationship with not just God—but with yourself as well is the first step to happiness. In your pursuit to happiness you must have these keys to unlock the doors to your own happiness. You must love yourself, know your worth, know who you are and know who you belong to.

It's okay to be single and if you are you shouldn't be embarrassed about it. When you have the right mind-set and you're content with who you are and you know where you are going, then you don't mind being single because you're happy with yourself.

Separation sometimes from the dating scene is good because of all the things that come with relationships. Some things are worse than others; like the emotional roller coasters, the STD scares. Not allowing that alone time is putting fire on top of fire. It forces you to see your faults as well, and then prepares you to be a better you in your future relationship.

When there are kids involved a parent has to take extra precaution. I also choose to be single and wait because I have kids. I have to set a proper example for them. Children are a product of their environment. They reenact what they see. I don't need them to see me with Johnny today and Tyler tomorrow. What I need them to see is Mommy happy, taking care of them, the house and staying focused on all my projects for now.

Being single for six years allows me to confront some issues I have and deal with them before I go into another relationship. I had to get my mind and my heart back. Now it may not take that long for you or it may be longer as I said earlier. Everyone has their own process they must go through. I was able to see who I really was and who God wanted me to become. I love myself so much that I am willing to remain single until God sends the man who He specifically designed for me who will know my worth and see my potential.

I am single and celibate so I don't put myself into situations where I can fall into temptation. I don't just casually date. I don't allow men to take me to dinner or to a show because it's a waste of my time if I know you're not man for me. Some asked, well if you don't date how will you know who is the right man for you?" Trust me you'll know but that's when you have to be in tune with God and yourself. If you are you'll be able to discern and you'll know. Don't get me wrong all women love to be pampered, wined and dined—but at what cost?. I am priceless and I am worth the wait. Again waiting can at times be a little challenging because I am human, but I get my mind right quickly and tell myself I'm worth the wait.

Get Focused & Stay Focused

If you are single that doesn't mean you are lonely or have to be. There are also benefits to being single. So enjoy them while you can, and enjoy you. Utilize that time to get in shape if you're not. Do some things you've always wanted to do. Go back to school, write a book, volunteer with various organizations, travel; hang out with your friends on a regular basis. That can be very fulfilling as well. Do you. Date yourself, and look good for yourself. At the appointed time love will find you. Until then it should be all about you and your kids if you have any.

Also what has helped me stay celibate is being involved in my projects and staying focused on my assignments and my destiny. When you're constantly busy there is no time left to lose focus. Some once said: "An idle mind is the devil's workshop."

So stay busy and stay focused because if you don't that's how you get yourself into trouble. You will know when you truly love yourself because you will not let anyone take advantage of your body because you know that is your temple and it should be treated with love and respect and maintained by the one God has chosen for you.

> *Finally brothers and sisters, whatever is true, whatever is noble, whatever is right, whatever is pure, whatever is lovely, whatever is admirable-if anything is excellent or praise-worthy-think about such things. Whatever you learned or perceived or heard from me, or seen in me-put it into practice. And the God of peace will be with you."*
> **—Philippians 4:8 (NIV)**

SEXUAL RISK AVOIDANCE

Freda McKissic Bush, MD, FACOG
www.fredabush.com

"If you could change your community to make it better, what would you do? If you knew your community was endangered near extinction, what changes would you be willing to make to save it?"

People often get caught up valuing "rights" and "freedom" more than the life of a human being, valuing the right to choose over the right to life. As a practicing OB/GYN for the past twenty-nine years and a health professional specializing in women's health for over forty years, I have become increasingly aware of an imminent threat to the survival of the Black race.

Initially presented as a way to help save women's lives and empower them to take charge of their own health, abortion was viewed as a "right." Now after thirty nine years, the truth is known. Abortion is a "wrong." Abortion not only hurts women, it also kills babies, families and communities.

Understanding this information empowers you to decide whether to continue down this path of death and destruction or turn and choose the path of life and liberty. With our history of slavery and disempowerment for generations, it was easy for us to latch on to the catchy phrases of "right to choose," "reproductive rights," and "freedom of choice." We quickly forgot that what is done to the least of us is eventually done to all.

Three consequences of our shortsightedness and ignorance that disproportionably affect Blacks will be addressed below. This does not include the physical consequences associated with abortion as hemorrhaging, infection, injury to the bowel and bladder, possible infertility, hysterectomy and death of the mother.

Consequences of Induced Abortion

First, according to the Institute of Medicine 2006 report on preterm birth causes, consequences and prevention, induced abortion is noted as an immutable risk factor for premature labor (Swingle, Colaizy, Zimmerman & Morris, 2009). Stated simply, if there's a history of a previously induced abortion, premature labor in future pregnancies is an unalterable risk factor. Black women deliver their babies prematurely three times as often as white women. We also obtain 35% of all abortions in the United States, although we are only 13% of the population.

The second consequence is the psychological affect evidenced most in the post-abortion syndrome. After the initial feelings of relief, there are long term studies that reveal a linkage between abortion and a woman's mental health resulting in depression, substance abuse, and suicide in young women (Coleman, 2011).

The third unintended consequence of abortion is the breast cancer risk. When this natural pregnancy process is interrupted abruptly by abortion, the breast cells are left in an immature state and vulnerable to develop cancer. The association between abortion & breast cancer has been documented by many studies (Laing et al, 1993).

Every organ system is affected and changed in some way by pregnancy. It is natural for the woman to nurture the child—the product of her womb. It is unnatural for a woman to sacrifice her child for herself. Without pregnancy and birth, the race becomes extinct. There is no one left to fight for rights.

A Scientific Reality

The scientific reality is that the instant a human egg and sperm unite (fertilization), the newly formed being contains the full complement of DNA in which hair and eye color, gender, and all other physical characteristics are determined. During its journey down the fallopian tube, the fertilized egg is actively growing and dividing. It will then implant in the uterine lining where it will continue to grow.

Body changes also begin immediately in the woman. The hormone progesterone prepares the endometrial lining in the womb to receive the embryo. Once implanted in the endometria, a special process occurs for the nourishments to be transported to the baby through a thin membrane without exchanging blood.

Estrogen grows the breast tissue and the milk glands. Progesterone matures the breasts for milk production to nourish the child after birth. Later, a brain hormone, oxytocin, stimulates the uterus for labor to evacuate the womb. After birth, when the baby cries or when it is time to feed, the oxytocin stimulates the milk to "let down" and the natural bonding of the mother and baby.

No Replacement Value

For every 100 Black babies born, there are seventy-seven other Black babies killed by abortion. That is a ratio of four to three. A fertility rate of 2.1 is needed to continue a race and replace the ones present who will naturally die. The 0.1 is needed for the expected miscarriages. Current fertility rate in Blacks is 1.9. We are not even at replacement value. As a race we cannot survive at that rate.

"Play It Forward" is a popular saying to evaluate future consequences of what we are doing now. Put aside labels like liberal, conservative, right, left, politically correct, Christian, Republican or Democrat. I read recently that the reason for a higher rate of abortion in the Black community was a function of healthcare disparity. The author proposed if Black women had access to birth control information and services including condoms, and if they had better healthcare and affordable healthcare for their children, then they would not have such a high rate of unintended pregnancies, and thus would not need abortions.

The fact is millions of dollars are being spent annually on Title X for free family planning services at health departments and Community Health Centers where they already dispense all birth control measures including condoms. The problem is that we have disconnected sex from procreation (reproduction) and we view sex mainly as a recreation seeking pleasure and stress relief.

Mistake . . . Intrusion . . . Burden?

When pregnancy occurs, even with the use of condoms and contraceptive measures, we are not prepared. We see the pregnancy as a mistake, intrusion and burden; thus, we treat it as such and seek to eliminate it. We are blindsided when we deny that the purpose of sex is not only for pleasure but also procreation and relationship or the 3 R's—recreation, reproduction and relationship.

The right of the woman to choose what to do with her body should be exercised *before* pregnancy is conceived. The right of the baby to life—to be born and exercise its rights to choose—is the first right after conception. If pregnancy is not desired, the woman has freedom and can exercise her right to avoid the risk of pregnancy by abstinence or birth control measures.

Pregnancy Resource Centers

Pregnancy Resource Centers (PRC) are nationwide to provide women with alternatives to abortion. They provide counseling, material services, referrals to financial assistance and medical services. PRCs also provide post-abortion counseling. I am the medical director for the two centers in Jackson, Mississippi. One is dedicated to the Black community since we obtain the largest number of abortions.

The thought process is to identify with the women and men of color and penetrate the communities with the information that would wake us up to the devastation abortion is causing. Being able to identify the root causes will help avoid the perceived necessity for abortion.

You have heard it said that to get a different result, one must do a different thing. I do not want to leave you hopeless or in despair after reading this article. Here are my proposals for action:

- We must come together and genuinely love each other—unselfishly, expecting nothing in return.
- We must practice the universal principles of self-control, self-discipline, respect and responsibility.

We have to take personal responsibility for our own actions first. Changing our worldview will save the children for they are our future.

Dr. Freda Bush is a board-certified OB/GYN in private practice in Jackson, Mississippi and a member of the American Association of Prolife OB/GYN.

REFERENCES

Coleman, P. (September 1, 2011). Abortion and mental health. *The British journal of psychiatry* (BJP).

Lazovich, D., Thompson, J.A., Mink, P. J., Sellers, T.A., Anderson, K.E. (2000). Induced abortion and breast cancer risk. *Epidemiology.* 11(1):76-80.

Laing, A.E., Demenais, F.M., Williams, R., Kissling, G., Chen, V.W., Bonney, G. E. (1993). Breast cancer risk factors in African-American women: the Howard University tumor registry experience. *Journal National Medical Association.* 85:931-9. http://www.ncbi.nlm.nih.gov/pubmed/8126744

Preterm Birth Report. (2006). Institute of Medicine.

Swingle, H. M., Colaizy, T. T., Zimmerman, M. B., & Morris, Jr., F. H. (2009). Abortion and the risk of subsequent preterm birth: A systematic review with meta-analyses, 54 J. *Reproductive Medicine.* 95-108.

HUMAN SEXUALITY AND GOD'S PLAN FOR MARRIAGE

Dr. Alveda King
www.kingforamerica.com

Scripture References: Genesis, Ruth, Esther, Psalm 51, Song of Solomon, Romans, Ephesians, Matthew, Mark, John, 1 John

Psalm 51:1 For the choir director: A psalm of David, regarding the time Nathan the prophet came to him after David had committed adultery with Bathsheba. Have mercy on me, O God, because of your unfailing love. Because of your great compassion, blot out the stain of my sins. 2 Wash me clean from my guilt. Purify me from my sin. 3 For I recognize my shameful deeds—they haunt me day and night.

Yes, the history about my two aborted babies (Phillip and Jessica) and one miscarried baby (Raphael) due to complications surrounding the abortions is becoming familiar. What many people haven't heard is the rest of the story, about my sometimes painful journey to sexual wholeness that has come full circle through forgiveness, the healing power of the Holy Spirit by the Love and Divine Mercy of my Lord Jesus Christ, and the grace of my ABBA Creator God.

Psalm 51:4 Against you, and you alone, have I sinned; I have done what is evil in your sight. You will be proved right in what you say, and your judgment against me is

just. 5 For I was born a sinner—yes, from the moment
my mother conceived me.

My grandfather, Dr. Martin Luther King, Sr. rescued me from abortion in 1950, when the Birth Control League (later known as Planned Parenthood) was trying to convince my mother that her "unplanned pregnancy" was just a "lump of flesh" and that she should try a procedure called a D&C which was a clever solution to many "mysterious female problems." Granddaddy told Mother that he had seen me in a dream three years before my birth, a "bright skinned baby girl with red hair." He convinced my mother to keep me, and on January 22, 1951 Alveda Celeste King was born.

As a cherished and beloved child in what would become the famous "King Legacy," I should have been protected from sexual predators. Without the knowledge of my parents and grandparents, I fell victim to a teenage neighbor when I was ten and he was seventeen. He touched me inappropriately when he walked me to the store and back, and brought me candy, and warned me not to tell "our secret." This was very confusing to me because I wasn't sure why I couldn't tell . . .

Two years later, I was still pretty confused about sexuality, but wasn't sure who to talk to and what to say. I did talk to another neighbor, an older girl who was my "babysitter." I told her what the boy had done, and she asked me to show her. The sad thing is, she ended up touching me too, leading to more confusion . . .

Today, we would call this "child molestation," and I would agree that as a child my innocence had been sorely violated. I even kept those experiences a secret when I became a "virgin" bride. At the time of my first marriage, I went to my honeymoon with my hymen intact. But I was far from innocent because of the previous violations.

Psalm 51:6 But you desire honesty from the heart, so you can teach me to be wise in my inmost being. 7 Purify me from my sins, and I will be clean; wash me, and I will be whiter than snow. 8 Oh, give me back my joy again; you have broken me—now let me rejoice. 9 Don't keep looking at my sins. Remove the stain of my guilt.

The sin of abortion was added to my list of guilty secrets. I became more "private" about my sexuality, adding secrets to secrets, pain on top of pain . . . In my twenties, after my divorce, I was a victim of "date rape."

It was painful and terrible . . . And a secret I added to my growing list of secrets . . .

Yes, I kept these incidents secret until many years later, when young victims of similar and worse incidents came to share their secrets with me. Needless to say, I remembered my pain, and was very careful not to continue the cycle of pain. I never did inappropriate touching of the little ones who were seeking my help. I also didn't advise any young women to get abortions. I thank God that He broke the cycle, and I didn't harm His little ones.

> **Psalm 51:10 Create in me a clean heart, O God. Renew a right spirit within me.**
> **11 Do not banish me from your presence, and don't take your Holy Spirit from me.**
> **12 Restore to me again the joy of your salvation, and make me willing to obey you.**
> **13 Then I will teach your ways to sinners, and they will return to you.**
> **14 Forgive me for shedding blood, O God who saves; then I will joyfully sing of your forgiveness.**
> **15 Unseal my lips, O Lord, that I may praise you.**

As the young ones came, I began to share my testimony of the violations of my soul and body by people I trusted. I added the molestation accounts and the abortion accounts, the adultery and fornication and rape episodes and finally the redemption trail that led to my being born again and healed. I was able to assure the ones who came to me that their victimization was not their fault, and to help them to forgive those who hurt them, and to seek forgiveness, restoration, redemption and inner healing for themselves.

> **Psalm 51:16 You would not be pleased with sacrifices, or I would bring them. If I brought you a burnt offering, you would not accept it. 17 The sacrifice you want is a broken spirit. A broken and repentant heart, O God, you will not despise. 18 Look with favor on Zion and help her; rebuild the walls of Jerusalem. 19 Then you will be pleased with worthy sacrifices and with our whole burnt offerings; and bulls will again be sacrificed on your altar.**

The bottom line is that too many people have been very ignorant of Satan's plan to destroy God's procreative plan for human sexuality. His evil tactics often lead to child molestation, human sex trafficking, porn addiction, adultery, fornication, abortion, rape, divorce and so many other forms and misuse of human sexuality and other destruction of God's procreative family units that are not life affirming.

The debate over human sexuality is as old as humanity. For ages, people have indulged in sexual expressions within and without of the foundational structure which was ordained for the procreation and longevity of the human family.

Is sex wrong? Is sex dirty? Is sex right? Is sex good? The answers lie in the perspectives of those asking the questions. Even the definition of sex is often unclear in these days and times.

For instance, someone might ask the question, "what sex are you?" Do they mean what gender? If gender determination is the desired outcome from the answer to the question, then, it would be better to ask, "what gender are you?"

This question often causes its own brand of confusion, because in the ongoing quest for enlightenment, some people are "gender confused." In essence, some people, born male, have early signs of "feeling more female than male." The same can be said of some women. As people approach puberty, their sexual identities mature, and heterosexual or homosexual tendencies become more apparent.

There are often testimonies from male homosexuals about how their parents tried to "beat it out of them." Girls who display male tendencies are generally labeled as "tomboys," and are not targeted for confrontation about their sexuality as early as boys are. Yet, the approach in any case should be compassionate and informed, rather than a form of attack. A question should arise: "If your son or daughter was born with or displayed early symptoms cancer, would you try to beat it out of your child?"

Some people believe that God creates homosexuals. They also believe that it is God's will that people have diabetes, or high blood pressure, or other forms of sickness and disease. They even feel that it is God's will that some be poor and hungry. Otherwise, they reason, "If God had wanted me to be straight, He would have made me that way. Since God is God, can't He change these things, if they are not His will?"

So if someone is born a certain way, the assumption would be that God made them that way. The good news is that God designs each of us to be whole and perfect. No matter how we are born, and what degree of sin and iniquity is part of our birth (including sickness and disease), the really good news is that we can be born again!

The bad news is that sin entered into our lives at the time of the fall of Adam and Eve, disturbing the perfect design of humanity, short circuiting the perfect plan of creation, all of which has been transmitted down from generation to generation through DNA and RNA.

A short lesson in history, or even a long BIBLE examination would reveal that God desires that we members of the human race **(Acts 17:26 Of One Blood, God made all people)** would all be whole, healthy and blessed in every way. Evil forces are the originators of sickness, disease and poverty; on the other hand, God is Love and God is good!

This leads one to consider the origins of sin, sickness, disease, poverty and all harmful influences that affect the procreative human family. We could turn to the Bible for answers, yet some people do not trust the Bible.

"The Bible was written by the white man," they say. "You can't trust their Bible because they used it to enslave us." While this is true, some slave masters often twisted the truths of the Bible, to their own dark purposes, this doesn't mean that the BIBLE is twisted, just the humans who did evil things were twisted. This is not just a Black/White thing; many people, no matter what their ethnic identities are, use the Bible to misinterpret the goodness of God.

Have you ever heard anyone say, "the white man used money to enslave us, so we can't use money?" Or, "the white man made us pick cotton, so we can't wear cotton?" Of course not. Like it or not, the Bible is an established source of divine law. Without the ten commandments, and all the commands of the Bible, especially the commandment to LOVE God, ourselves and our neighbors, we are a lawless people.

So why do we reject the Bible which is full of truth, and still cling to other much less perfect tools that were used in our days of misery?

Some even try to use the Bible to justify certain lifestyles, whether in the realms of sexuality, money, relationships, no matter. If a human being can interpret or misinterpret the Bible to fit a personal desire, the temptation will be there. People do this all the time, no matter what color they are.

Mark 11:22 Then Jesus said to the disciples, "Have faith in God. 23I assure you that you can say to this mountain, 'May God lift you up and throw you into the sea,' and your command will be obeyed. All that's required is that you really believe and do not doubt in your heart. 24Listen to me! You can pray for anything, and if you believe, you will have it. 25But when you are praying, first forgive anyone you are holding a grudge against, so that your Father in heaven will forgive your sins, too."

When people went to Christ for healing, He taught them to forgive others. Then, He would forgive their sins, and they would be made whole. Of course, some people were offended when Jesus said "your sins are forgiven, be whole." They didn't want to forgive those who had hurt them; and they didn't want to admit that their own sins and sickness were related.

Matthew 9:_1Jesus climbed into a boat and went back across the lake to his own town. 2Some people brought to him a paralyzed man on a mat. Seeing their faith, Jesus said to the paralyzed man, "Be encouraged, my child! Your sins are forgiven."3But some of the teachers of religious law said to themselves, "That's blasphemy! Does he think he's God?"4Jesus knew what they were thinking, so he asked them, "Why do you have such evil thoughts in your hearts? 5Is it easier to say 'Your sins are forgiven,' or 'Stand up and walk'? 6So I will prove to you that the Son of Man has the authority on earth to forgive sins." Then Jesus turned to the paralyzed man and said, "Stand up, pick up your mat, and go home!"7And the man jumped up and went home! 8Fear swept through the crowd as they saw this happen. And they praised God for sending a man with such great authority.

Sins and iniquities are ancient, so are sickness and disease (which originated with sin and iniquity.) Let's just say that one more time. Sin and iniquity are partners with sickness and disease. We are born into a world of sin, with the ravages of sin translated into sickness and disease (generational curses) imprinted in our DNA and RNA. Think about it. Mama was diabetic, so is the child. Papa had high blood pressure, so does the child.

Sickness and sin entered into the human family with the fall of man. It is interesting to note that if someone has cancer, or diabetes or hypertension, he or she will run to the doctor. Sickness feels bad, so we try to get rid of it. Sin feels bad too, but we are not so quick to look for deliverance or healing from sin. It just seems easier to try to find a way and a reason to keep doing it as long as it feels good in the beginning before it turns bad.

Some people even try to get rid of lust, various addictions, and gluttony, which is why there are so many seven step deliverance programs out there. Lust, substance addictions and gluttony can lead to many other problems either physical or financial. The temporary good feelings that come from indulgence vanish in the long term, leaving their victims with the sad and unfortunate results and consequences of the indulgences.

> *1 Corinthians 6:9 Don't you know that those who do wrong will have no share in the Kingdom of God? Don't fool yourselves. Those who indulge in sexual sin, who are idol worshipers, adulterers, male prostitutes, homosexuals, 10 thieves, greedy people (gluttons), drunkards, abusers, and swindlers—none of these will have a share in the Kingdom of God.*

When we burn for drugs, or harmful foods (weight loss and body building = big business), society shows compassion and offers solutions to help us. Even lust for money is recognized as a problem, and there are programs for compulsive gamblers, or people addicted to money schemes. Yet, when our flesh burns for sexual release from someone else's spouse, or a child, or a same sex partner, we fight to protect these categories of human sexuality.

For example, why is homosexuality a protected category, when it comes to examination of what is good for us and what is not? Perhaps for the same reason that there is one category of protected murder in our communities. Think about it, abortion kills babies, yet abortion is legal. (Remember, we are speaking on what "is good" for us, and not necessarily what "feels good" to us.) In other words, to keep from hurting people's feelings, should we fight to uphold homosexuality and kill babies?

My uncle, Dr. Martin Luther King, Jr. addressed both homosexuality and abortion in an advice column he wrote for EBONY Magazine in the 1050's:

Question: My problem is different from the ones most people have. I am a boy, but I feel about boys the way I ought to feel about girls. I don't want my parents to know about me. What can I do?

MLK: Your problem is not at all an uncommon one. However, it does require careful attention. The type of feeling that you have toward boys is probably not an innate tendency, but something that has been culturally acquired. . . . You are already on the right road toward a solution, since you honestly recognize the problem and have a desire to solve it.

Question: About two years ago, I was going with a young lady who became pregnant. I refused to marry her. As a result, I was directly responsible for a crime. It was not until a month later that I realized the awful thing I had done. I begged her to forgive me, to come back, but she has not answered my letters. The thing stays on my mind. What can I do? I have prayed for forgiveness.

MLK: You have made a mistake. . . . One can never rectify a mistake until he admits that a mistake has been made. Now that you have prayed for forgiveness and acknowledged your mistake, you must turn your vision to the future. . . . Now that you have repented, don't concentrate on what you failed to do in the past, but what you are determined to do in the future.

Consider this, homosexuality and abortion share a common denominator; they both attack the foundations of procreation and the human family. The sex act between two men or two women cannot result in conception of another human being. Abortion cuts off/kills the life of the person in the womb. Add to this deadly formula pornography, child pornography, sex trafficking, fornication and adultery; what do you get? The destruction of humanity.

There are obviously destructive forces at work to attack the procreative human family; and these forces are not readily and easily perceived by the human senses. Any force that short circuits the life span of a person, and/or circumvents the procreative energy of a person cannot be good.

So what is a decent, kind hearted sexually challenged person to do? The same thing that a decent, kind hearted victim of any problem would do. Seek truth, resist the evil forces. The funny thing about all of this is that if we don't have sex, we won't die.

Think about it. The person addicted to food, resulting in life threatening illness, also has a problem. He or she needs to modify her lifestyle. This is often very hard, because we just can't say, "I'll never eat again." We have to eat something, or we will die.

Such is not the case with sex. We can abstain from sex for a season, or a lifetime, and not die. So, someone just can't stomach having sex with someone of opposite gender; or feels like he or she can't live without having sex with a child or someone else's spouse . . . Then, why have sex at all? Remember, we won't die if we don't have sex. Love and sex are really two different things. Yet, we are such a "feel good" society, such a "gratify me now" society, that we often indulge in things that ultimately make us sick, and often even kill us.

"So, God is so mean that He will deprive us of sex, if we don't follow His rules," some ask? It might be better to ask what draws us to partaking of forbidden fruit of any type?

The Christian Church has the best kept secret around. "Christians do it better!" Any sex outside of God ordained marriage is somehow counterfeit and often unfulfilling. This includes adultery, homosexuality, pornography, sex trafficking and fornication.

The thing is, we need to realize that sex between one man and woman in marriage is liberating. Neither the "redeemed" husband nor his "redeemed" wife is under the curse of Adam and Eve. The man is not trying to "have the rule over his wife," as he was cursed to do in Genesis because of Adam's and Eve's sin. Instead, the redeemed husband loves his wife as he is taught in the book of Ephesians. The woman's/wife's desire is not directed towards her husband as in the curse of Eve, but rather she is at liberty to express her godly desire, and to love and respect her husband as is also taught in the New Testament. Together, they can enjoy their mutual sexuality in the bonds of Holy Matrimony, as God always intended.

So, why has the devil been able to sell illicit sex on such a grand scale? We as Christians have not effectively taught our young people about the procreative plan of God and the rewards that come with fulfilling God's plan.

Song of Solomon 6:_1 Young Women of Jerusalem: "O rarest of beautiful women, where has your lover gone? We will help you find him." Young Woman: 2 "He has gone down to his garden, to his spice beds, to graze and to gather the lilies. 3 I am my lover's, and my lover is mine. Man: 4 "O my beloved, you are as beautiful as the lovely town of Tirzah. Yes, as beautiful as Jerusalem! You are as majestic as an army with banners! 5 Look away, for your eyes overcome me! Your hair falls in waves, like a flock of goats frisking down the slopes of Gilead

The most romantic love stories in the Bible are between married people. Sensual love is approved within marriage. The marriage bed is undefiled! Spread the good news!

Hebrews 13:4 Let marriage be kept honorable in every way, and the marriage bed undefiled. For God will judge those who commit sexual sins, especially those who commit adultery.

My grandfather, Daddy King used to preach a sermon: NIBBLING SWEET GRASS. It was a parable about a beloved little sheep that ignored the loving rules of his master, to stay in his own protected pasture. Next door, the grass in the sheep slaughter's field appeared to be greener and sweeter. So the little sheep edged closer and closer to the fence, nibbling in ignorant bliss, till one day he slipped into the slaughter pen. The rest was history!

This reminds us of people today. Fornication, adultery, divorce, sexual "preference" and so many other lifestyle occurrences have us out to pasture and in danger. Our sons and daughters value their CD players, their gold chains, their cars, their clothes much more than they value their own bodies which are the temples of the Holy Ghost.

1 Corinthians 6:19 Don't you know that your body is a temple that belongs to the Holy Spirit? The Holy Spirit, whom you received from God, lives in you. You don't belong to yourselves.

Lack of understanding of the purpose of our lives, and the purposes for which God intends for our bodies leads to curiosity akin to that Satan stirred within Eve, causing her to sin. An example of this is pornography which entraps so many of our children, and even unsuspecting adults; whether it be on the Internet, or magazines or television, or wherever they get it, porn is often at the root of sexual exploration. Pornography encourages unholy images and soul ties which are very difficult to break. Porn also leads down the deadly spiraled path to human sex trafficking. Only the Blood of Jesus can wash away the ungodly images and influences from this influence.

Let's talk about the Blood of Jesus for a moment here; that pure DNA of Christ the Lamb that can never lose its power! Whew! There is a plausible explanation for the origin of iniquity, sin, sickness and disease, including misuse of human sexuality. Our original bodies were not designed to accommodate the DNA of demons, nor of sin! We need the blood of Jesus, which flowed into the earth from which our natural bodies are formed, to deliver us from this situation!

> *1 John 8: (Jesus) the Son of God came to destroy these works of the Devil. 9 Those who have been born into God's family do not sin, because God's life is in them. So they can't keep on sinning, because they have been born of God.*

Without being born again, the human race is subject or slave to sin and iniquity. Sin breeds in iniquity, and once grown, sin leads to spiritual and physical death. Iniquity is like the soil or fertilizer or fodder. Sin is the seed, which once grown, brings death. Sin is an evil fruit, and must be pulled up from the roots, and destroyed by the Word of God, the Blood of Jesus, and the Power of the Holy Ghost. Too often we attack the symptoms, without dealing with the root problems. We "mow the grass" as it were, topping off the weeds, without killing their roots. Redemption in Christ is needed to free humanity from the curse which results from iniquity and sin!

We are not just talking about Christian conversion here. We can be converted, saved, and at church every Sunday, while still indulging in sin and sickness. Yes, indulging in sickness, doing those things that will result in sin, and ultimately death. This includes what we eat, who we have sex with, what we do in and away from home.

> *John 3:16 God so loved the world that He gave His only begotten Son (Jesus) so that everyone who believes on Him will not perish, but will have eternal life!*

The bottom line is love. Everybody needs (Agape) love. We must never condemn, only share the truth in love. Love never fails. Notice that we say love never fails. Love and sex are two different things. Love never fails! Ungodly sex does fail, and if the sex is outside the Divine Plan, it will fail to truly satisfy, it will fail to deliver.

We need to graduate from conversion to deliverance. We need to be free from the generational curses of sin! We need to know the truth, which will set us free! Sexuality is just one part of the picture. The topic is broad, and we need full understanding of the purpose of sex, and the benefits.

> *Song of Solomon 9:11 Come, my lover, let us go to the countryside, let us spend the night in the villages. 12 Let us go early to the vineyards to see if the vines have budded, if their blossoms have opened, and if the pomegranates are in bloom—there I will give you my love. 13 The mandrakes send out their fragrance, and at our door is every delicacy, both new and old, that I have stored up for you, my lover.*

As we can see in this Bible passage, a conversation between King Solomon and his bride, sex in marriage is desirable and good. This is something that should be taught to our children, and remembered among adults.

It is so much easier to teach human sexuality the Bible way from the beginning than to have to undo the work of the devil once the influences of ungodly sex take hold. Godly sex is the real thing. Godly sex, some ask? Who do you think created sex in the first place? Sex in marriage between one man and one woman is ordained of God, and can be very fulfilling and rewarding.

Our people perish for lack of knowledge. Don't be afraid to teach your children about sex and marriage. There are great benefits and rewards!

GOD'S PURPOSE FOR MARRIAGE (RESTORING THE MARRIAGE AND FAMILY)

Genesis2:21-25; 3:16 MATTHEW. 19:3, TIMOTHY 2:9-13, TITUS. 2:4-5, ROMAN. 1:2, PETER 3:6, PROVERB. 24:3

Marriage is a creation ordinance. God is the author of marriage. God puts marriage on the books, while man puts marriage on the rocks.

Some forms of Families recognized by society today:

1. Christian (Bible) type marriage
2. Common Law (Shacking)
3. Companion Union or Civil Union (can include other than heterosexual relationships)
4. Disintegrate Union (visiting relationships from one woman/ man to another)

Three factions that have altered the Bible way of families in the Black family:

1. African Retention: polygamy or multiple wives.
2. Plantation system: stud or breeding system, which does not allow the husband to be the father. The modern day welfare system has been a modern day derivative of this system, with the Government being the master.
3. Socio-economic-political factors: i.e. crime, abortion, education, finances, divorce.

Marriage precedes sin. God ordained marriage in creating the union between Adam and Eve. Christ approves of marriage, and compares marriage of man and woman to His marriage to the church.

One primary purpose of marriage is for couples to procreate (have sex and conceive and birth) and/or raise up godly seed (either natural children, adopted children or spiritual children).

Another purpose of marriage is for conjugal companionship, friendship and fellowship between man and wife. Partners in marriage should help each other to realize their dreams, to birth their visions.

Marriage is three faceted.

1. Public whereby a man publicly leaves his family and takes a wife.
2. Permanent in that the husband and wife cleave to each other.
3. Private in that they join together in spirit (mutual submission to God, agreement in prayer and worship), soul (in submission to each other, intellectually and emotionally) and body (sexually) to become one. (In-laws must respect God's order, and follow the word, or in-laws become out-laws. My pastor's wife is fond of saying, be equally yoked or you run the risk of having the devil for a father-in-law.)

In order to experience this God kind of marriage, we must go back to the beginning and rediscover God's plan and purpose for marriage. We must learn to govern ourselves and agree with this plan rather than to stubbornly cling to independence, which cannot work in a marriage.

Human sexuality should or indeed must be reserved for the marriage bed. In the love song, Song of Songs, chapter 3, "do not awaken love until it desires." In other words, do not pursue sexual love outside the marriage bed, because you will open up all kinds of inordinate soul ties, since the sex acts ties you to your lover in a deeper expression than mere friendship. Everyone we join with in a sex act becomes a part of us. 1 Corinthians 6:16 Do you not know that he who unites himself with a prostitute is one with her in body? For it is said, "The two will become one flesh."

In sex outside of marriage, you also expose yourself to many evils such as STD's, unwed pregnancy, abortion and emotional turmoil. Satan is after the seed! In marriage, the seed, the fruit of the womb is protected. Children are a gift from God.

Also, there is the trauma of triangle love affairs, and the potential for domestic violence. Have a standard of discipline, and trust God for the passionate love affair between a husband and wife, that He designed for you!

THE PURPOSE OF MAN—MALE AND FEMALE (MAN AND WOMAN)

In the beginning, God created Man; Male and Female created He them. (Genesis 1).

So (hu)man appears on the planet in two forms, male and female. The church world as we know it has taken the fallen doctrine of the church (men ruling over women, according to the curse of the law from which Jesus has redeemed all believers) and attempted to make it a Divine Order. Going back to Genesis, God cursed Adam and Eve by causing Adam to rule over Eve, and for Eve to bear children in painful childbirth. God then turned Eve's desire away from Him (God) towards Adam. When Eve lost the blessing of having her desires fixed on God, and not her husband, this caused a longing and emptiness within Adam and Eve, because Adam was never designed to meet Eve's needs. Only the Messiah Jesus can satisfy a longing soul, male and female. So, fallen, unredeemed Adam was given the position to rule over fallen, unredeemed Eve. Prior to the fall, Adam had the rule over birds and animals. After the fall, Adam was cursed to rule Eve. Unredeemed men rule other people. Redeemed men lead other people.

God doesn't operate by gender, but rather by anointing. The prophet Joel plainly reminded us that in the latter days sons and daughters of man would prophecy.

> Acts 2:17—"'In the last days, God says, I will pour out my Spirit on all people. Your sons and daughters will prophesy, your young men will see visions, your old men will dream dreams.

We all are Spirit However some of us are housed in female bodies, some in male bodies. Yet, there is no gender in the spirit. The first evangelist after the death and resurrection of the Messiah Christ was a woman named Mary Magdalene.

The husband is truly the priest of the home, as it is biblically recorded. It is also written that we are all royal priests and priestess; a chosen generation. It is clearly understood that the husband is the head of his home. God has specific realms of authority here on earth, and none of them overlaps or contradict any of the other.

The husband is the pastor in the family, being the authority over his home, but not necessarily having any authority over the church. Women who are not going to church, or who attend church sporadically shouldn't ever use the excuse: "My husband won't let me go to church." Suppose a woman is driving a car, and her husband is on the passenger side, demanding her to speed because he's in a hurry. It happens that the woman, who was not in agreement with speeding, obeyed his demand anyway. However, when the police stopped her, he never asked for her husband's license, but only her license. The emphasis here is that at that very moment, the woman had to answer for her own actions, and not her husband's. We must follow our husbands as they follow Christ, but not if their directives are illegal, inaccurate, or go against the will and Word of God.

Men and women must seek deep relationship with God, to comprehend more of God's character and nature in order to know what is proper or not proper. In Isaiah 32, women are warned not to be complacent. In the book of Titus, women are charged to be godly.

In the second chapter of Colossians we as men and women of God are reminded of our rightful positions. Verses 11-14 state: "When you came to Christ He set you free from your evil desires (your unfulfilled longings.) You were dead in sins, and your sinful (cursed) desires were not yet cut away. Then, He gave you a share in the very life of Christ, for He forgave all your sins, and blotted out the charges proved against you (by the curse of Adam and Eve and the breaking of God's commandments).

He took the list of sins (and curses) and destroyed it by nailing it to Christ's cross." Jesus reached His maturity and ministry during His life on earth, whereas Adam and Eve never reached maturity because they allowed rebellion to hinder them. Their basic sin derived from an act of wanting to be independent or separated from God, automatically caused disobedience.

God designed us in order to pour himself into us. He gave us breath. Then, He prepared a way for us to be redeemed and given eternal life. In a unique covenant among the Trinity, God made arrangements for us to live with Him forever. If we are to be included in the covenant, we must first surrender unto God.

The tree of good and evil included humanism, atheism, skepticism, communism, new age, women's lib, sexual depravity, and every other Christ-less thought that we can imagine. Eve was named after the fall, but she was redeemed so that she could bring seed that would eventually destroy the Devil.

God drove Adam out of the garden along with his companion Eve. God didn't directly command Eve to leave the garden. Eve followed Adam because she had to. Her desire was now towards Adam. She too was cut away from God.

The next supreme battle and attack from Satan is also couched in more deception. Satan first stole Eve who was God's first son's bride. Satan now pursues the second bride, Christ's bride which is the church. Now the only difference is that Adam was not God-Jesus, who has the power to protect His bride. When Adam's bride sinned, Adam followed suit. When Christ's bride sins, He leads her to repentance, and back to God.

We must continue to resist Satan, who was cursed to crawl on his belly, while eating dust. Christ reminds us:

> John 16:33—"I have told you these things, so that in me you may have peace. In this world you will have trouble. But take courage! I have overcome the world."

Jesus overcame and defeated Satan for us. We don't have to fight with carnal weapons. We have the armor of God! (Ephesians 6). Yet, man's physical frame is also a composite of dust, and we must remain covered by the Word, in order to be protected from Satan's devouring tactics.

As for Eve's desire (we are not speaking of sexual desire, which is God ordained, and covered in the marriage bed between a man and a woman. See Hebrews and I Corinthians:

> *Hebrews 13:4 Marriage should be honored by all, and the marriage bed kept pure, for God will judge the adulterer and all who are sexually immoral.*

> *1Corinthians 7: 5—Do not deprive each other except by mutual consent and for a time, so that you may devote yourselves to prayer. Then come together again so that Satan will not tempt you because of your lack of self-control.*

Sexual intimacy between a husband and a wife is God ordained. This special connection, called Eros is designed to be incredible. It has nothing to do with store bought perfumes and negligees, although such accents can be "fun," much like icing on a cake. Our natural body essences are much more "sexy" than what we can buy. Our birthday suits are designed to be more attractive to our mates than anything we can buy.

The Song of Solomon in the Bible is the perfect example of God's plan for love and sex between a man and his wife. Consider the language between Solomon and his Bride:

> *The Bride to her Husband—1:1 The Song—best of all songs—Solomon's song! 2 Kiss me—full on the mouth! Yes! For your love is better than wine, 3 headier than your aromatic oils. The syllables of your name murmur like a meadow brook. No wonder everyone loves to say your name! 4 Take me away with you! Let's run off together! An elopement with my King-Lover! We'll celebrate, we'll sing, we'll make great music. Yes! For your love is better than vintage wine.*

> *The Husband to his Bride—4: 1 You're so beautiful, my darling, so beautiful, and your dove eyes are veiled By your hair as it flows and shimmers, like a flock of goats in the distance streaming down a hillside in the sunshine. 2 Your smile is generous and full-expressive and strong and clean. 3 Your lips are jewel red, your mouth elegant and inviting, your veiled cheeks soft and radiant. 4 The smooth, lithe lines of your neck command notice—all heads turn in awe and admiration! 5 Your breasts are like fawns, twins of a gazelle, grazing among the first spring flowers. 6 The sweet, fragrant curves of your body, the soft, spiced contours of your flesh invite me, and I come. I stay until dawn breathes its light and night slips away. 7 You're beautiful from head to toe, my dear love, beautiful beyond compare, absolutely flawless.*

Note that we say love and sex. The two are not the same. We can love someone and not have sex with that person. We can have sex with a person, and not love that person. These two lovers had permission to mate sexually in marriage. This is God's way. For a man and a woman to marry, mate sexually, and have babies. That's the purpose. Pleasurable purpose is God's way for us.

When a woman's desire is demanding fulfillment from her husband, other than within God's plan for her life, she should become even more alert concerning the curse, and focus more toward the Savior, rather than looking to a human being to be her source of protection and fulfillment. Think about it! God provides all that we need, and sets the stage for our enjoyment!

My Pastor, Allen McNair explains it this way: God gave woman a special influence with her husband. He needs her because she came out of him. (. . . And God said, "it is not good for man to be alone . . . I will make a suitable helpmeet for him . . . and Adam called his wife Eve." Eve was taken out of Adam's own DNA.)

So, woman's influence should be used for good, as in the example of Queen Esther, rather than the wicked example of women like Jezebel. A woman's influence should be God centered. A man's strength should be God ordained.

Therefore, Man's (and woman's) inner man (being, or inner self) wasn't designed to be satisfied by human fulfillment. Everyone needs to become God sufficient, rather than self sufficient. A man or a woman must first find sanctuary in God's care. It is a curse for a woman to desire or turn to follow a man outside of the principal of marriage. We are to love our husbands but live for God.

Fallen man rules, while a redeemed man leads. When the inner man is controlled by God, for the man and the woman, then the husband can be an effective leader of his home. The wife can take her rightful place. When we return, or become redeemed from the fall, God comes to live within us, and we by His grace become submissive, to Christ and to each other. This way, a home is not ruled by a two headed monster, with the wife competing with the husband for authority. Even the children line up. Everything is in order, under Christ.

Everything is easier when God rules and reigns. God's hands are tempered with love and mercy towards those who love and obey Him. Let us realize that even work and tasks of vocation are easier in countries where the love of God is preached.

Women are the carriers of the Seed which has surely crushed Satan's head. Mary bore Christ. It is the church (feminine form) who is married to the Son of God.

Men in the arms of God are not domineering men. They are powerful, yet meek, gentle and kind. Two examples of this kind of power and authority are Jairus and the centurion. Both were men of authority who sought after Jesus for healing of a loved one. Jesus responded to their submission, not their earthly power and titles. It is important for men and women to know who we are in Christ Jesus, and to live according to the pattern He establishes for us.

God grants grace to all who desire to fulfill His purpose for their lives:

> 2Co 9:8—And God is able to make all grace abound to you, so that in all things at all times, having all that you need, you will abound in every good work.

Submission is required by God, and is actually attractive, in both women and men. Godly married women are truly the reflections of their husbands and of Christ. Godly unmarried women reflect Christ. Godly men reflect Christ. A Godly woman will never attempt to rule over their husband. A Godly woman will always submit to her husband as he submits to Christ (I Peter 3:6). A Holy woman becomes God's expression, who allows God to express Himself within her. On the other hand, godly men submit to Christ and love their wives.

What about sexual desires when we are not married? Pray to marry if you are burning with a desire for sex, for the Bible truly says that it is better to marry than to burn with lust. Until marriage comes along, pray for strength to abstain, and for enough water to take a cold shower.

THE NATURAL FAMILY AND NATURAL MARRIAGE: THE KEY TO THE AMERICA DREAM—LIFE, LIBERTY AND THE PURSUIT OF HAPPINESS

By Alveda King and Larry Jacobs
(Credits also to Allan Carlson and Paul Mero)

In 21st Century, the "American Dream of Life, Liberty, and the Pursuit of Happiness" is mortally threatened in this dark time of moral and social disorder. Not from poverty, debt, unemployment, or the global financial crisis, but from the attacks and continued assault on the "natural family (*see definition below)." The last two generations of children in America have been born into a nationalized culture of self-indulgence and of abortion—a culture embracing death. More than all the generations before, these children have known the divorce of parents and have lived too often in places without fathers. These children have been taught to deny their destinies as young women and men. They have been forced to read books that mock marriage, motherhood, and fatherhood. Persons who should have protected these children—teachers, judges, public officials—often left the children as prey to moral and sexual predators. Many of them are in fact the victims of a kind of cultural rape: seduced into early sexual acts, and then pushed into abortion and sterility.

True happiness and real freedom comes from the power of Americans to engage in "the pursuit of happiness" which the American founders properly understood to mean 'domestic happiness,' the real joys of marriage and home life. The American Dream has always depended on the <u>natural family</u> as the fundamental social unit to exercise and guarantee these most basic human rights of "Life, Liberty and the Pursuit of Happiness" granted to us by God. Dr. Martin Luther King, Jr. (Alveda's uncle) embraced this concept in his famous "I Have A Dream" speech. As he declared in Washington, D.C., "In a sense we have come to our nation's capital to cash a check. When the architects of our republic wrote the magnificent words of the Constitution and the Declaration of Independence, they were signing a promissory note to which every American was to fall heir. This note was a promise that all men, yes, black men as well as white men, would be guaranteed the unalienable rights of life, liberty, and the pursuit of happiness." Unfortunately, at the same time that new civil rights were being granted to blacks, the secular culture was attacking their Faith, families, and new found civil freedoms with increasing divorce, promiscuity and out-of-wedlock births.

As part of the King Family Legacy, Alveda can testify that the married-parent, natural family is a necessary component to achieve the American dream for African-Americans and for all of God's people. "I know firsthand the importance of a strong family brings to overcoming difficulties; as a child as I was jailed, my house was bombed, and my daddy and uncle were killed in the Civil Rights Movement of this great nation. If it had not been for the safety and security provided by my father and mother, we their children would have been severely if not irreparably traumatized."

Alveda also speaks often of her grandfather (MLK's father), Daddy King, "who always taught me and my family to have faith in God, and to value life, liberty and justice for all. I frequently share editions of my Uncle M. L.'s Ebony Magazine Advice Column that was based upon the same values espoused by my family."

Opponents of the <u>natural family</u> continue today to attack all aspects of "Uncle Martin's Dream" through destruction of natural marriage and family: from the bond of marriage, to the birth of children, to the true democracy of free homes. More and more families show weaknesses and disorders. There are growing numbers of young adults rejecting the fullness of and joy of marriage, instead choosing cheap substitutes or standing alone, where they are easy prey for the socialist state. The American marriage rate has fallen from 61.4 (per 1,000 unmarried women) in 1980 to 39.2 in 2007, a decline of 36 percent. Too many children are born outside of wedlock, ending as wards of that same state. More than 40% of American children are now born into single-parent households. Too few children are born inside married-couple homes, portending depopulation (even the entire world now has at least 10 million fewer children [under the age of 5] then it did in 1990). In summary, for the first time in American history we are a society of mostly single, non-family

----

What is the "Natural Family?"

The definition of the natural family comes from a working group of the Howard Center for Family, Religion & Society and the World Congress of Families, crafted in May, 1998, in a Second Century B.C. room in the ancient city of Rome. It is supported both by the Universal Declaration of Human Rights (United Nations, 1948) and by the findings of social science. This definition is consistent with Article 16:3 of the Universal Declaration of Human Rights which states, "The family is the natural and fundamental group unit of society and is entitled to protection by society and the State."

The natural family is the fundamental social unit, inscribed in human nature, and centered around the voluntary union of a man and a woman in a lifelong covenant of marriage for the purposes of:

1. *satisfying the longings of the human heart to give and receive love;*
2. *welcoming and ensuring the full physical and emotional development of children;*
3. *sharing a home that serves as the center for social, educational, economic, and spiritual life;*
4. *building strong bonds among the generations to pass on a way of life that has transcendent meaning;*
5. *extending a hand of compassion to individuals and households whose circumstances fall short of these ideals.*

Why Use the Term "Natural Family" vs. "Traditional Family" vs. "Nuclear Family?"

Our use of the term "natural family" is significant in many respects.

-   *First, the term signifies a natural order to family structures that is common across cultures, historical, and overwhelmingly self-evident.*
-   *Second, the term signifies a wholly defensible expression. "Natural" is not "nuclear," which would limit its scope, nor is it "traditional,"*

which would burden its utility in public discourse. It is what it is, a totally self-evident expression.

- *Third, the term "natural" precludes incompatible constructs of the family as well as incompatible behaviors among its members.*
- *Fourth, the "natural family" is a positive expression. It does not require a discussion of negative incompatibilities to define itself.*

----

households instead of married-parent households with children and financial, physical, and emotional health has gotten worse as a society.

Furthermore, the American principles of family established by the Founding Fathers and echoed by Dr. Martin Luther King, Jr. have been largely forgotten. These principles are wonderfully articulated in the book, "The Natural Family: Bulwark of Liberty" by Allan Carlson and Paul Mero. We add our agreement to them here and encourage you to do the same.

"OUR PRINCIPLES

To advance this [King Dream for America], we advocates for the natural family assert clear principles to guide our work in the new century and millennium.

- We affirm that the natural family, not the individual, is the fundamental unit of society.
- We affirm the natural family to be the union of a man and a woman through marriage for the purposes of sharing love and joy, propagating children, providing their moral education, building a vital home economy, offering security in times of trouble, and binding the generations.
- We affirm that the natural family is a fixed aspect of the created order, one ingrained in human nature. Distinct family systems may grow weaker or stronger. However, the natural family cannot change into some new shape; nor can it be re-defined by eager social engineers.
- We affirm that the natural family is the ideal, optimal, true family system. While we acknowledge varied living situations caused by circumstance or dysfunction, all other "family forms" are incomplete or are fabrications of the state.

- We affirm the marital union to be the authentic sexual bond, the only one open to the natural and responsible creation of new life.
- We affirm the sanctity of human life from conception to natural death; each newly conceived person holds rights to live, to grow, to be born, and to share a home with its natural parents bound by marriage.
- We affirm that the natural family is prior to the state and that legitimate governments exist to shelter and encourage the natural family.
- We affirm that the world is abundant in resources. The breakdown of the natural family and moral and political failure, not human "overpopulation," account for poverty, starvation, and environmental decay.
- We affirm that human depopulation is the true demographic danger facing the earth in this new century. Our societies need more people, not fewer.
- We affirm that women and men are equal in dignity and innate human rights, but different in function. Even if sometimes thwarted by events beyond the individual's control (or sometimes given up for a religious vocation), the calling of each boy is to become husband and father; the calling of each girl is to become wife and mother. Everything that a man does is mediated by his aptness for fatherhood. Everything that a woman does is mediated by her aptness for motherhood. Culture, law, and policy should take these differences into account.
- We affirm that the complementarity of the sexes is a source of strength. Men and women exhibit profound biological and psychological differences. When united in marriage, though, the whole becomes greater than the sum of the parts.
- We affirm that economic determinism is false. Ideas and religious faith can prevail over material forces. Even one as powerful as industrialization can be tamed by the exercise of human will.
- We affirm the "family wage" ideal of "equal pay for equal family responsibility." Compensation for work and taxation should reinforce natural family bonds.
- We affirm the necessary role of private property in land, dwelling, and productive capital as the foundation of familial independence and the guarantor of democracy. In a just and good society, all families will hold real property.

- And we affirm that lasting solutions to human problems rise out of families and small communities. They cannot be imposed by bureaucratic and judicial fiat. Nor can they be coerced by outside force."

A few decades ago, it was not necessary to articulate these principles as they were passed to each succeeding generation by families and resulted in shared values among all nations and races. In 1948, the United Nation's Declaration of Human Rights even reaffirmed these principles in Article 16(3), "The family is the *natural* and *fundamental* group unit of society and is entitled to protection by society and the State."

Anthropology, medicine and science all confirm these simple truths about the natural family (as reported quantitatively for more than 20 years by the founding editor, Dr. Allan Carlson and the current editor, Bob Patterson, in *The Family In America: A Journal of Public Policy:*

- "Children do best when born into and reared within a household composed of their two natural parents who are married; any deviation from this model—single parenting, step-parenting, divorce, remarriage, cohabitation, same-sex households, adoption—raises the risks of negative outcomes for children.
- Conventional marriages of men to women produce abundant positive results—from better health and more wealth to greater happiness—for both husbands and wives.
- Healthy and stable families who worship God are essential to the preservation of a free society. They limit the size and intrusiveness of government, promote public engagement, stabilize neighborhoods, and build the institutions of civil society.

Empirical research studies in the social sciences point to the natural family and natural marriage as the single most important factor in promoting economic justice, fighting poverty, and decreasing dependence on welfare. Perhaps President Obama has said it best. In his words, "We need families to raise our children. We need fathers to realize that responsibility does not end at conception. We need them to realize that what makes you a man is not the ability to have a child—it's the courage to raise one."

In fact, this is the one time we agree with President Obama's words where he has cited the same research to highlight the importance of natural family in his father's day speech, "Of all the rocks upon which we build our lives, we are reminded today that family is the most important . . . We know that more than half of all black children live in single-parent households, a number that has doubled-doubled—since we were children. We know the statistics—that children who grow up without a father are five times more likely to live in poverty and commit crime; nine times more likely to drop out of schools and twenty times more likely to end up in prison. They are more likely to have behavioral problems, or run away from home, or become teenage parents themselves. And the foundations of our community are weaker because of it."

Unfortunately our media and our government spend time ridiculing those who advocate for the "child-rich, married-parent" family and then criticize and de-value mothers and fathers who choose to "stay at home" with their children. Instead the media should be highlighting the <u>natural family</u> as the solution to poverty, drop-out rates, and crime.

From these principles that have shared with you, we lay out a new platform of actions and solutions for Society and the Civil Rights Movement based on the natural family and natural marriage. Again these action statements are drawn from the book, "The Natural Family: Bulwark of Liberty" by Allan Carlson and Paul Mero.

"OUR PLATFORM

From these principles, we draw out a simple, concrete platform [for action] for the new century and millennium. To the world, we say:

- **We will build a new culture of marriage, where others would define marriage out of existence.**
- **We will welcome and celebrate more babies and larger families, where others would continue a war on human fertility.**
- **We will find ways to bring mothers, fathers, and children back home, where others would further divide parents from their children.**
- **And we will create true home economies, where others would subject families to the full control of big government and vast corporations.**

To do these things, we must offer positive encouragements, and we must also correct the policy errors of the past. Specifically:

To build a new culture of marriage . . .

- We will craft schooling that gives positive images of chastity, marriage, fidelity, motherhood, fatherhood, husbandry, and housewifery. We will end the corruption of children through state "sex education" programs.
- We will build legal and constitutional protections around marriage as the union of a man and a woman. We will end the war of the sexual hedonists on marriage.
- We will transform social insurance, welfare, and housing programs to reinforce marriage, especially the marriage of young adults. We will end state incentives to live outside of marriage.
- We will place the weight of the law on the side of spouses seeking to defend their marriages. We will end state preferences for easy divorce by repealing "no-fault" statutes.
- We will recognize marriage as a true and full economic partnership. We will end "marriage penalties" in taxation.
- We will allow private insurers to recognize the health advantages of marriage and family living, according to sound business principles. We will end legal discrimination against the married and child-rich.
- We will empower the legal and cultural guardians of marriage and public morality. We will end the coarsening of our culture.

To welcome more babies within natural marriage . . .

- We will praise churches and other groups that provide healthy and fertile models of family life to the young. We will end state programs that indoctrinate children, youth, and adults into the contraceptive mentality.
- We will restore respect for life. We will end the culture of abortion and the mass slaughter of the innocents.
- We will create private and public campaigns to reduce maternal and infant mortality and to improve family health. We will end government campaigns of population control.
- We will build special protections for families, motherhood, and childhood. We will end the terrible assault on these basic human rights.

- We will celebrate husbands and wives who hold open their sexual lives to new children. We will end the manipulation and abuse of new human life in the laboratories.
- We will craft generous tax deductions, exemptions, and credits that are tied to marriage and the number of children. We will end the oppressive taxation of family income, labor, property, and wealth.
- We will create credits against payroll taxes that reward the birth of children and that build true family patrimonies. We will end existing social insurance incentives toward childlessness.
- We will offer tax benefits to businesses that provide "natal gifts" and "child allowances" to their employees. We will end legal incentives that encourage business corporations to ignore families.

To bring fathers and mothers home . . .

- We will ensure that stay-at-home parents enjoy at least the same state benefits offered to day-care users. We will end all discriminations against stay-at-home parents.
- We will encourage new strategies and technologies that would allow home-based employment to blossom and prosper. We will end policies that unfairly favor large, centralized businesses and institutions.
- We will favor small property that reintegrates home and work. We will end taxes, financial incentives, subsidies, and zoning laws that discourage small farms and family-held businesses.

To create a true home economy . . .

- We will allow men and women to live in harmony with their true natures. We will end the aggressive state promotion of androgyny.
- We will encourage employers to pay a "family wage" to heads of households. We will end laws that prohibit employers from recognizing and rewarding family responsibility.
- We will craft laws that protect home schools and other family-centered schools from state interference. We will give real control of state schools to small communities so that their focus might turn toward home and family. And we will create measures (such as educational tax credits) that recognize the exercise of parental responsibility.

We will end discriminatory taxes and policies that favor mass state education of the young.

- We will hold up the primacy of parental rights and hold public officials accountable for abuses of their power. We will end abuse of the "child-abuse" laws.
- We will encourage self-sufficiency through broad property ownership, home enterprise, home gardens, and home workshops. We will end the culture of dependency found in the welfare state.
- We will celebrate homes that are centers of useful work. We will end state incentives for home building that assume, and so create, families without functions.

ON LIBERTY

Through all these tasks, we seek to advance true freedom. The partisans of a "post family" world have taught that liberty means freedom from tradition, from religious faith, from family, from community. They also hold that freedom is a gift of the state. We deny these statements. Rather, true liberty comes from the ability of human beings, of women and men, to find their real destinies, in their ability to live in harmony with the created world. Real freedom lies in holding the power to engage in "the pursuit of happiness," which the American Founders properly understood to mean "domestic happiness," the joys of marriage and home life. True liberty rests on family ownership of real, productive property. Political liberty includes freedom from the modern social engineers, who would create their own artificial orders based on social class, or racism, or the violence of androgyny (the negation of woman and man). In truth, human beings are made to be conjugal, to live in homes with vital connections to parents, spouse, and children. Authentic freedom comes in and through the natural family.

THE USUAL CHARGES

We know that certain charges will be leveled against us. Some will say that we want to turn back the clock, to restore a mythical American suburban world of the 1950's. Others will charge that we seek to subvert the rights of women or that we want to impose white, Western, Christian values on a pluralistic world. Still others will argue that we ignore science or reinforce patriarchal violence. Some will say that we block inevitable social evolution or threaten a sustainable world with too many children.

So, in anticipation, let us be clear:

We look forward with hope, while learning from the past.

It is true that we look with affection to earlier familial eras such as "1950's America." Indeed, for the first time in one hundred years, five things happened simultaneously in America (and in Australia and parts of Western Europe, as well) during this time: the marriage rate climbed; the divorce rate fell; marital fertility soared; the equality of households increased; and measures of child well-being and adult happiness rose. These were the social achievements of "the greatest generation." We look with delight on this record and aspire to recreate such results.

However, we also know that this specific development was a one-generation wonder. It did not last. Some children of the "baby boom" rebelled. Too often, this rebellion was foolish and destructive. Still, we find weaknesses in the family model of "1950's America." We see that it was largely confined to the white majority. Black families actually showed mounting stress in these years: a retreat from marriage; more out-of-wedlock births. Also, this new suburban model—featuring long commutes for fathers and tract homes without the central places such as parks and nearby shops where mothers and youth might have found healthy community bonds—proved incomplete. Finally, we see the "companionship marriage" ideal of this time, which embraced psychological tasks to the exclusion of material and religious functions, as fragile. We can, and we will, do better.

We believe wholeheartedly in women's rights.

Above all, we believe in rights that recognize women's unique gifts of pregnancy, birthing, and breastfeeding. The goal of androgyny, the effort to eliminate real differences between women and men, does every bit as much violence to human nature and human rights as the old efforts by the communists to create "Soviet Man" and by the Nazis to create "Aryan Man." We reject social engineering, attempts to corrupt girls and boys, to confuse women and 25 men about their true identities. At the same time, nothing in our platform would prevent women from seeking and attaining as much education as they want. Nothing in our platform would prevent women from entering jobs and professions to which they aspire. We do object, however, to restrictions on the liberty of employers to recognize family relations and obligations and so reward indirectly those parents staying at home to care for their children. And we object to current attacks on the Universal Declaration of Human Rights, a document which proclaims fundamental rights to family autonomy, to a family wage for fathers, and to the special protection of mothers.

We believe that the natural family is universal, an attribute of all humankind. We confess to holding Christian values regarding the family: the sanctity of marriage; the desire by the Creator that we be fruitful and multiply; Jesus' miracle at the wedding feast; His admonitions against adultery and divorce. And yet, we find similar views in the other great world faiths. Moreover, we even find recognition of the natural family in the marriage rituals of animists. Because it is imprinted on our natures as human beings, we know that the natural family can be grasped by all persons who open their minds to the evidence of their senses and their hearts to the promptings of their best instincts. Also, in the early 21st century, there is little that is "Western" about our views. The voices of the "post family" idea are actually today's would-be "Westernizers." They are the ones who largely rule in the child-poor, aging, dying lands of "the European West." It is they who seek to poison the rest of the world with a grim, wizened culture of death. Our best friends are actually to be found in the developing world, in the Third World, in the Middle East, Africa, South Asia, and South America. Our staunchest allies tend not to be white, but rather people of color. Others seek a sterile, universal darkness. We seek to liberate the whole world—including dying Europa—for light and life, for children.

We celebrate the findings of empirical science.

Science, honestly done and honestly reported, is the friend of the natural family. The record is clear from decades of work in sociology, psychology, anthropology, sociobiology, medicine, and social history: children do best when they are born into and raised by their two natural parents. Under any other setting—including one-parent, step-parent, homosexual, cohabitating, or communal households—children predictably do worse. Married, natural-parent homes bring health, learning, and success to the offspring reared therein. Science shows that these same homes give life, wealth, and joy to wives and husbands, as well. Disease, depression, and early death come to those who reject family life. This result should not really cause surprise. Science, after all, is the study of the natural order. And while the Creator forgives, nature never does.

We seek to reduce domestic violence.

All families fall short of perfection and a few families fail. We, too, worry about domestic violence. We know that people can make bad choices, and that they can fall prey to selfishness and their darker instincts. We also know that persons can live in places or times where they have few models of solid homes, few examples of good marriages. All the same, we also insist that the natural family is not the source of these human failures. The research here is clear. Women are safest physically when married and living with their husbands. Children are best sheltered from sexual, physical, and emotional abuse when they live with their married natural parents. In short, the natural family is the answer to abuse. We also know that all husbands and wives, all mothers and fathers, need to be nurtured toward and encouraged in their proper roles. These are the first tasks of all worthy social institutions.

We believe that while distinct family systems change, the design of the natural family never does.

Regarding the natural family, we deny any such thing as social evolution. The changes we see are either decay away from or renewal toward the one true family model. From our very origin as a unique creature on earth, we humans have been defined by the long-term bonding of a woman and a man, by their free sharing of resources, by a complementary division of labor, and by a focus on the procreation, protection, and rearing of children in stable homes.16 History is replete with examples of distinct family systems that have grown strong and built great civilizations, only to fall to atomism, vice, and decay. Even in our Western Civilization, we can identify periods of family decline and disorder, followed by successful movements of renewal. It is true that the last forty years have been a time of great confusion and decay. We now sense a new summons to social rebirth.

We seek a sustainable human future.

With sadness, we acknowledge that the new Malthusian impulse has succeeded in its war against children all too well. Fertility is tumbling around the globe. A majority of nations have already fallen into "the aging trap" of depopulation. As matters now stand, the predictable future is one of catastrophic population decline, economic contraction, and human tragedy. Our agenda actually represents the earth's best hope for a sustainable future [and good stewardship of the earth's resources].

OUR ALLIES

How do we relate to other movements or campaigns to protect the family? The conservative intellectual and political movement in America, for example, has claimed in recent decades a philosophy of "fusionism": economic conservatives holding to free market capitalism "fused" to social conservatives focused on "life" and "family" questions, or "traditional values." At times, this fusionist approach has worked well politically. And it has shown real economic results in those family businesses that successfully balance the pursuit of profit and the integrity of homes (including the homes of their employees).

However, we also see that the interests of "big business" and of families are not always compatible. Unless guided by other ideals, for example, the great corporations seek cheap labor wherever it can be found and an end to all home production, from clothing to meal preparation to child care. The whetting of appetites commonly takes precedence over family integrity in corporate advertising. As "globalization" now shows, families are not immune to capitalism's "creative destruction."

We admire and support truly free markets and equitable trade. We praise companies that grasp their long-term interest in strong homes and that craft advertising with positive family images. But we also indict legal privileges and special benefits bestowed on large corporations that buy political access and power to the damage of families. In addition, we point to an inherent dilemma in capitalist economics: the short-term interests of individual corporations in weak homes (places focused on consumption rather than productive tasks) and universal adult employment (mothers and fathers alike) versus the long-term interest of national economies in improved human capital. This latter term means happy, healthy, intelligent, and productive young adults, "products" that cannot be shaped by day-care centers, let alone by childless homes. "Fusionist conservatism" tends to paper over such inherent tensions. We put families first. We see any economy and all of its components—from financial markets to rules of trade to the setting of wages—as servants of the natural family, not the other way around.

We also claim an alliance with the "pro family" and "pro life" movements of recent decades. Indeed, we might be called part of them (in modest ways). But we also see (and so confess to) weaknesses that have marred their effectiveness. Too often, individual ambitions and squabbles have prevented movement success. A narrowness of vision has led, at times, to a focus on petty questions, while the truly important battles have been ignored, and so lost by default. Strategic thinking and bold moves that could transform key debates have been undone by timidity on the part of leaders and funders. Sustaining large institutions, rather than encouraging swift and effective agents, has been too common. Money, particularly "direct mail" money, has become the measure of too many things. Doctrinal and sectarian differences on important, but tangential, questions have been allowed to obscure unity on the central issues of family and life. Our foes have celebrated as old fears and suspicions between religious groups have trumped potentially powerful new alliances. The initiative on most questions has been left to the other side.

At this juncture, we do insist on "pro-family" integrity. Our true allies will accept the whole case for the natural family, not just parts. One cannot affirm the natural family while also defending serial divorce or infant day care. Our real allies will be those who, as far as possible, align their own lives in accord with the created order.

We also believe that victory for the natural family will come only as we change the terms of debate and open ourselves to fresh coalitions. It is not enough to stop public recognition of "gay marriage," nor to oppose "safe sex education" in the public schools, nor to ban partial birth abortion, nor to create optional "covenant" marriages. These gains will have no lasting effect unless the natural family is freed from the oppression of the post-family ideologues, unless we build a broad culture of marriage and life.

LOOKING FORWARD

That large task requires new ways of thinking and acting. Our vision of the hearth looks forward, not to the past, for hope and purpose. We see the vital home reborn through startling new movements such as home schooling. We marvel at fresh inventions that portend novel bonds between home and work. We are inspired by a convergence of religious truth with the evidence of science around the vital role of the natural family. We see the prospect of a great civil alliance of religious orthodoxies, within nations and around the globe; not to compromise on doctrines held dear, but to defend our family systems from the common foe. With wonder, we find a shared happiness with people once distrusted or feared. We enjoy new friendships rooted in family ideals that cross ancient divides. We see the opportunity for an abundant world order built on the natural family.

We issue a special call to the young, those born over the last three to four decades. You are the children of a troubled age, a time of moral and social disorder. You were conceived into a culture of self-indulgence, of abortion, a culture embracing death. More than all generations before, you have known the divorce of parents. You have lived too often in places without fathers. You have been taught to deny your destinies as young women and young men. You have been forced to read books that mock marriage, motherhood, and fatherhood. Persons who should have protected you—teachers, judges, public officials—often left you as prey to moral and sexual predators. Many of you are in fact the victims of a kind of cultural rape: seduced into early sexual acts, then pushed into sterility.

And yet, you are also the ones with the power to make the world anew. Where some members of our generation helped to corrupt the world, you will be the builders. You have seen the darkness. The light now summons you. It is your time to lead, with the natural family as your standard and beacon. Banish the lies told to you. Claim your natural freedom to create true and fruitful marriages. Learn from the social renewal prompted by "the greatest generation" and call on them for special support. You have the chance to shape a world that welcomes and celebrates children. You have the ability to craft a true homecoming. Your generation holds the destiny of humankind in its hands. The hopes of all good and decent people lie with you.

THE CALL

A new spirit spreads in the world, the essence of the natural family. We call on all people of goodwill, whose hearts are open to the promptings of this spirit, to join in a great campaign. The time is close when the persecution of the natural family, when the war against children, when the assault on human nature shall end.

The enemies of the natural family grow worried. A triumph that, not so many years ago, they thought complete is no longer sure. Their fury grows. So do their attempts, ever more desperate, at coercion. Yet their mistakes also mount in number. They misread human nature. They misread the times.

We all are called to be the actors, the moral soldiers, in this drive to realize the life ordained for us by our Creator. Our foes are dying, of their own choice; we have a world to gain. Natural families of all races, nations, and creeds, let us unite [together a new civil rights movement to guarantee the life, liberty and happiness of every person]."

The totality of human knowledge and experience points to the importance of the natural family, natural marriage and having a Mommy and Daddy at home for every child. This is the American dream that Alveda's uncle had and it is deeply rooted in the natural family; where children are allowed to be born and raised by parents who understand the value of our most cherished national institution—the natural family. So let us remember Dr. Martin Luther King, Jr.'s words, "And so even though we face the difficulties of today and tomorrow, I still have a dream. It is a dream deeply rooted in the American dream."

Dr. Alveda C. King
Civil Rights Activist and Pro-Life Warrior
Founder, King for America and Pastoral Associate Gospel of Life Ministries

Lawrence D. Jacobs
Vice President, The Howard Center for Family, Religion & Society
Managing Director, World Congress of Families

BIBLE STUDY—REBUILD

Dr. Alveda King
August 2009

Ezra 8:22—For I was ashamed to ask the king for a band of soldiers and horsemen to protect us against the enemy on our way, since we had told the king, The hand of our God is for good on all who seek him, and the power of his wrath is against all who forsake him.

Nehemiah 1:3—The remnant there in the province who had survived the exile is in great trouble and shame. The wall of Jerusalem is broken down, and its gates are destroyed by fire. *4* As soon as I heard these words I sat down and wept and mourned for days, and I continued fasting and praying before the God of heaven.

Nehemiah 2:8—for the good hand of my God was upon me.

During personal Bible study time, it came to me that we should be ashamed to say that we are trusting God, then turning to the world's solutions for our problems. I don't mean that we can't use what is available to use, because the wealth of the wicked is laid up for the just. But—are we trusting God to guide us in taking possession of the "spoils," or are we relying on getting the goods by our own strength? For example, the stimulus package surely has some "hidden treasures" in it for us, but do we rely on God to direct our approach for the solutions or are we looking to God while using earthly tools? I can't say that God will never instruct someone to do something that we as Christians would ordinarily not try, because Peter had a dream to eat "unclean" food and God told him not to say what was clean or not, but to let God make those decisions. But do we come up with schemes on our own and then say God blessed us if we happen to win? I think not.

When Nehemiah and his company were rebuilding the city, there was an order to the process. We would do well to operate in these days according to the pattern of the WORD of GOD—Hebrews 8:5). ABBA Creator Father God, Lord Jesus and Holy Spirit must be our answers to every need! There is much to be learned for today's battle in the book of Nehemiah.

First, they rebuilt the Sheep Gate (recovering the Sheep of The Shepherd of Psalm 23 for this present season). Then, they rebuilt the Fish Gate (for the Fishers of men of Mt. 4:19 and Mark 1:17). Next, they rebuilt the Gate of Yeshanah (the Old City, representing biblical foundations). After that, the Dung Gate (self explanatory).

Then, it's on to repair and open the Fountain Gate (the flow of Holy Spirit and the washing of the WORD and the cleansing of The Blood of Jesus. Next, Repair the pool of Shelah (which means leading—being led by the Spirit of God), into the Kings Garden (where we should find the fruit of the Spirit of Galatians in manifestation in the Saints), on to the artificial (manmade) pool (as in manmade solutions such as grants, stimulus plans, etc. which are not all bad, but are not to be relied upon, simply used as we are led by Holy Spirit). Next, repair the houses of the Mighty (prayer warriors and worshippers) Men (and women since in the Spirit there are no male and female, bond or free, only Christ, Lord of all). Then we repair the districts (under the guidance of evangelists, prophets, teachers, preachers, and the ministry gifts assigned to local church bodies in their dominion territories).

Then, the branch ministries, supported by the Armory (spiritual warfare) which through prayer buttresses the Door of the High Priest (here prayer is a buttress or support and reinforcement for the work of the Ministry of the Saints of GOD) so the imagery and reality of prayer supporting and leading up to the Door of the High Priest is very profound! This path here leads around the Houses of the Servants of ABBA to the Tower of the Court of the Guard (prayer watches)!

Then there is repair of the Water Gate, (living water that Jesus speaks of in John 4:10, 4:11, 7:38 and Revelations 7:17) with the Water being brought in daily, hourly and breath by breath through the labor of Prayer! Often it was the women who carried the water because the men were so encumbered with worldly affairs during the day. Yet the hour is here now where all must worship ABBA in spirit and in truth (John 4:23-24). For me, this revelation coincides with 2 Chronicles 7:14). If my people, which are called by my name, shall humble themselves, and pray, and seek my face, and turn from their wicked ways; then will I hear from heaven, and will forgive their sin, and will heal their land.

After this comes, the Horse Gate (jobs, promotions, prosperity, etc.) to every house and every chamber. All of this process affects the restoration of the House of the Temple Servants, and finally to the Muster Gate which means the inspection or judgment gate and for some the prison gate, but for many the victory gate. What an opportunity for healing and restoration this process brings, for spirit, soul and body!

Men like Ezra and Nehemiah realized that they could accomplish nothing on their own. Indeed, in John 5: 19 and 30, Lord Jesus says of Himself, He can do nothing. He goes on in John 15:5 to reveal Himself as the Vine and us as the branches.

This particular lesson ended with me realizing that one thing that is needed today is much prayer and devotion to ABBA, our mighty Father Creator God! Nehemiah was wise to set the workers to laboring with one hand and doing spiritual warfare with the other hand, while half worked, half prayed nonstop! (Nehemiah 5:6).

The thing is, today, while many are going around to Town Hall meetings, screaming and yelling, bringing about envy and strife and every evil work (James 3:14), we as The Body of Christ are called to prayer and worship where we will find answers and strength for victory. Yes, we can go to a Town Hall meeting, but go in the love and grace of GOD, and people will hear HIM in this hour!

So, our Kingdom work today includes restoring, reviving and feeding the Sheep (people of God), catching the Fish (the lost souls in the world) through evangelism and salvation for the lost, reinforcing the Bible foundations (though mature Christians need milk and meat, the new Christians need to know the foundations, we can all use the WORD), and then, once people are restored, revived, saved and taught, the dung (waste, sin, etc.) needs to be carted out of the Kingdom. On to the Fountain, the Leading of the Holy Spirit, the King's Garden, the Artificial Man Made solutions, rising of the Mighty Warriors, Prayer and Service Districts, Prayer Buttress at the Door of the High Priest, our homes, The Prayer Tower, Prayer Watches, then to the Horse Gate, or our jobs, and our prosperity from which we tithe and give for the Kingdom, and we are blessed, and healed and full of joy!

Today, in our nation and across the globe, we are threatened by concepts and forces that would like to advance abortion, the destruction of the Bible Model for Marriage and Family, the euthanasia of the elderly and infirm, racism, poverty, crime, famine, drought, a crashing economy, I don't need to rehearse the list.

My own testimony, being healed after the destruction of abortion on my own life and the lives of my preborn children. Being a victim of the population control genocide eugenics campaign that is still prevalent today. How can the Dream Survive if we murder our children? Acts 17:26 teaches us that we are one human race, designed and created of "one blood." If we want to see another race of people, we will have to look to Star Trek!

Yet, are we looking to GOD for deliverance? Or are we looking to human ability? The Bible also warns us of naysayers like Sanballat and Tobias, and the doubters and scorners of the New Testament. Everyone who offers assistance or sympathy is not your friend! Use discernment, try the spirits by the Spirit of the Living God!

GOD wants to deliver us! He wants to repair the breech and rebuild our communities. Let us pray!

Alveda
Shalom

THERE ARE NO GLASS CEILINGS IN GOD'S KINGDOM 3/18/2012

Dr. Randy Short

There are essentially two kinds of human beings: those that are mostly secular in their worldview; and, those of a sacred orientation. The secularist view of adversity is irregular mishaps that exist for no reason other than these must be surmounted. Somehow the secular man or woman must confront bad luck or rough situations with the mind to overcome these unrelated difficulties attributed to bad luck, enemies, or the irrational outcome of fate. On the other hand, the sacred-minded person views adversity, obstacles, challenges, and barriers to their achieving goals and objectives are spiritual tests and/or divinely-inspired character-building exercises that will glorify God when the individual undergoing trials is able to succeed.

I am of the latter persuasion, and I believe that the same God that created the universe governs the most infinitesimal matters of my life—even my problems and my barriers. While the secular man or woman sees adversity as a glass ceiling, believers in God see these times in life where things are not going the way we think they should as opportunity for God to make them better and more faithful human beings. As a Christian when in trouble or feeling denied advancement or stymied be unknown forces, I find myself turning to find answers in my Faith's Holy Book the Bible and, there, are hundreds of inspiring stories of the deliverance of those who sought God's help when the storms of life or a glass ceiling arched over their lives.

I trust in the scriptures that attribute the name Jehovah Jireh (the Providing God) to God Almighty who is able to break all glass ceilings, yokes, barriers, and solve all problems. Even more than that, we have the consolation that of Romans 8:28: "all things work together for the good of those that love God and are called according to his purpose". Our life's walk is about breaking the many "ceilings" that would deny us the fulfillment of our divine purpose to be like Jesus Christ.

Men and women who lack the faith to achieve their foreordained purpose too often overlook the privilege of worshiping a God that is omnipotent, Omni state, and omniscient. We lose focus of the might and majesty of Jesus Christ when our fleshly minds and eyes only see "ceilings" and "barriers" and "dead-ends". This writer would humbly suggest that the greatest pitfall in life is faithlessness. The absence of faith and hope precludes all resolutions to human problems. In fact unbelief and faithlessness in God is a wanton act of rebellion, self-deification, rejection and negation of the Almighty. Even believers who claim with their mouths to be in relationship with God are afoul with the Almighty without unconditional faith and belief in their Lord it is written in Hebrews 11:6: "Without faith it is impossible to please God". Those who complain about the challenges in life ignore the reality that God seeks to prove himself to us by rescuing his people when they are in dire circumstances Psalms 50:15: "Call on Me in your times of trouble. I will save you, and you will honor Me". Perhaps we devote too much time to feeling sorry for ourselves than to realize that God wants us to know that there is no situation from which he will not rescue us, and it is His divine will to break the fetters that bind us so that we will give him the glory.

In these troubled times of economic woes, we let the media and the vain rhetoric from the mouths of those out of relationship to God cause us to fear for our material lives but if we are faithful to the Word of God it reminds us in Proverbs 37:25: "I have ever seen the righteous forsaken nor their seed begging bread". If we walk in a life of faith we have intergenerational promises of divine intervention on our behalves. My question is do we thank God even in our difficulties? Have we realized that these challenges allow God to demonstrate both his love and power for us? Everyone's glass ceiling was broken when Jesus Christ rose from the dead and conquered death, sin, and suffering. I believe that our lack of faith is a bigger problem than any glass ceiling. Furthermore, we think of glass as something breakable. All of us have seen shattered glass, but none of us have seen mountains of stone move, and yet Christ told us in Matthew 17:20: "I tell you the truth if you have the faith as small of the mustard seed, you can say to this mountain 'Move from here to there' and it will move. Nothing will be impossible for you". If a mountain can be ordered to move why would a glass ceiling be a major concern to us?

I want to remind those of your reading this that God, as a deliverer of His people is a continuous theme in the Holy Bible. First, we need to remember problems are a part of life itself. Job 14:1 says, "Man born of woman is of few days and full of trouble". We can expect difficulties with the assurance that no weapons formed against us can prosper according to Isaiah 54:17. Every saint of the Old Testament came out on top: Joseph, Elijah, Ruth, Esther, Hannah, Mary, David, Job, Gideon, Joshua, and countless others. We live in an age where we run to psychotropic drugs to alter our moods and self-help books to appeal to our egos, but these come with built-in-man-made-shortcomings.

The Bible is replete with stories of people overcoming incredible glass ceilings and death-defying challenges that only divine intervention could provide. Only God's grace working on the inner man of Joseph, who had been sold into slavery by psychopathically jealous brothers, empowered him to receive them in love and give them a conciliatory word of forgiveness exclaiming, "As for you, you meant evil against me, but God meant it for good, to bring about that many people should be kept alive, as they are today "(Genesis 50:20). Slavery and long prison sentences are among the high-ticket and big box glass ceilings that modern mankind complains about. Joseph's response was to look to God and eschew the pity-party doldrums that ensnare so many today.

In the 6th century B.C., Belteshazzar, Shadrach, Meshach, and Abednego were four Judean men who held high government appointed positions for the King Nebuchadnezzar of Chaldean Babylonia. These young men, of noble birth, witnessed the total destruction of their native Judah by the armies of the very man they were forced to serve as officials running a kingdom founded on warfare and social inequality. Further, Babylonian soldiers depopulated Judah by forcibly deporting the defeated survivors of war back to Mesopotamia.

These young men of noble birth had been selected to become assimilated Babylonians stripped of their culture, families, language, and faith. Even today we know these men by their "conquered names" for their real names were Daniel, Hananiah, Mishael, and Azariah. Many people like me of African ancestry carry the names of people who once owned our ancestors, but the hand of God can break any yoke in all situations throughout history. Some folks look down on these names that came through conquest without giving thanks that names given to human beings claimed as chattel, now, belong to people able to struggle for a free and just world.

All that Shadrach, Meshach, and Abednego had been accustomed to coming-of-age in Judah had been eliminated by war, forced migration, and the destruction of their family units. Under their new rulers, these men were privileged hostages expected to gratefully 'fit in' and 'go along to get along' and conform to the ways of Babylon. Nothing about these Hebrew experimental boys was left to chance; they were subjected to many tests and examinations as a form of quality control especially designed by the men in service of the Nebuchadnezzar.

In addition, the finest of clothes, food, drink, and activities—including palace courtesans were placed before these men to alter their morals and beliefs. It was expected of them to eat ritually profane foods, but they refused. God rewarded their faithfulness with high civil service examination scores. Moreover, once they completed their three-year academic training Nebuchadnezzar employed them in managerial positions in the Province of Babylon. The king himself adjudged them ten-times greater than their peers, and their exemplary service resulted in regular promotions.

During the reign of Nebuchadnezzar, he constructed a nine-story golden statue erected in the Plain of Dura in his image or that of the Babylonian god of wisdom Nabu. To celebrate his narcissistic achievement, Nebuchadnezzar decreed a national day of dedication and celebration to honor his statue and he made it a capital crime for observers of the idol to not prostrate and worship it when the royal orchestra played the call to worship. According to the Code of Hammurabi Code burning criminals was an accepted practice, and ancient Babylonians used kilns to make bricks, pottery, and cuneiform books, and these ovens were used on people. As suddenly as the Hebrew Golden Boys had climbed to the heights of public service, a glass ceiling caused by a wicked man who arrogated to himself the divinity of God seemingly stymied forever the dreams of Daniel and his three friends.

The royal orchestra played its Faustian fugue and thousands bowed before the idol of gold. They wanted to keep their good jobs and everyone else was doing the same thing—almost. Others from other lands figured that due to theomachy (the war of the gods) their deities lost so they might as well bow down to the god of the hour. Others reasoned why burn-up in the furnace trying to be different or militant. Just like the people of today there is always an excuse to disobey God and seek unrighteousness. The excuse is the earthly cost of the present outweighs eternal reward at the side of God the Father. In real time in Dura, yes-men idolaters who bowed down noticed the three minority folks who refused to worship, ad word got around quickly and jealous peers of Shadrach, Meshach, and Abednego informed the so-called king of kings Nebuchadnezzar about his affirmative action employees 'dissing' him. A sated and irate Nebuchadnezzar, in furious rage thinking about all he had done for these ungrateful minorities, had Shadrach, Meshach, and Abednego arrested and brought to him therewith. He knew these men because Daniel (who interpreted his dreams accurately) had incessantly told him of their high abilities and character, and on the account of their friend they would be accorded a second chance to worship the king. Thus, these men would have to explain their perfidious treason.

Before Nebuchadnezzar the man who controlled their careers, their homes, their freedom, and plausibly their temporal lives, the three Hebrew men were under arrest were expected to show remorse for their actions; however, these men felt that nothing done by a man—even one of considerable might and wealth—could note trumped by God. Nebuchadnezzar reminded the men that the penalty of their refusal to obey him was death, and they for the first time since taken from their homes in Judah let the king know how they understood the universe stating[Daniel 3:16], "O Nebuchadnezzar we do not need to defend ourselves before you in this matter. If we are thrown into the blazing furnace, the God, which we serve, is able to save us from it, and He will rescue us from your hand, O King. But even if He does not, we want you to know, O King, that we will not serve your gods or worship the image of gold you have set up."

They were tossed into the furnace heated seven times the standard level of heat, and soldiers were ordered to place these men into the furnace. While the men of Nebuchadnezzar who threw the prisoners in the fire died from the intensity of the great heat, onlookers could see the three Hebrew men walking around in the furnace unbounded and accompanied by a fourth person. Even the wicked Babylonian King realized God was working on behalf of the men he tried to kill and beckoned that they leave the furnace. The glass ceiling of the world's most wealthy and powerful man could not harm those faithful to God.

Job who was the most righteous and wealthiest man in the world, when he was alive faced perhaps the most incredible glass ceiling known to a human being. Everything that he owed or took pride in children, reputation, health, cattle, land, friends, crops, possessions, and love and affection of his wife was stripped of him in a matter of a New York minute. His suffering endured for years and there was none to comfort him. Job broke his glass ceiling caused by Satan by being faithful. Believers too often forget the precious promise of Revelations 2:10, "Be Faithful unto death, and I will give you the crown of life." We cannot control our days or moments on this earth. God must be trusted to help us in our good and bad times. Moreover, Job's glass ceiling shatters when he finds his strength in faith growing despite all his earthly loses and he says in repentance Job 42:2, "I know You can do everything and that no purpose of Yours can be withheld from you". Job was restored with 7 sons and 3 daughters, and lived more than 120 years afterwards.

Jonah found himself trapped inside a great fish for disobeying God. There is no more thorough example of being trapped than his. Imagine unemployed, God angry with you, single, surrounded by decaying fish and swimming in gastric acids of an animal intent on digesting you? Many people have a sense of having burned all their bridges and exhausted their credit. They look to everything but God as their liberator. Moreover, Jonah tired of being trapped in the great fish got on his knees and prayed. Jonah 2:7-9 reads, "When my soul fainted within me, I remembered the Lord: and my prayer went up to You, into Your holy temple. Those who regard worthless idols forsake their own mercy. But I will sacrifice to You with the voice of thanksgiving: I will pay what I have vowed. Salvation is the Lord".

The great fish let the wayward prophet go at that very second.

In real time today, there are people who feel forgotten or overlooked covered by a glass ceiling. I want to tell them especially those in minority or smaller ethnic groups that faithlessness and unbelief and the refusal to love one's neighbors are the greatest impediments to God releasing them from their trials. Seek first the kingdom of God and all the other things are forthcoming.

As an African American, I find my people incredibly estranged from the God that has helped them endure and advance in a situation where racism, economic injustice, endemic cult-of-personality-prosperity-false Christianity reigns, ubiquitous black-self hatred is commonplace in families and communities, a popular culture that enshrines materialism hedonism, self-worship, sexual perversion, veneration of porn, substance abuse, ignorance, and rejection of Jesus Christ, and even indifference mixed with envious hatred inflicted on them from other black people in the world who come to America. Through it all God has held us in his hands. Our glass ceiling is completely linked to our failure to trust in God and put into practice the teachings of Jesus Christ. If people pooled their moneys they would have fewer worries about the people who will not hire them. If we learned to love one another the rates of violent crime and assault and rape and battery would drop like stones falling from a skyscraper. If we honored our bodies the illegitimacy, the venereal diseases, the bastardy, the abortions, the broken hearts and minds due to infidelity and wanton promiscuity would retreat like an ebb tide. If God is all powerful the challenges and issues that we attribute to the bad other people would be so diminished that those injustices that do exist would be plainly manifested and they would be put down in a fortnight.

There is no glass ceiling in God. We can do all things with God on our side. Remember the miracles of Jesus Christ did not stop at Golgotha! We must return to God. We must believe and trust God, and make how we treat each other the living evidence that we know God and walk with him. God never changes. It is our faith and trust that rises and falls, and we must always struggle to keep our hearts and souls in remembrance of God. We must learn to keep the cross before us as a guide. 2 Corinthians 4:18 gives us a cautionary admonition: "So we fix our eyes not on what is seen, but on what is unseen. For what is seen is temporary, but what is unseen is eternal".

Whatever obstacles are in your life must be recognized as temporary and serve a godly purpose of refining your character. God is always with us and we must remember the word tells us Psalms 84:11 "For the Lord is a sun and a shield: the Lord will give grace and glory: no good thing will he withhold from them that walk uprightly". Be strong in the Lord for his promises in Matthew 16:19 "and I will give unto thee the keys of the kingdom of heaven: and whatsoever thou shall bind on earth shall be bound in heaven: and whatsoever you loose in earth shall be loosed in heaven". Don't sweat the small things and rough patches in life's road they are for us to overcome 1Thessalonians 3:3, "That no one be moved by these afflictions. For yourselves know that we are destined for this". Finally, we must never discount in our lives the many blessings that we take for granted and even in struggles we owe God praise 1Thessalonians 5:18,"In all things give thanks in all circumstances, for this is the will of God in Christ Jesus for you".

God Bless You
Dr. W. Randy Short, M.Div., Baltimore-Washington SCLC

Dr. Short is a Harvard Graduate, Executive Director Youth Commission at County Council Prince George's County, Writer/Curator at West Tennessee Cultural Heritage Association and Consultant-Researcher at Christian Methodist Episcopal

CLOSING WORDS

Dr. Alveda King
www.kingforamerica.com

King for America—Where Jesus Christ is Lord

In the 1990's my Pastor, Allen McNair encouraged me to develop a ministry. Not being sure where to start, I first began proclaiming the Gospel of Jesus Christ. That message alone is enough to fill all of my waking hours. Yet, God has been gracious enough to allow many creative expressions to spring forth and become King for America, where Jesus Christ is truly Lord.

I am deeply grateful to each of the contributors who have shared their testimonies and missions in this book. They are all ministers in their own rights, and together we are seeking to bless our readers with a broad representation of our ministries of services to the masses.

Due to the variety of messengers, it was difficult to choose just one voice and one theme. So, we began with love and ended with the pursuit of happiness. Between the beginning and the end, we added faith, hope, life and liberty.

Because King for America is not just Alveda King, this book is written by many and not just the one. Our goal is to touch hearts of our readers, and to illuminate the shadows of death and destruction that have plagued the world for far too long. We pray to see the captives free.

Consider this: you can lock someone in chains, but you must watch over your prisoner lest he or she escape. So both the oppressor and oppressed are bound until a force more powerful than either sets the captives free.

Jubilee

American slave traders and slave masters often misquoted the Bible as justification for slavery. I often ask those who point to the Bible as justification for slavery why then, if the Bible is to held up as a standard for slavery, why the slave masters didn't honor the command the set the slaves free and give them wealth and property after seven years of service? The Bible describes this process as *Jubilee*.

Obviously the ancient bondages of slavery and racism still exist in the 21st Century. Now, along with oppression due to skin color, babies in the womb are counted in the masses of the oppressed. The sick, infirm and elderly are not far behind in the onslaught.

It will take yet another brief history excursion to discover why the African American or Black communities of America are being targeted by racism, segregation, genocide and the onslaught of social ills. Please take a deep breath and hold on to your hat. What you are about to read may shock you.

Possibly, many African Americans are the biological and spiritual seed of Abraham. This is what makes the mandate of Jubilee as cited in Leviticus 25 relevant to Black people in America. Consider this excerpt from the book, *Who We Are in Christ Jesus*:

> God wants us to have a greater knowledge of who we are, and how we fit into His eternal arrangement. By coming to understand God's heavenly plan, we will be able to conceptualize how we as a nation of people came to be known as "The Black Man," also known as "The Slave," "Nigger," "Colored," "Negro," "Black," "Afro-American," and "African American."

> Here in America for over 400 years, we Black Americans have longed for a name and home, and yet our destiny lies in two covenants. The term remnant in the Old and New Testaments, reveals that we, like our oppressed Hebrew brothers of old, have been living in bondage, but have been a major source of energy in the building of our country (like Joseph in Egypt.). Also like Joseph in Egypt, we came in as slaves, but have risen to the top of the political and social platforms of our great nation, as we ourselves are critically entrenched in the mechanisms of its influences.

If we consider how the Hebrews ran into all parts of Africa just after the massive slaying by the Roman Empire, we can also discover how the Hebrew nation came into captivity at the hands of African nations (Deut. 26:5-8; Ps. 105:32-27; 106:19-22; Isaiah 11:11; Amos 9:7; Zeph. 3:10Mi. 5:7-8; Acts 2:5). The Hebrew nation was no stranger to bondage on the continent of Africa. Moses, in the dramatic Exodus of the Bible, answered God and led the people out of Egypt. But once again, in the first century A.D., Israel returned to Africa seeking refuge, only to find themselves in certain situations causing them to be re-enslaved!

The children of Ham largely accepted the children of Shem, as they intermingled into one people (Judges. 3:5-6; Ezra 2:1-2; Ezek. 16:1-3). Remember, the God of Israel also embraced the children of Ham. At that time in history, the Afro-eastern religions had a toehold in every aspect of the African society. For fourteen centuries, the blood of Abraham mingled with the blood of Ham. Now if we could keep in mind that God knew before day one, just what would occur, would definitely help us to understand that He knew that Abraham's seed would mingle with the African people of Ham.

Religious differences made the now Black skinned, broad nosed Israelites easy prey for their Hamitic relatives, who sold them into the profitable slave trade of the 16th century. It would be some time before people of conscience such as Wilberforce and the abolitionists leaders in America would rise up against the forces of darkness, and once again echo the cry of Moses: "Let my people go!" The wheel was set in motion, and slavery had a course to run.

At the height of the more recent oppression, when the slave traders reached the "dark continent," they attained help from the native Black people in order to "capture" the Black Jews, then placed them on the treacherous slave ships to a "new land."

Here, we can observe how the "Black Jews" went into bondage for another 400 years, which lasted from the 1500's to the 1900's. These Black Jews carried with them their heritage in their music. The old "Negro Spirituals," "Go Down Moses," "Joshua Fit De Battle of Jericho," "Jordan River Crossing," and many others give credence to a history that the Black Israelite slaves in America did not learn such rituals in Africa, nor from their slave masters in America. These children in a strange land had carried those songs from their Mother Land Israel, to their Mother Land Africa, then to the remote regions of the earth.

Later, during this same period, the blood of Abraham crossed with the blood of Japheth, when the "White" slave masters, took the Black slave girls into their beds. These acts irrefutably initiated a breeding system that would alienate the slaves from each other by forming a system of color differentiations; a system that taught the darker skinned slaves to resent the lighter complexions; a practice that did not avoid consequential preferences.

Then, another spiritual Exodus, similar to the times and experiences of Moses, which occurred hundreds of years before Martin Luther King, Jr., certainly brought Blacks up from the dregs of oppression. Like Moses, Dr. King did not "reach the promised land." God has raised up another "Joshua generation" to lead the people into another spiritual warfare, toward possessing a promise land.

Unlike our Hebrew brothers of old, we are not seeking milk and honey, even though the stakes are the same, since we want the richest of God's promises. We, as Blacks who have accepted the heritage offered by the Salvation of the Messiah, are heirs to an unlimited source of power and wealth. Naturally, God's promise is for everyone, regardless of color or gender. Yet, while God's promise is not limited, it is certainly for us as well as others, since we are a special people. It is plainly understood that the Word acknowledges that God has vested interest in us, and that all people, including African-Americans are definitely members of the family tree of Adam (Acts 17). People around the globe acknowledge this truth. Yet, it appears that the American Blacks still stumble in unenlightened confusion, leading many to cry out that we must discover who we are in Christ Jesus!

In light of the context of the ancestry of the African American "nation" or "village" living in America in the 21st century, many are connected to ancestors of the ancient Hebrew bloodline. Following this trail of evidence, we can conclude that descendants of slaves in America are entitled to the Jubilee Mandate of Leviticus 25:39-55:

If any of your Israelite relatives go bankrupt and sell themselves to you, do not treat them as slaves. Treat them instead as hired servants or as resident foreigners who live with you, and they will serve you only until the Year of Jubilee. At that time they and their children will no longer be obligated to you, and they will return to their clan and ancestral property. The people of Israel are my servants, whom I brought out of the land of Egypt, so they must never be sold as slaves. Show your fear of God by treating them well; never exercise your power over them in a ruthless way . . .

So, according to the Bible, our "foreign" slave masters were required to release us after seven years, and give us land and gifts as we departed from the years of slavery. They were not supposed to hang us, lynch us, bomb us and otherwise abuse us. They were not supposed to enslave us for generations, even into the 21st century, and keep us on "the plantation."

So, can we then conclude that greed and manipulation caused American slave masters to disregard the Bible mandate of Jubilee? Is this same spirit of greed and rebellion at the basis of racism, genocide and other atrocities of man's inhumanity to man at the root of America's social ills today?

This is a question that must surely be considered in the next edition of our Anthology. We want to hear from you as we prepare to launch our next volume. Please send your questions and feedback to Blackprolifeanthology@gmail.com.

Friends, there is a cry for revival in the land. There is a longing for a Jubilee. Set the captives free we cry. At the time of this publication, we are months away from the 50th anniversary of Dr. Martin Luther King, Jr.'s 1963, "I Have a Dream" speech. The number 50 marks the time of Jubilee. As we approach or, as some say, as we are in the era of the end of a dispensation, we look towards the new where liberty and freedom will take on heaven's appearance.

We long for liberty and redemption, not just for some, but for all, regardless of skin color, gestational condition, age or physical restraints. Yet, there can be no revival without repentance. This is a season to cry out for repentance and revival. Oh Lord, send revival. LET FREEDOM RING! Amen.

THIS SAME JESUS CHRIST: FINDING COMPASSION IN 21ST CENTURY BABYLON

By Dr. Alveda C. King

Seek ye first the Kingdom of God and His righteousness,
and all these things, (better than Utopia) will be added to you.
Matthew 6:33

On Wednesday, May 9, 2012, President Barack Hussein Obama, known by many as the first "Black" President of the United States of America, also became the first Black President to endorse homosexual marriage. This startling decision came as no surprise to some who already knew him as the "most abortion minded president in the history of America." A few days after President Obama's announcement, the National Association for the Advancement of Colored People also endorsed homosexual marriage.

Amid the controversy of these seemingly contemporary 21st century policies, the question repeatedly arises: How can we show compassion to those who believe that homosexuality and abortion are civil rights? My now deceased and beloved Aunt Coretta Scott King supported both the homosexual agenda and the abortion agenda. She even accepted the 1966 Planned Parenthood "Maggie" award in her husband's stead. Uncle M. L. was prolife. Aunt Coretta was the first to ask me the compassion question in the mid-1980's. Many have since posed the compassion question to me.

The homosexual lobby likes to point to the professional relationship between Uncle M. L. and Bayard Rustin, his openly gay staffer who left the movement at the height of the campaign. Rustin attempted to convince

Uncle M. L. that homosexual rights were equal with civil rights. Uncle M. L. did not agree, and would not attach the homosexual agenda to the 20ᵗʰ century civil rights struggles. So Rustin resigned. He was a brilliant strategist and was hired by Uncle M. L., not because he was gay, but because he was a capable strategist. He also was not fired, he chose to resign. My uncle was not a bigot, and he didn't judge people for the color of their skin nor their sexual orientation. Neither do I. As compassionate Christians who won't be forced to sit on the back of the bus as far as our spiritual commitments are concerned, we can be compassionate without endorsing sin.

As to the relationship between Mrs. Coretta Scott King and the homosexual lobby, Mrs. King was a very compassionate woman. She and I shared conversations regarding misplaced compassion. When her daughter, my cousin Elder Bernice King marched for family, education, economics, Criminal Justice and traditional marriage early in this century, the homosexual lobby demanded that Mrs. King publicly rebuke her daughter for her stance. Mrs. King did not rebuke her daughter. The issue here is compassion, and how to show compassion in the face of controversy.

As one who is unabashedly unashamed of the Gospel of Jesus Christ, I must admit that when the question first came to me, I sought for a humanly wise response. I struggled and groped in my finite mind for something my Daddy A. D. King might say; or my uncle M. L. King, or my Granddaddy King. At first, I didn't even remember their sermons, just thought about what their answers might be from a civil rights perspective. After all, I knew that they all preached the Bible, and like David, did their best to obey God in spite of their human frailties. I knew that they were pro-life and believed in procreative marriage. After all, I'm the one who coined the now popular slogan: "I have a dream, it's in my genes."

I wanted to express to the world that my great-grandfather, Dr. A. D. Williams, a Baptist preacher was an original NAACP founder. I wanted to express that my Granddaddy, also a Baptist preacher, was an early NAACP leader. Following in their footsteps, my Daddy A. D. King and Uncle M. L. King founded the 20ᵗʰ century Civil Rights Movement in the Name of Jesus.

Thank goodness my good friend Day Gardner helped me to get back on track quickly. In a joint press release from the African American prolife community regarding President Obama's decision, Day wrote: "The NAACP was founded by Blacks who had an understanding and strong faith in God. They were people—pastors and congregations who knew that the Bible, God's final Word—was very clear on the immorality and wages of homosexuality and abortion. It is appalling that this one time super hero 'civil rights' organization supports the breakdown of traditional marriage and the ruthless killing of our unborn children as a civil right. In its decision to please the world, the NAACP has turned its back on the things of GOD and in doing so it has become irrelevant. We must encourage those who know the truth to speak out—to stand firmly on the solid rock—to not look to the right or to the left. Dr. Martin Luther King, Jr. once said: "Our lives began to end the day we become silent about things that matter."

Day's thoughts lead me to the answer to the compassion question. How can we show compassion for people who want to legitimize sin? If we love them, shouldn't we try not to hurt their feelings by pointing out that things like abortion and homosexuality are against the Word of God? No matter how many new Bible translations that people come up with, God's Word isn't going to change.

My answer came not from what would Daddy do, or Uncle M. L. do, or Granddaddy do? The answer will always be "what would Jesus do?" Living on the edge of a 21st century Babylon with the stench of Sodom and Gomorrah stinging our nostrils, we need to know that the question is relevant and the answer is imperative. Not only what would Jesus do, but what did Jesus do when confronted with sinners? Jesus extended compassion in the form of "ye shall know the truth and the truth will set you free."

Right now the anti-procreative marriage community is in league with the anti-life community, and together with the NAACP and other sympathizers, they are seeking a world where homosexual marriage and abortion will supposedly set the captives free. To the contrary, it is the Word of God on these and all human issues that sets people free. As Christians, we must have the compassion of Jesus Christ and tell the truth and shame the devil. We must not allow false compassion to force truth to take a seat on the back of the bus.

As a young woman, sitting in the pews of the congregations of my elders, I must admit that I questioned God and the Bible, seeking inconsistencies in the Word. I wanted to enjoy sin, and was looking for loopholes. My Daddy and Uncle M. L. had similar experiences before they were "transformed" by God's light and love through Jesus Christ.

I guess the best example of the transformation or born again experiences in my family would be my Uncle M. L.'s conversion testimony which came to him in 1956. As was previously stated, Uncle M. L. belongs to a long line of preachers, and during his early years, he depended on the faith of his fathers. Then, in 1956, Kin experienced his first personal encounter with God.

On page 59 of BEARING THE CROSS (Garrow), there is an account of the experience. At around midnight on Jan. 27, 1956, at the height of the bus boycott in Montgomery, Ala. Uncle M. L. was discouraged by death threats, exhaustion, and the heavy burdens of organizing the community. He also feared for his wife and babies. He was praying at his kitchen table, h "It seemed at that moment," he later told an interviewer, "that I could hear an inner voice saying to me, 'Martin Luther, stand up for righteousness. Stand up for justice. Stand up for truth. And lo I will be with you . . . . 'I heard the voice of Jesus saying still to fight on."

The link between Christian faith and the 20th Century Civil Rights Movement was genuine and indistinguishable, in that you could not have one without the other. It was the vision and reality of Christian love that strengthened the Christian warriors. Uncle M. L. had a love for all humanity, that one race of people created by God. Agape love is not easily attained, but Uncle M. L., my Daddy A. D., Daddy King, our hold family legacy has always embraced Agape. God is Love. The Bible teaches us to walk in love, even as my Uncle M. L. was taught. The Bible was Martin Luther King Jr.s' best textbook, always.

Not long after his conversion, Uncle M. L. wrote the following to a youth seeking advice:

From 1950's Ebony Advice Column

QUESTION: My problem is different from the ones most people have. I am a boy, but I feel about boys the way I ought to feel about girls. I don't want my parents to know about me. What can I do?

MLK: Your problem is not at all an uncommon one. However, it does require careful attention. **The type of feeling that you have toward boys is probably not an innate tendency, but something that has been culturally acquired.** . . . You are already on the right road toward a solution, since you honestly recognize the problem and have a desire to solve it.

Uncle M. L. showed the compassion and love of Jesus in his letter to this youth. He didn't help the young man embrace a position contrary to God's Word, rather he extended God's loving compassion in his response. We have a sure example of this type of compassion from Jesus Himself:

In the case of "the woman caught in the act," Jesus said to her accusers: "Ye who are without sin, cast the first stone." As one by one her accusers dropped their stones, and walked away, Jesus wrote in the dirt. He then asked Mary Magdalene, "woman, where are your accusers?" She realized that her accusers had dispersed. Then, Jesus spoke the startling words of liberation to the woman who would become his first female disciple. "Neither do I accuse you. Go and sin no more."

Yes friends, Jesus acknowledged the woman's sins, and he still loved her. He set her free, not just from those who would stone her, but from the behavior that bound her. Loving someone who is bound by sin, dismissing their sanctimonious judges and then setting the captives free by showing them a way out of sin is the answer to the compassion question. Show compassion by showing people the liberty and love of This Same Jesus Christ: yesterday, today and forever.

To do this, we must be transparent, admit to and repent of our own sins first, and then be the examples traveling the road of repentance and redemption. There is love, mercy, compassion and grace in what we have to offer. We just have to be bold enough and strong enough to love.

REFERENCE

Preserving families of African Ancestry. (January 2003) Retrieved March 5, 2010, from http://nabsw.org/mserver/PreservingFamilies.aspx

A Prayer for Revival

Dear Heavenly Father, because you are my Creator and my Judge, I want you to be my Father. Please forgive me for my sins, and show me the way to you as my Father through Christ Jesus. Teach me Your ways, and fill me with Your Holy Spirit. Help me to forgive my oppressors, and all who have sinned against me and hurt me and my ancestors, so that you can forgive and heal me. You are LOVE Father and YOU never fail! Lord, send revival to my heart and life, and to our families, our communities, to America and to the world. In Jesus' Name I pray. Amen.—Dr. Alveda King

AFTERWORD: A WORD OF ENCOURAGEMENT

"Doc" Ed Holliday
Winter 2012

Alveda,

I want to simply send you a note of encouragement. Your reminder to all Americans that your Uncle Martin promoted change through non-violence and your words of strength in a day when wimpish words create conditions for less than our better angels to act, are both beautiful words of healing. You speak with a voice founded in faith, experience, and hope. You, Bishop Harry Jackson, Dean Nelson, Rev. C. L. Bryant, Rev. Bill Owens, and so many other friends of yours are so important to our nation.

You are 21st century pioneers for freedom. Just as Daniel Boone helped find a passage through the Appalachian Mountains so, too, are you seeking to trailblaze a path through the mountains of despair. Your Uncle Martin's new monument on the Mall in Washington D.C. is a testament that mountains can be moved and real change can happen to make the lives of all Americans better.

When your Uncle Martin told us that he had been to the mountaintop, and he had seen the other side I have always assumed that America was on that mountain and we just had to go down the hill into the valley and cross the Jordan River into the Promised Land. I have been so wrong for so long, because I now realize that only Martin had the God-given strength to prophetically get to the mountain top more than 40 years ago. Alveda, you and your friends must carve out a passage for America to get through the many mountains of despair before "we as a people will get to the Promised Land."

As you carve out the passage I am reminded of what the humanists have given our nation. Over the last forty years the false promises like fool's gold have devastated our inner cities as children born out of wedlock have exploded, abortions have skyrocketed, and our young people are killing each other and being jailed in numbers that numb us to the reality. And now these same humanists are telling us what we need now is the ability for men to marry men and women to marry women. The road that leads to destruction is wide.

Alveda, please continue to carve out of the mountains of despair the straight and narrow road that will lead us to the Promised Land. Our nation needs a new moral leader, one that is not afraid to stand on the Judeo-Christian principles that have guided this nation since its birth. Indeed, the path through the mountains of despair may be narrow. Just as the Democrat, Rev. Diaz in New York has warned the Democratic Party there that the Democrats have lost every special election since they forced through the legalization of gay marriage last year, and now former President Jimmy Carter is telling the Democratic Party that they need to be more Pro-life, something is happening here in America.

God wants to move mountains!

Alveda, I pray for God to give you wisdom and grace, discernment and passion, and the strength to blaze a path through the mountains of despair for Americans everywhere. May your words be words that heal, may you take the stumbling blocks in peoples' lives and teach us how to build a better nation.

Allow God to use you to help to lead us to life, liberty, and the pursuit of happiness in a land of abundance where all Americans will be privileged to say we as a people have made it to the Promised Land—thank God.

God bless you,
Ed "Doc" Holliday

APPENDIX ONE

(Note: On May 8, 2012, President Barack Obama became the first President of The United States to openly endorse "Gay Marriage.")

OPEN LETTER

Dear President Obama: Americans Prayerfully United to Advance the Culture of Life

"For Life, Liberty and Family"

To sign on to this letter, please visit www.africanamericanoutreach.com where you can print a PDF of the letter and encourage your elected officials to sign the letter. Once you and/or your elected official have signed the letter, email to aao@priestsforlife.org or mail to Priests for Life, c/o African American Outreach, PO Box 141172, Staten Island, NY 10314

Adapted from original letter posted January 7, 2009

<u>Dear President Obama</u>, Members of the U. S. Congress, Governors of State and Legislative Bodies, All Political Candidates and all elected and appointed leaders of the people of the United States of America:

Objective: To restore respect for human life, liberty and family, as a means of reducing crime; America's grossly disproportionate prison inmate population; and the number of pregnancies ending in abortion.

Violent crime reflects a basic disrespect for the lives and liberty of other individuals. Crime often destroys human life or the liberty to enjoy freedom or pursue happiness. As crime has skyrocketed in the United States, so has the cost of defending one's freedom be it as a criminal defendant or as a community burdened by the cost of law enforcement and imprisonment of those convicted of crimes so that others may enjoy the freedoms promised by the Constitution. Abortion is an act of violence against God and humanity. Life and Liberty are joint partners, anchored by the family. The challenge of this country has been to balance the freedom of one individual against the freedom of others. The essential duty of protecting the lives of its citizens must not be subjugated to the protection of the liberties of a few.

We the undersigned respectfully submit for your consideration the following strategic plan with the desire to accomplish the betterment of all Americans. We would appreciate the opportunity for open dialogue at town hall meetings, or at any venue you so choose.

1) Remove all federal and state funding including Title 10 funding that is used to promote or commit acts against the family.

2) Remove all federal and state funding that is used to support, promote or commit acts of genocide, abortion and prenatal murder, including Title 10 funding.

3) Support legislation and allow funding for development of a Human Life Curriculum for schools; youth detention; centers and prisons. Said curriculum would include pertinent information regarding nutrition; natural family planning; the link between fertility, breast feeding and continuation of the species and other non-invasive prevention strategies. The race issue would be addressed with information regarding the knowledge that all human beings are one race rather than the currently accepted concept that there are separate races of human beings on the earth. Essential parenting concepts, fatherhood and motherhood principles and other information regarding human life and development would be included.

4) Support legislation and provide funding for enabling mothers and fathers to be actively involved in the educational choices of their children.

5) Provide legislation, funding for and support of Public Service Announcements heralding the benefits of embracing family life as opposed to practicing the use of harmful chemical and surgical procedures such as artificial birth control and abortion.

Such announcements would be similar to those of those Surgeon General's warning that smoking is hazardous to your health.

6) Support legislation and provide funding that enables provision of Birthing and Crisis Pregnancy Centers throughout America.

7) Support legislation and provide funding for Re-establishment of the Federal Parole System:

8) Support legislation and provide funding for Municipal Transition Centers: (The Clinton Administration directed funding to local government for the funding of new prisons and jails. Similar funding should be directed to local governments for the funding of locally operated transition centers for newly released prisoners)

9) Provide funding for and support the development of Local Parole Advisory Boards: made up of local citizens who assist state parole boards in making parole decisions.

10) Support legislation and provide funding for Re-established Prisoner/ Parolee Exchange Programs to maintain balance in state and federal prison population with parole population and to limit the growth in prison population.

11) Provide funding, legislation and plan for utilizing Parolee Labor to rebuild America's infrastructure as opposed to privatizing prisons.

12) Provide legislation and funding for federal and state establishment of a commission made up of civil rights advocates, spiritual and community leaders, lawyers, law enforcement etc. for a "jubilee release project" to review individuals for release first considering those who may have been wrongly convicted, unjustly sentenced and then those who have demonstrated rehabilitation, targeting a reduction in federal and state prison populations.

As leaders and lay members of the populations you serve, we welcome the opportunity to assist and support efforts such as those outlined above in this letter. We commit ourselves to communicating this information to you through the channels you provide, and expect to find other creative, loving and non-violent ways of communicating with you, respectfully acknowledging your authority to govern, with the expectation of fostering a better life for all human beings.

Your signature here represents your commitment to this pledge and to a better America.

Signed: _____ (Political Leader)

We are looking forward to your response.

Prayerfully and sincerely,

Americans for Advancing the Culture of Life, Liberty, Justice and Family in America

Signed: _____(US Citizen)

APPENDIX TWO

Selected Poetry by Alveda King

FOR GENERATIONS TO COME

Our family tree
means more to me, Than silver
or gold,or a
Rolls Royce.

I can rejoice and be glad,
that Mother and Dad, loved each other
—and GOD
Who blessed their union.

From one to another, we are linked
to each other . . .
Through the blessings and mercy of our awesome
CREATOR

Our Creator, the Artist, Who reminds us of
ETERNITY

In the smiles of our children, who have the
Spirit of our ancestors—
Twinkling out from their eyes . . .

Reminding us
Of GENERATIONS to COME.

SJ Forevermore
SJ, today
You lift me up.

Yesterday, you filled my cup.
Tomorrow and forevermore,
You are my keys to Heaven's door.

Praise to
Father
Son
and Spirit.
Thanks, S.J.,
Forevermore.

P.S. Thanks for breaking bonds and curses.
Sunshine feels real good.

Politics Can Make You . . .

Mad
Powerful
Excited
Politics can shape you, Politics can break you
Politics can woo you—to spend and WIN
Politics can make you. GOD. Don't let it TAKE you
Body
Soul
Spirit
or politics can make you
a political animal.

Money

Don't tell me that money is the root of all evil. That may be so.
Sometimes I feel that the White man, knowing that Blacks (having no

want to be evil) would believe the myth that the possession of money can cause evil deeds. However, lack of money causes many more evil situations, like little children with sagging skin and swollen bellies; families living in matchbox houses, literal fire traps; victims of poverty forced to steal because they feel there is no other way out.

Yes, I like money. Not only because it can buy things for me, but because one day, if I get enough money, I can help others.

There is one class in our society who thinks more about money than the rich, and they are the poor. They can think of nothing else, which is the misery of being poor. Poverty produces degradation.

For me, money will always be an instrument to be handled, a weapon to fight poverty—not a deity to be worshiped.

Voices

You gave life voice
    To sing sweet psalms.

Life sings of degradation.

You gave life ears to hear
    your music

Life listens to pagan drums.

Life has many voices Lord.
    We need to only listen.

Of all the voices in my life
    Yours is sweetest.

Where Is Passion?

We crave a passion, hot and burning
We long for love, forever yearning

Our flesh deceives us, our loins mislead us
The path of throbbing passion calls us

Where is the joy of love? Nay, lust
leaves us crawling in the dust

Panting, wanting, needing, pleading
Forever searching, not succeeding.

Until submission, sure and lasting,
leads us to the source of power.
      Power, pleasure, joy; Yes Passion
Wait for us behind the door. When we yield
we know forever, love yes love,
Forevermore.

Ripples (In Time and Space)

Libations, fluids rippling on the sands bringing time and space together;
Bringing souls and spirits together . . . pebbles on the water, water making ripples,
Ripples in time.

"Behold I show you a mystery; We shall not all sleep, but we shall all be changed
In a moment, in the twinkling of an eye, at the last trump;
For the trumpet shall sound, and the dead shall be raised
Incorruptible
And we shall be changed."

II

Libations, shadows rippling on the sand
The earth beneath my feet changes from my dark and musky
Mother, becoming red and alien, harsh,
As the waters ripple and the great ship rolls.

III

I am carried away from my familiar jungle of fruits and passion flowers,
wild animal friends and even wilder beasts;

Four legged animals, predators and yet, magnificent creations of God, with
skins and furs . . . and fangs.

IV

Yet, change carries us over waters that no longer
Ripple.
The water becomes an awesome, rolling jungle of waves
That carries us on in the Middle Passage
Washing us away from our home ground to a new land of tears and sorrow,
Our newfound home in a new world.

V

And yet, wherever we were bought,
Beaten and scattered, over continents and islands,
New blood was added to our veins; and yet the Blood of our Motherland
remained,
True and deep.
In our new world, we learned to harvest new crops;
Some not quite so different from our jungle fruits and vegetation.
We tamed fields of cotton and tobacco
Even as our wild, free spirits were tamed by the new predator; Two-legged
beasts, still creatures of God, yet not quite so magnificent in their borrowed
skins and furs. But still their fangs, though changed Remain deadly.

VI

The libations continue
The spirits that were summoned bring new birth to memories
Reflections of time itself.
We see ourselves in a new jungle—still a part of God's creation,
And yet, the earth has changed.
The soil is not dark and musty between our bare and braceleted feet,
Nor is it red and cracked beneath our chained and callous feet.
It has become rock, concrete,
A machine-made improvement on nature,
And yet still part of nature.

VII

The tribal dancers before the sun, the wind, the rain and the Moon have become whirling disco bodies beneath a myriad of simulated starlight, Lightning and thundering electro phonic sounds.

VIII

The hunter's spears and darts have become a mania for Money;
And guns bring down men and the bloodthirsty prey upon the weak who become Homeless, Jobless, and
Dreamless.

IX

The savagery continues, though times and methods change. The lie of racism causes us to forget that we are all of one blood. Slaughter begins in the womb, and the terror rains down across the ages. Humanity seems to have forgotten why we are here.

Humankind has changed, and yet has not changed, only
Shimmered and rippled in the reflections of time.

X

For though one generation passeth away, another generation cometh.
As the sun rises, it sets only to rise again.
The wind goes to the south only to return to the north,
Whirling continually, returning again according to its circuits.
And the rivers run to the sea, yet the sea is not full,
For the rivers return again to that place from which they came.
For that which has been, shall be again, and that which has been done,
Shall be done again.
For as all things change, they remain because: "There is no new thing under the sun." There are only rippling images of change, all belonging to the universe, The Old, the New created by the Omnipotent
The Lord GOD! Who changes not.

The Companions

BIG MOMA

It's yo' show, Big Moma.
At least, that's what they call you, ain't it.
With yo' minks, and lynx, and diamond studded sphinx,
You strut round like some reincarnated Nefertiti.
If someone were to ask you bout the Virgin Birth,
(you've given birth befo', but y'aint no virgin.)
Would you say, "VIRGIN?" How unfashionable,
Virgins went out with the bite from that passion fruit, back there.
In the Garden, all those years ago.
Where, in the world,
Can you find a virgin these days?
I sure would like to sink my fangs . . .
Excuse me. Teeth
Into
A Virgin
Does this turn our mind to blood covenants? Occult violations?
Blood spilled out and sucked up over the centuries?
Blood untold, blood washing away the sins of the world?
The covenant Blood of the LAMB?
Maybe this is a dream. A fantasy.
A motion picture slice from the mind of a dreamer
Seeking eternity in the arms of
Her Savior
Where yo gonna go?
I don't know
It's yo' show,
Big Moma.

BIG DADDY

And what about you,
Big Daddy?
Forgetting wife,
And life,
And family, chasing dreams, making schemes

To out so
Slew
Foot.
Your master plan is to beat the odds
Play the game, make a name
For yourself.
After all, you grown ain't you?
Old Slew Foot can't possibly get one up
On you.
What you got to do is to make enough to buy yo' way out
Of that six foot deep dirt lined condo
Watin' for you down the way.
Say . . .
The possibility of power; faith Shields.
Spirit Swords, seems
Ridiculous. Doesn't it?
Like seeking HIM while HE'S findable?
Unrighteous acts can be bindable. You know?
Anyway, who is HE? You can't see HIM, or touch
HIM.
Although some nuts say they can actually feel HIM.
Cain't rightly claim to know HIM, huh?
Lord of rejection, jealousy, murder . . .
Satisfy, gratify, the master of the flesh.
LOVE, family joy, peace, must all be sacrificed on
Slew Foot's alter.
Witch's Brew, Occultist whispers
Drown out the sound of
Angel's wings.
Demonic voices, offer choices.
Porn and lust, and angel dust.
The mark of the beast appears on the souls
Of our nearest and dearest . . .
Friends?
Be for real There Is a way out,
You know.
HIS Word is food.
HIS Word is drink.
HIS Word is power.

The price? Your Pride,
Laid aside. Cleansed by the
Blood of the Lamb.
Who Is HE?
Old Slew Foot Knows.
What you gone do? Big Daddy.

On the Way to Becoming Who I am

Just the other day, I caught myself judging others
Oh, brother
I can't begin to tell you the pitfalls of such folly
Oh golly!
There was the young lady with the weave of purple hair
How can she dare?
I wondered, with my skirt split up my thigh,
Oh, my. I had an excuse of course, the thread just popped, you know.
Surely that wasn't the same as the young hussy in the hall.
What gall!
Just then, a still small voice
Reminded me of my purple rain spree years ago
Pregnant was I no less
Purple hair and purple dress
What was I thinking, God bless?
Suddenly the purple girl was revealed as who she is
From the reality of who I once was!
All fire and passion and potential to become
A wonderful woman of God.

Oh beware of the snare of judging others
There are usually little green monsters lurking
Behind the self righteous indignation that
Creeps into our awareness as we wonder
And reflect upon the sins of those other
Fellow human beings that cross our paths
In the ever increasing years of our earth journey.

As I continue along the road of becoming
Who I am, and what I'll be

I can't help wondering if others
See my Lord Jesus Christ in me?
Lord help me not to judge, and keep me free from sin
And wrap your children in your love
And life that never ends.

Amen